Paul Howard

Driven to Murder

Author: Paul Howard

Copyright © Paul Howard

Email: paulhoward109@btinternet.com

Website: www.paulhowardwriter.com

ISBN: 978-1-909655-03-4

First published 2013

Published by Peppermint Books

Unit 2B, Church View Business Park,

Coney Green Road,

Clay Cross,

Derbyshire S45 9HA

www.peppermintbooks.co.uk

e: sales@peppermintbooks.co.uk   tel: 01246 866165

Acknowledgements

Thanks to Hannah, Dan C, Nick, Chris and Jillian, for taking the time to read and comment on early drafts and a big thank you to Dan Reason for the cover design.

Thanks also to Norman and Becki at Peppermint Press for their expert guidance through the publishing stage.

Last but not least, special thanks to my wife, Helen, for her patience, encouragement and critical friendship during the 'few' ups and downs between my having the germ of an idea and bringing it to fruition.

1

The scissors moved precisely around the edge of the picture. You couldn't be too careful with newspaper cuttings. One slight deviation from the vertical and the blades would rip and pull at the paper leaving the finished article unfit for the scrapbook. The new entry was now firmly in place. What a fine collection! What a fine man! Such charm, here presenting a cheque to a local hospice, there winning the President's cup at the golf club, the next with him showing schoolchildren some historical artefacts and now standing proudly as a racehorse owner in the winner's enclosure at Fontwell. A life full of giving, for which the material well-being was just reward. A human being without blemish.

"Bastard!"

The scrapbook was closed in anger.

2

Detective Inspector Steve Reason however, was not without blemishes either in the present or the past. He emerged from his shower and stood in front of the bedroom mirror with a towel wrapped around his middle. If he wasn't exactly *admiring* his own body, nor was he displeased by the shape he was in. Sure, he was carrying a few pounds, but nowhere near as many as the dark weeks immediately after he and Rebecca had separated. She had been the initiator of proceedings. He hadn't had an affair, not in the conventional sense at least, but he had been wedded to his work. From the outset he had been up front with her about his belief that public service meant making sacrifices. She had accepted this in the early years, perhaps harbouring a hope that his commitment to the force would fade over time and to her relief the birth of their two delightful children had put a temporary brake on his work ethic. But this had been short-lived. Family and friends, his as well as hers, marvelled that she stood by him for as long as she did and Steve himself felt more resignation than anger over the split.

For a while he had gone into a tailspin, drinking more heavily than before, eating badly and exercising hardly ever. At a routine check-up, the police doctor had been shocked by his condition and fortunately had managed to instil the same sense of shock in the detective. Since the doc's earnest warning that he was heading at best for early retirement and at worst for an even earlier grave, Steve had taken a grip of his life and the results of the rescue mission were there to see in the mirror. In his forties, he looked almost as good as he had when half that age. In his bare feet, he stood a shade under six feet tall, was reasonably muscular although missing the six-pack of his younger days, and had had often been told that he had good features, apart from the twice broken and permanently disfigured nose. He recollected the two very different events behind this blot on his facial landscape. On the first occasion, he had been fielding in a charity cricket match. To this day he swore blind that he had had the shot under control, when the ball hit a stone and bounced past his welcoming hands into his face. From time to time, his so-called friends ribbed him mercilessly, convinced that it had simply been a poor piece of fielding. For the second break, he had never received anything but genuine admiration, the injury being the result of his bravery in apprehending a bank robber armed with a baseball bat. "A sporting connection," he smiled as he yanked his nose from side to side, in the vain hope of placing it even if only temporarily where it would not appear so incongruous.

Over five years on, there were times when he still missed Rebecca and he hated the infrequency with which he saw the children, Ellie now twelve and Liam fifteen. Northampton wasn't the other side of the world, but Reason felt as if it might as well be. His work and their lives had an unhappy knack of seldom aligning with each other and, with most of the school holidays spent with Rebecca's family in Ireland or her new husband's parents in Yorkshire, his contact was limited to the occasional rendezvous in London. He would have loved for them to take holidays with him, but Rebecca had consistently opposed this on the grounds that he would never be able to give them his undivided attention with his job on the doorstep. Deep down, he knew that hers was the voice of experience.

Reason had managed to cling on to some aspects of his past. When Eastbourne's new police station was built out at Cross Levels he had been determined to remain at Grove Road nick for as long as he could. His official reason was an unwillingness to move until all the systems at the new base were not only up and running but of proven reliability.

4

This was not without foundation, because the force had only just out-sourced the system to a new contractor. As an occasional reader of *Private Eye*, he knew something about the repeated failure of public sector IT projects. However a stronger, unstated factor drove his determination to delay his transfer to the new station, the Fiesta cafe and restaurant, just a stone's throw from his office. Although never mentioned in official despatches, the Fiesta had played a role in several of his successful cases, providing him with sustenance and thinking space at critical stages of his investigations. Reason took one long, last look at himself in the mirror and sighed. He couldn't put the move off for ever, but he would hold on for as long as possible.

3

Unbeknown to him, he was being watched. Twenty years old, skinny, pale skinned, a couple of tufts of dyed black hair escaping from under his baseball cap which he was wearing back to front. His clothes were shabby and grubby and although his face was hidden, in profile he resembled a weasel. From a vantage point a few yards away, the watcher looked him up and down before calling out,

"Danny Young?"

"Who wants to know?" the skinny youth snarled. He didn't lift his gaze from beneath the bonnet where he was working but slowly moved his hand to take hold of a large wrench that was lying on the air filter. Just in case.

"A potential customer."

"Nuttin' doin'," Young said in mimicry of a black youth that was so popular among some white kids, "I got too much on me plate."

His visitor didn't say anything, but remained rooted to the spot.

Danny was irritated by the continuing presence, "Look, once I've fixed this, I've got two others to work on. I can't fit you in," he snapped, unable to sustain his Jamaican accent.

"I'm not looking for a motor mechanic."

"Then what the fuck are you botherin' me for?"

"I understood that I could get other services from you."

For the first time Danny looked up from the car. The stranger was framed by the open garage door, silhouetted against the sun.

"Dunno what you're talkin' about," he said nervously.

"A little something to take away the worries of modern living."

It was Danny's turn to say nothing.

"Some weed or a couple of tabs of e," the shadowy figure explained in a whisper.

"You tink me tick or someting? I don't do any of that shit."

"According to my sources..."

"Just as I thought, a fuckin' pig," Danny interrupted.

"Relax," the visitor said soothingly, "I'm as far away from the police as you are"

"You're probly lyin'"

"If I was, there's not a lawyer in the land who couldn't get you off. Count one: entrapment, count two: the quantities found were clearly for your personal use, count three; some cock and bull story about me threatening you if you didn't give me some dope."

Danny smiled. He couldn't see any holes in the logic, but nevertheless, he remained cautious- he knew you couldn't be too careful in this line of business.

*"Suppose I could help you, you'll have to wait. It's too risky here."
"I agree."*

"Give me your number and I'll text you mine," Danny said.

"I've come out without my mobile. Can you write it down for me?"

Danny fished around on one of the garage shelves, found a pen and a scrap of paper. He wrote awkwardly with the paper pressed against the car roof. "Here," he said handing it over.

The visitor peered at the scrawl, "Is the last number a three or a five?"

Danny made a noise through his teeth, "A fuckin' five. Can't you read?"

"I'll give you a ring later today and arrange a safe place to meet."

"Fine," Danny said nonchalantly as he bent back over the engine, "Now, piss off and leave me alone."

4

As she lay in bed, Gemma Gilligan heard the familiar crunch of the gravel as her husband drove towards the exit of their house, then the pause as he carefully checked that the road was clear. A smile started to form on her lips as she awaited his trademark departure, a roar of the engine and tyre noise as he launched into his day. He only did this to annoy the next door neighbours, a stuffy middle-aged couple who tutted and moaned their way through life; once clear of their drive, he would ease to a silky smooth pace.

Her smile turned to a frown as she tried to fathom why the ticking over of his Merc's engine was continuing. "It can't be traffic," she mused. Even at its busiest, only a handful of cars used the road. At this time of the morning, there was seldom another vehicle to be seen or heard. "Perhaps he's forgotten something." But she hadn't heard him come back into the house.

Then a terrible thought came to her, "Oh God, I hope he hasn't got a puncture. He'll be in such a foul mood if he's late for his meeting." Her concern was not only for her husband and the pressure he was working under. She knew that she would bear the brunt of his agitation for days if things went wrong. It wasn't a matter of physical safety - he was never violent towards her – but something worse, the sense of disconnection from him while he remained buried in his pit of frustration and anger.

She slipped from the bed and walked over to the window. As she drew the curtain back a few inches, she was surprised that he wasn't kicking a tyre or ranting through his mobile at the AA operator. The engine was still running and his door was still shut, so he had not returned to the house. Perhaps he was taking a call. Normally he didn't give a damn about using his mobile while driving, but at the start of a journey, he'd probably answer the phone before going on his way. Then another panic, "Who the hell would be phoning him at this hour? Shit, if I find out he's having an affair, I'll kill him."

She picked up her silk dressing gown and tied the belt as she raced downstairs. Her progress slowed as her bare feet hit the gravel and she hobbled the last few yards to the car, like a child picking her way down a pebbly beach to the sea. As she approached, through the rear window she saw him sitting stock still at a strange angle. She took the last awkward steps towards the driver's door, the window of which was wound down.

"What's the mat...?" she started, but guillotined her own question as her brain took in the scene in front of her. A small dark circle on his temple signposted the entry point of the bullet, the blood splattered over the front seats its exit. She staggered back, her hand clamped across her mouth. She could feel a scream welling up from deep inside, withdrew her hand and threw up.

5

Steve Reason stepped from his car and gazed around at the large detached houses that held sway over this part of Lower Willingdon. As a Detective Inspector, he could never hope to own a property like these. He didn't even mix with anyone in this bracket. When he came to think of it, he hadn't so much as set foot on these streets in the twenty years he'd lived and worked for the Sussex force. Whatever the truth about the politics of envy, he knew that most offences were committed by the poor against the poor. He doubted whether crime had visited this area any more than he had himself. Yes, the rich had most to lose, but they also had the resources to protect what they had, state of the art alarms and surveillance, well hidden safes, private security patrols and gated estates. Reason didn't hanker after these, but he wouldn't have minded some respite from the hand-to-mouth existence that had resulted from his expensive divorce from Rebecca. At the sound of someone clearing his throat Reason emerged from his reverie to find his assistant, DC Peter Dawson holding up the blue and white incident tape for him to pass under.

Dawson was in many ways the polar opposite of Reason in appearance. The epitome of a modern detective, there was a thorough crispness about him. His thick brown hair was styled fashionably without being ostentatious and his clothes were perfectly fitted and coordinated in terms of colours and shades. Today, he wore a dark navy suit with a light pink tie and white shirt. Even his eyebrows were never allowed to stray from a neat, carefully clipped state. As Reason passed beneath the tape, the contrast between the two men was complete. Reason's brown trousers were one size too big- bought when he had put on all that weight and he had not managed to find the time to replace them. They were not the right shade to match the old blue jacket he had thrown on. He wore no tie, preferring to keep his shirt open at the neck. Although he was aware that critics of his turn out would describe it as scruffy, Reason's defensive explanation was one of pre-occupation. It wasn't so much that he didn't care about how he looked, rather that the extreme demands of his job and his commitment to it, left him with precious little time to worry about such niceties.

A Scene of Crime team was busily unloading equipment, including a tent for setting up over the car.

"Give me a few minutes before you put that thing up," Reason called over to them. "I want to take a look at things as they were."

One of the SOC Officers wasn't happy with this, "Given the proximity of the murder scene to the road, the Super ordered that we shield it from public gaze without delay."

"At the risk of sounding insensitive, Mr ..." he turned to Dawson, who responded without hesitation, "Gilligan, Conrad Gilligan..." "That's it," the DI continued, "Mr Gilligan wasn't killed on a camping trip. Your erection will change the context."

He waited a beat, to allow his colleagues time for a snigger, then added reassuringly, "I won't take long and if you get any grief from the Super, put my name in the frame."

"Don't worry, Steve," the SOCO retorted, "I will."

True to his word, Reason conducted his initial observation quickly.

"What do you make of the open window, Peter?" he asked his sidekick when they had completed their perusal.

Driven To Murder

As a young and impatiently ambitious detective, Dawson found his immediate boss's approach much too slow and laborious. "It's obvious," he sighed, "Assuming that he wasn't clearing dew from the glass, Gilligan knew his killer and wound down the window to speak to him."

"I was thinking along similar lines" Reason smiled, "although without your level of clairvoyance."

Dawson was irritated by this, "What the hell do you mean?"

"I mean we don't know for certain that they knew each other or that the assailant was a man."

He waved to the SOCOs to indicate that they could proceed and headed towards the front door, where a uniformed bobby stood guard. Dawson followed a couple of paces behind with a face like thunder.

"Good morning, Brian," Reason greeted the PC, "how are Jenny and the boys?"

"Fine thanks, sir."

"How long have I known you, Brian? Since you were at school doing a project for citizenship. So, you can cut the 'sir' nonsense, at least while we're not in earshot of the top brass. Now, where can I find Mrs Gilligan?"

"She's in the dining room, second on the left. Wendy Puttick's with her."

The young PC, who was sitting next to the victim's wife, made to stand up when the two detectives entered the room. DI Reason beckoned to her to remain seated, skirted the table and sat down opposite them. Dawson hovered uncomfortably between them and the doorway.

"Mrs Gilligan," Reason spoke softly.

The woman didn't respond, but continued to stare into the mug of tea that she was nursing. She was still dressed in her silk gown, which revealed her naked breasts as she sat hunched over the table.

Over the years, there wasn't much that Reason hadn't seen and he had learned to sustain a professional detachment from both the gruesome and the beautiful. Fleetingly noting that Mrs Gilligan's breasts definitely fell into the second category, he repeated his address, this time in a whisper, "Mrs Gilligan, I know that this is a terrible time for you. In your state of shock, you won't feel like facing anything, my questions least of all, but in my experience, it is in these first minutes that we gather some of our most important information … while things are fresh."

Gemma Gilligan wearily raised her head and looked across at the DI. Her face was ashen, in stark contrast to the dark tear-drained redness of her eyes. Although not well versed in these matters, Reason could tell that her hair, despite its current distressed appearance, was expensively coiffured. Even in her current dishevelled state, Mrs Gilligan dripped class or, at least, wealth.

"Can you start by telling me what happened?"

"I've already told this officer," Gemma screwed her eyes as she spoke and her head dropped again.

"You've taken a statement already, Wendy?"

16

"No, sir, not formally, but Mrs Gilligan blurted it all out when I came in to look after her."

"I understand." He turned his attention back to the distraught woman, again in a gossamer thin voice.

"Mrs Gilligan, I can see how painful this is for you, but I need you to take me through this morning's events again." He gestured to Dawson to take notes.

Slowly and unsurely, Gemma recounted how Conrad had left the house for an important meeting. She didn't know where it was or who it was with, but he expected to be away all day and would be back too late for dinner. She revisited her bemusement when the car didn't pull out of their drive and relived the panic about his having a puncture or an affair. Finally, the horror of finding him dead. Murdered.

"Do you know of anyone who had a grudge against your husband?"

A startled look spread across Gemma's face. In the midst of her emotional turmoil, she hadn't given a moment's thought to the possible motive for Conrad's death. Confronted by the policeman's question, her memory span into overdrive.

"What? You mean an enemy? Someone who Conrad had crossed in business? Or someone he owed a lot of money to?" She halted the flow of rhetorical questions, then shook her head as she regained a sense of reality.

"No, I can't think of anyone. My husband's a good and generous man. He does a lot of work for charity, Rotary Club and all that, a member of the Royal Eastbourne Golf Club. He's a well-respected and successful businessman and his success was achieved without hurting anyone. Don't you think I'd know if he was up to no good?"

Reason suppressed the observation that he had known many a wife, husband, mother and father who had lived in blissful ignorance of their loved ones' shady dealings. With Mrs Gilligan in such a bad shape and clinging to the flotsam of her shipwrecked marriage, now was not a good time to pursue the question of motive.

"OK, let's leave it there for now, although I may want to ask you some more questions later, even repeat some of these."

Gemma nodded her understanding.

"Have you someone you can stay with for a few days?" Reason continued.

The PC answered for her, "I've already asked, sir. Mrs Gilligan doesn't want to leave the house and her sister is on her way."

"Good," Reason said. He got to his feet and placed his card on the table, "If you think of anything, just give me a ring, day or night. My mobile number's on the card."

Gemma stared blankly at the card and said nothing as the two detectives left.

"Well, that didn't get us far," Dawson bemoaned as they stepped outside.

"Every journey starts with the first step, Peter," Reason responded.

That was another thing that got the DC's goat; DI Reason could be so bloody philosophical. Not for the first time, Dawson surmised that this went hand in hand with his boss's slow, methodical approach.

In their absence, The SOC team had swung into full action. The murder scene was now safely inside the tent and the forensic search and recording of the car and its surroundings were well underway.

"We'll see if the neighbours saw or heard anything, Keith," Reason told the officer leading the Crime Scene team, "then we'll head back to the station. Give me a ring once you've finished here. Oh, and while you're at it, can you see what's on the rich folk's security cameras?"

Enquiries in the immediate neighbourhood proved fruitless. As Dawson had predicted, no-one else was up and about at the time of the attack on Gilligan. Mrs Eddie, from three doors away, was sure that she had heard what could have been a gunshot, but when pressed to say when this was, she had confidently pinpointed a time almost an hour after the murder, by which time the police investigation was already in full swing.

On their return to the station, Reason directed Dawson to get his notes typed up without delay and set about appropriating sufficient space for the conduct of a murder investigation. There was some discontented murmuring from those officers who had been displaced; however, no-one doubted the need for additional resources. "You'd better pull out all the stops on this one, Steve," quipped Frank Graham, the ageing sergeant responsible for the office, "The deceased was a regular golfing partner of the Assistant Chief Constable and others among the great and the good."

"No pressure, then," Reason responded, his grin matching Graham's.

"Just let me know what you need and I'll sort out the requisitions."

"I don't want my investigation bogged down with bureaucracy, Frank," Reason issued a mock warning, winking as he did.

"It won't be," Graham reassured him, "You can count on my own unique approach to requisition," he winked back and left the detective to make a start on his case board.

There was a knock at the open door and he turned to see the dark, smoothed-back hair, chiselled face and tall thin body of Superintendent James Shaw. Although he hadn't served for as long as Reason, Shaw had been ambitious and had progressed rapidly up the ranks. Steve smiled as he imagined Peter Dawson in the same uniform at a future date. He didn't have a lot of time for Shaw, not because he envied his seniority but because he resented what the fact that his promotions appeared to owe as much to arse licking and who he knew as to his skill as a policeman. There was no questioning his intelligence, but in Reason's view it would have been better applied to politics than policing. Then, there were times when he had difficulty telling the two apart. Given Conrad Gilligan's connections this could be one of those occasions.

"Nasty business," Shaw announced as he stepped over the threshold.

"Murder is, sir," Reason observed.

"Yes, but this is particularly nasty, Reason."

The DI shared this view as a reference to the rarity of gun-related crime, but he sensed that Shaw was on a different tack.

"I suppose you know that the victim was a pillar of the local community," Shaw proceeded.

"I had heard."

"Friends in high places," the Superintendent added.

"Including at headquarters."

"Quite," said Shaw, "I am glad we understand each other."

Reason seized the opportunity to have some sport, "I don't understand, sir," he lied.

"This case must be afforded the highest priority, Reason."

"Because the deceased played golf with the Assistant Chief Constable?"

Shaw's face reddened. "So the people of this town can rest safe in their beds at night!" he thundered. "How dare you imply that there is something untoward in my requiring this matter to be given priority?"

"With due respect," Reason parried not unduly respectfully, "how dare you imply that I wouldn't throw everything I've got into *any* murder investigation?"

"You know that's not what I was…"

He was cut off by Peter Dawson appearing at the door, "Sorry to interrupt, sir, but Keith Jeffries is on the line. He's on his way back and wants to know if you're ready for him?"

"Yes, I am," Reason replied, then as soon as Dawson had gone he turned to the Super, "If that's everything, sir?"

Shaw was flustered, because he didn't want to let Reason have the last word, but nor did he want to get in the way of business that he himself had insisted was a priority.

"We'll leave it there for now, Reason," he said, moving towards the door, "but you may not have heard the end of it yet."

"No, sir," Reason mumbled distractedly, already turning his attention back to his fledgling case board.

6

The initial feedback from the SOCOs didn't add a great deal to the information on display. Conrad Gilligan had been shot once at close range with a hand gun. The bullet, which had passed through his head, had been retrieved and was on its way for analysis. Unless his wife was concealing something or, in her understandable state of shock, had been unable to recall, there was no indication as to who might want him dead.

Although it was evidently the norm for Gemma Gilligan to know little or nothing about her husband's movements, Reason was surprised that she was unaware that he was carrying tickets for a return trip to Spain. It seemed odd to him, but then he did recall how, towards the end of their marriage, Rebecca had become obsessive in wanting to know his whereabouts and that this may not be how other wives react to their husbands.

"Nothing much to go on, is there?" Dawson said ruefully as he and his boss went over what little information they had.

"No, Peter," Reason replied, "Are you a keen angler?"

"What?" Dawson was taken aback, "No, I can't stand the bloody sport, if you can call it a sport."

"Pity," Reason quipped, "because I think we're going to have to spend a lot of time fishing around before we make a breakthrough on this one. If Mister Gilligan kept a diary, that might shed some light on his Spanish jaunt, but we'll need to wear kid gloves, given the state that his wife is in."

7

The DI had a reputation for accurately predicting the shape and duration of a case, but the appearance of Superintendent Shaw with a female colleague left him feeling his nose had let him down on this occasion.

"Dawson," Shaw gave the DC perfunctory acknowledgment as they entered the room. Dawson nodded in response.

"DI Reason, this is DCI Owen, head of the Serious Crimes Unit."

Steve looked at the visitor. Harriet Owen. She was wearing smart jeans, designer t-shirt and an expensive looking leather jacket. Her hair, already naturally dark, Reason guessed, had been given even more depth by the introduction of reddish purple highlights. It formed a neat, smooth bob around her face whose features were a little hard but undeniably attractive. He recalled having met her on a couple of courses some time back, but their paths had rarely crossed. Another 'straight liner', his personal nickname for colleagues who have advanced their careers in the shortest possible time. By all accounts, she was a smart cookie, who was where she was on merit, unlike some of the others in the force. He glanced momentarily at Shaw as he reflected on this. The DCI's intellect matched her appearance.

"We have met," Reason said, extending his hand to welcome the DCI.

Her small hands belied the power of her grip as she shook his hand confidently.

"Last year at Bramshill, wasn't it," the DCI recalled.

Reason didn't answer. He was anxious to know what business she had in his office. "To what do we owe this honour?" he smiled.

Shaw stepped in, "DCI Owen has an interest in the Gilligan case."

"News travels fast," Reason mused.

Shaw closed the door and gestured to everyone to sit at the table.

Owen spoke crisply "We suspect that Conrad Gilligan had links with organised crime."

"On what grounds?" Reason was genuinely curious and hoped his enquiry had not sounded incredulous.

"We've been tracking his movements for some time. He's had meetings with one or two interesting characters who are on Europol's radar."

"Known heavies?" Reason asked.

"No, lawyers and accountants, but our continental colleagues are building up a picture of their association with the *really* big players."

"He was on his way to Spain when he was killed," Peter Dawson said helpfully.

Reason had no right to hold back the little intelligence they had gleaned, but he wished that Dawson would think more carefully when it came to the timing of his contributions.

"Really?" Shaw sneered, "You didn't tell me this, Reason."

Reason knew the Super was performing for the DCI's benefit. He was usually only interested in the detail of cases when they were done and dusted and he could bathe in the reflected glory that illuminated the media conference.

His inclination was to ignore his senior, but found himself driven to justify the situation. Perhaps he too was playing to the visiting audience. "We've only just found out ourselves," he replied, looking at Owen, not Shaw.

"Malaga?" she frowned.

"Yes," Dawson confirmed, "How did you ...?"

"He's made two other trips there in the last month. Out and back on the same day both times."

"Ditto today," Dawson added.

"So, we'll be working together on this one?" Reason surmised. He was looking forward to the opportunity to watch Owen in action at close quarters. Not that he had any conscious designs on her; he wanted to see for himself if she really was as clever as he'd been led to believe.

Shaw was quick to deflate his bubble of anticipation, "No, Reason, this isn't a joint operation. DCI Owen and her team will be taking the case over. Obviously, you'll co-operate with her, give her all the information you have, that sort of thing. What shall we say? Twenty four hours to wrap up the hand-over?"

Reason was seething inside, but somehow managed to retain an outward calm. "Isn't it a bit early for that? Have you really got enough to go on to link Gilligan's death to a criminal gang operating out of Europe?"

"I can't go into details, but the murder certainly fits out hypothesis," Owen spoke confidently.

"If you can't share what you know, how can I help rule out other possible explanations?"

The DCI was intrigued, "Such as?"

Shaw didn't allow Reason to answer. "None of us likes letting go of an important case, but when it's apparent that it's more appropriate in someone else's hands .... You can't deny that Gilligan's death fits the picture that the DCI has been developing."

"My point is," Reason protested, "that I need to see more of that picture, to be sure that we're not barking up the wrong tree."

"You're actually missing the point, Reason," Shaw said sternly. "It is not for you to judge the Serious Crimes Team. They are taking this case on, whether you like it or not and you are to expedite the transfer of authority by this time tomorrow. Do I make myself clear?"

Reason remained silent.

The Superintendent got to his feet, "Good" he announced with characteristic pomposity.

"DCI Owen," he said as he opened the door and waited for her.

Owen knew that Reason would be bruised and simmering, "Is it OK for us to meet here at three o'clock?" she asked softly, "I'd really value your assistance."

Reason grunted his confirmation and followed the two senior officers' path to the door, which he slammed so fiercely behind them that a number of his neighbours reacted like startled meerkats.

"I'd really value your assistance" he exaggerated Owen's gentle voice as he stomped angrily around the room.

Dawson once again demonstrated his inability to know when to keep his thoughts to himself, "You've got to admit, boss, it does look like the Serious Crimes squad is onto something."

"I'll admit no such fucking thing," Reason fumed. "I don't give a damn about their fucking *hypothesis*," he emphasised the word sarcastically while making inverted comma signs with his fingers, "the murder happened on my patch and I should be given a crack at solving it."

He stomped some more and banged his fist on the table, "I can't believe that a supposedly intelligent highflyer like Owen can do something like this. I bet that prick Shaw's behind this. Everyone knows we hate each other's guts and there's more fucking kudos in it for him with the Serious Crime Team at the helm."

"It didn't sound that way to me, boss," Dawson tried to pour oil on troubled water. He failed.

"When I want your bloody opinion, I'll ask for it, right?!"

The Detective Constable held both hands his hands out in submission, "I think I'll go and grab a coffee."

By the time he had returned with two coffees, the storm had abated. "That's good of you," the DI said as Dawson handed him his mug.

"Yes, it is, isn't it?" the junior officer replied.

"I shouldn't have laid into you earlier."

"Agreed."

"It wasn't your fault I was being shafted."

"Agreed."

"I was just pissed off with Shaw and Owen, mainly Shaw."

"I know, I was there."

Feeling he had done enough to work off his penance, Reason changed tack, "I've been thinking."

"Dangerous!" Dawson laughed.

"If the DCI isn't coming back until three, we've got time to make a copy of anything we've got on the case so far."

Dawson stopped laughing, "Now that really does sound dangerous. Shaw will throw the book at you if he finds out you've been running a parallel investigation."

"That's a fact, but that's not what I have in mind. I haven't had time to quench my curiosity about the Gilligan murder. All I want to do is have the chance to give it further thought, while off duty of course."

"Doesn't sound all that different from a parallel investigation to me," Dawson observed.

"Of course it is," Reason reassured him. "All I'll be doing is reading through a few notes over my cocoa, instead of tackling a Sudoku puzzle."

Dawson seemed surprised, "I didn't know you did them."

"I don't, it was just by way of illustration. So, are you going to lend me a hand with this?"

Dawson hesitated.

"Or are you going to grass me up to Shaw?" Reason continued.

"No way, boss. I'd never do anything like that. I'm just a bit worried about getting caught. I've got my career to consider."

"Fair shout, Peter. I'll do it myself, but I'd appreciate you covering my back while I do."

Dawson sighed, "I'd be in as much shit as your look-out man as I would by doing the copying for you." He paused, "Go on then, I'm in."

"I knew I could count on you," Reason said.

"If that's the case, why have you just uncrossed your fingers?"

"How very observant of you."

"Yeah, I reckon I'll be a great detective like you one day!"

The two men laughed and set about gathering together Steve's homework.

8

When DCI Owen appeared on the dot of three, she was in a conciliatory mood, affirming Reason's suspicion that the haste of the handover was Shaw's doing.

"I know how shitty it is to be bounced off a case," she said, "it's happened to me often enough."

Reason wasn't entirely convinced that the upwardly mobile Owen had experienced anything like his loss, but he was willing to give her the benefit of the doubt.

"I'd appreciate it if you could take me through what you've got."

"For obvious reasons, there's not a great deal yet. Limited evidence and no previous, apart from a charge of dangerous driving. Needless to say, he was acquitted, thanks to some sharp London lawyer."

"I don't just mean the concrete pieces," Owen replied, "I'm interested in your thoughts on the case, your hypotheses."

That word again!

"OK, but I prefer to call them hunches."

As they worked their way through the still slender file, Reason found himself warming to his senior colleague and grafting onto his respect for her record and reputation the real enjoyment of her company. As far as he could tell, this feeling was reciprocated.

"So, Steve," she said, "What are your takes on this one?"

Reason smiled mischievously, "Well, firstly, this could be a professional hit. I have it on good authority that Gilligan may have been mixed up with some nasty criminal types in Spain."

"Touché," the DCI smiled too.

"Even if it's nothing to do with organised crime, it could still be a professional   job."
"Any leads on who might want to take a contract out on him?"

"Not leads but hunches, er, I mean hypotheses," he answered playfully.

"All right, you can stop taking the piss now, DI Reason," Owen said with mock rank-pulling.

"A business competitor perhaps. Although the world of importing and exporting antiques and artefacts might not seem a likely setting for murder, there's big money wrapped up in it."

"And his legitimate business and involvement with organised crime might not be mutually exclusive," Owen affirmed.

"It sounds as if you already have something."

Owen didn't respond.

"Which you are apparently not prepared to share with me."

"Sorry, I can't."

"OK, if we can continue our stroll down this one-way street," Reason said huffily, "the next possibility is that he was having an affair and his lover's husband or Mrs Gilligan herself took their revenge."

Owen looked sceptical, "A contract killing is a bit of an extreme response in those circumstances."

"Maybe, but if we can see that he might be killed for crossing someone in business, why not for cheating in his personal life? They're not that dissimilar."

"But Mrs Gilligan? You really think she would be capable of arranging a hit on her husband?"

"I don't know, but what do they say about a woman scorned? Anyway, this isn't about me knowing anything, just about possibilities. Shall I go on?"

The DCI gestured to him to continue.

"If we put the professional hit to one side, what else might have been played out early this morning? We can probably rule out theft. His ipad was on the passenger seat beside him and he had a wallet full of euros and cards."

"What about a failed burglary attempt?" Owen probed, "He's about to drive off when he disturbs someone trying to break into his castle."

"No," Reason was emphatic, "He'd've got out of the car."

"What if he didn't have time, or the burglar had an accomplice?"

"At the very least, he'd have started to get out of the car. His door would've been open when his wife found him and he would have fallen backwards across the passenger seat when shot. Obviously," he stressed the word to demonstrate his superior reasoning, "the blood pattern would've been different too."

"I'm convinced."

"And to make sure that we've kicked that one into touch, given the levels of security and surveillance in that neighbourhood, any self-respecting burglar would know he wouldn't have a chance."

"What if it was a novice?"

"I thought you said you were convinced! No-one in their right mind embarks on a burgling career by carrying a gun, which brings me to the next thought. Are we looking at the random act of a psychopath who's escaped from a maximum security hospital? I can't recall any recent warnings, but didn't have time to follow that up before your earlier visit."

"How likely do you think it is?"

"As someone who likes the occasional flutter, I reckon it's an outsider compared to the others."

"We will check, though," Owen said. "Personally, I am convinced that this is linked to Gilligan's shadowy side, but I can't afford to be blinkered in my approach. Any other theories?"

"There are one or two other possibilities at even longer odds, someone who's been hurt by Gilligan without him being aware of their existence, maybe?"

"That sounds very speculative."

"In my book, that's where all good detective work starts. Hypothesis and speculation have the same number of syllables!"

They had exhausted their trawl of the Gilligan material and Reason's various hunches, when Owen adopted a conspiratorial posture, glancing around the room furtively to check that they were not being overheard.

"Whatever the Superintendent thinks, I know that you're very good at what you do. As I see it, I could do with you on the team."

"I'm happy where I am thanks," Reason jumped in, "even with Shaw to deal with."

"You may have got the wrong end of the stick," the DCI countered, "There aren't any vacancies in Serious Crime."

"I thought I just received a job offer."

"You did, sort of."

Reason looked puzzled.

"What I'd like is for you to lend me an unofficial hand."

Steve chuckled, "I think people in both our teams might notice if I kept popping over to Lewes."

"That's why this would have to be an off duty, out of hours commission. I know it's a big ask, but it's the only way I'll be able to carry on picking your brains."

Steve thought for a few moments, "I suppose it would be some consolation for being mugged by you. When do I start?"

Harriet Owen got to her feet and picked up the file, "Over dinner this evening. Eight o'clock at my place."

"Which is where?" the DI asked as he stood up.

"Written on the back of the business card I've left on the table."

"Do you want me to bring wine?"

"That sounds good. I'll be cooking fish. You do eat fish don't you?"

Reason nodded.

Owen continued, "But I'm not stuffy about what wine goes with what, so bring something you like."

With that she swept from the office.

Reason picked up the card, checked the address and toyed with it between his fingers.

He was excited about his next meeting with Harriet Owen and not only because of the opportunity to keep in touch with the Gilligan case.

As their shift was coming to an end, Dawson asked the DI if he fancied a drink and something to eat with a few of their colleagues. "We're going to Lloyd Lanes for a spot of ten-pin bowling then on to Simply Italian in the harbour."

Reason declined the invitation, "Nice of you to offer, but I've got a few things to sort out at home."

"You're not on a promise, are you?" the DC smirked.

"Of course not, although I promise you I'll kick your arse from here to Brighton if you don't watch your step."

9

Reason finished shaving. "My hair could do with a make-over," he said to his reflection and smiled at the oddity of his caring what his hair looked like. He had always gone to 'Roger the Bodger', as his son had called the barber. He already knew that Harriet Owen was impressed by his professional expertise. Now it seemed to matter that she might be interested in his personal appearance too. Since the divorce, he had steered clear of anything resembling a serious relationship and the not so serious ones hadn't exactly been numerous. As he reflected on how good Harriet looked, he wondered whether he was at last emerging from the wreckage of his former life and whether he had a cat in hell's chance with her.

Shortly before eight, Reason parked his car outside Harriet's place in Glynde village, walked to the front door and rang the bell. Although a similarly modest size to his own house in Hailsham, the relationship between the two properties was otherwise one of contrast, his a featureless semi-detached box in a recent development on the edge of town, hers a monument to a rural idyll. Steve didn't know a great deal about architectural styles, but he reckoned that the cottage dated from the eighteenth century, perhaps earlier. Its external features had a charming irregularity. As he waited, Reason wondered whether his selection of wine, a 2008 pinot noir from New Zealand, would pass muster.

When Harriet answered the door, she was dressed in a t-shirt, a knee-length skirt and moccasins. She also sported an apron and from her uncharacteristically flustered demeanour, Reason sensed that things might not be going according to plan in the kitchen.

"Can I help?"

"No, everything's under control, but you'll find glasses through there in the cabinet in the lounge." She darted back into the kitchen, from where she heard a thud and a curse.

"Sorry," she called through, "I forgot to warn you about the open beams."

Reason joined her in the kitchen, a glass of wine in each hand.

Harriet accepted hers and hastily took a sip. "Mmm," she cooed, "New Zealand pinot if I'm not mistaken. One of my favourites. Is it an 09?"

"08," Steve responded, wondering whether she really did know a lot about wines or had simply caught sight of the label when he had first entered.

"Cheers!" he said raising his glass.

"Cheers!" Harriet echoed, "Now, go and make yourself at home in the lounge. Dinner will be ready in a few minutes. I hope you're hungry."

"Ravenous!"

"Good."

As he melted into a comfortable period sofa, Reason pondered Harriet's instruction to make himself at home. From all angles it seemed inappropriate. Firstly, this neat, colourful treasure trove of a room was a universe away from his untidy, sparse and magnolia-dominated living room. Secondly, he doubted whether his host would appreciate finding him lolling around in his boxers, which is how he liked to unwind in the privacy of his own place.

He sipped his wine and cast his trained eye over the room, as if looking for something significantly out of place. He didn't know what that something might be, but if it existed, he couldn't find it. . Everything - furniture, fittings, pictures, books - seemed just so.

His investigation was ended abruptly by Harriet's appearance at the door holding two plates laden with steaming food. "Through here," she directed, before disappearing into the dining room, "Bring the bottle and mind your head!"

Inwardly, Steve thanked her for the warning. With his attention distracted by his surroundings, he had forgotten about the exposed wood in the low ceilings.

The centrepiece of the dinner was a whole sea bass, stuffed with prawns and mushrooms, and as he tucked in, Reason was rapidly heading towards the conclusion that DCI Owen was perfect.

"Where did you get this lovely fish?" he enquired through a mouthful of succulent meat.

"Southern Head," she replied, "I make a point of calling in there whenever I'm in Eastbourne. You're so lucky to have them on your doorstep."

Reason knew where the seafront fishmonger was, but had never taken the trouble to try it. He wondered whether to busk his way through an appreciation of halibut and mackerel, but decided that discretion and honesty should be his guides on this occasion.

"On the few occasions I cook fresh fish, it's from a supermarket," he confessed, slightly sheepishly.

Harriet tuned into his discomfort, "Nothing wrong with that. When I'm not in Eastbourne, which is most of the time, I buy from supermarkets. Most have decent fish counters ... and a good selection of wines" she added, noting that they had polished off the bottle that Steve had donated.

She wiped her mouth with her napkin and stood up, "I'll fetch another bottle," she said heading off to the kitchen, leaving Steve cursing himself for not having been more generous.

When she returned, Harriet had *two* bottles, holding them with the labels towards her, "Do you want a blind tasting?"

"No, I'll pass on that, thanks," Steve said humbly, "My specialism is in knowing where the wine's going not where it came from."

Harriet laughed and charged his glass. "Another Kiwi pinot, same year, different area," she explained.

"Same effect!" Steve beamed as he lifted the glass to his mouth and took a draught.

Dinner over, Steve offered to wash up.

"That's kind of you, but I'll throw everything into the dishwasher later. Go through to the lounge while I make some coffee."

Taking the remainder of the wine and their glasses with him, Steve narrowly avoided another encounter with the beam, before settling down into what had already become his favourite sofa.

When Harriet joined him she sat in one of the two armchairs that flanked him.

"I really appreciate the help you gave me this afternoon, Steve," she said as she pushed the down the cafetiere's plunger.

"Just following Shaw's orders."

"You know I'm not talking about the part you had to do. Your hunches were invaluable in ensuring that I wasn't stuck in a rut and blissfully unaware of what lay either side of it."

"Very wise, although your rut still may be leading you in the right direction. You've clearly got more than hunches to go on when it comes to Gilligan and criminal gangs. If I'm going to be of further assistance, perhaps you can start showing me what you've got."

"A very attractive face and gorgeous body for starters," Steve said to himself as he stared across at his colleague. He had drunk enough wine to have overtaken mellow and was now driving in the lane marked 'potential embarrassment ahead'.

Owen's drive through Marlborough's vineyards had been more leisurely than his, leaving her capable of both lucidity and relaxation.

She started to describe the points at which Gilligan had come into contact with the known criminal underworld and to recount some of the more significant journeys, both by plane and on the expensive boat that he kept moored in Sovereign Harbour. But after a few minutes, she sensed that Reason was no longer assimilating her intelligence through his glazed eyes and inane smile.

"I'll tell you more later," Harriet said, making a note that if their collaboration was going to get her anywhere the next time it would be business first and socialising second. "Let's get you to bed."

Reason's smile grew bigger and more inane looking. As the evening unfolded, he had grown more and more attracted to Harriet and mentally had been rehearsing the moves he would make to convert that attraction into action. He certainly hadn't expected her to take the initiative like this.

"I always keep a bed made up in the spare room," she added.

Steve lurched out of the room behind her. He could feel his smile being eclipsed by pouting disappointment.

Harriet's expression headed in the opposite direction, as she heard the familiar thud of head on wood and Steve's cursing his way upstairs.

10

Although Reason continued to curse the loss of such a high profile case, he was at least spared the torrent of media interest in the death of the prominent local figure. After the initial burst of activity by the local press, the town was crawling with journalists and photographers from the nationals as well as TV and radio crews.

In police circles, Shaw pronounced that the invasion ran the risk of jeopardising their investigation, but Reason knew that privately the Super enjoyed the attention. "Like a pig in shit," he said to Dawson as they stood at the back of the hall hastily commandeered for the first press conference.

"He's certainly in his element, guv'" Dawson added, "Spouting on at length and saying next to nothing in the process."

Reason nodded and smiled, "Come on, Peter. We're going to learn nothing new here."

Most of the media army behaved with sensitivity and their business gave an unexpected, welcome boost to the coffers of Eastbourne's restaurants and bars. The more intelligent among them weren't remotely interested in the theories with which some locals, eager to get in the papers or on the telly, bombarded them during their down time, but they listened with good grace and on the whole proved to be popular visitors.

The exceptions were some of the newsmen and women from the gutter tabloids, who established camp outside the Gilligan residence, where they hatched the most salacious explanations for the murder that they could come up with and from where they launched a photographic assault through high powered lenses.

With her distress amplified by their behaviour, Gemma asked her sister to 'phone DI Reason and insist that the siege be lifted. "I'll do my best," he had reassured her, even though he knew he had little immediate influence over the situation. He decided to bypass Shaw and took the problem straight to Owen. This worked and a couple of hours later, the wolf pack had been dispersed, bleating about the destruction of the freedom of the press as they departed. To Reason that was a good result, which would help strengthen Mrs Gilligan's confidence in him and well worth the bollocking he was bound to receive from the Super when he realised that he had been side-lined.

11

As he turned into the car park that is overlooked by Firle Beacon on the South Downs, Reason was starting to rue his acceptance of an eight a.m. meeting on a Sunday. Although he sometimes had a shift on Sundays, usually this was the one day when he had a chance of a lie in, when the world and its woes could be forgotten.

DCI Harriet Owen had been as insistent as she had been logical. "There won't be many other people about, so we can talk openly."

"For 'many' read 'any'" Reason muttered out loud as he surveyed the deserted tarmac area.

Whilst he waited for Owen to join him, he reflected on the last time he'd been near to this spot. Could it really have been six years ago? Maybe even longer! He and Rebecca had brought the children up near here to fly kites. She had protested that they could have accessed the Downs much nearer to home without the need to use the car, but he had insisted that the short drive would be worth the marginal additional pollution. He had led them on the short walk from Firle Beacon back towards Eastbourne, just above the Long Man of Wilmington, the locally famous image cut into the Downland chalk, where they had come across a group of overgrown boys playing with radio controlled aeroplanes. Liam had been thrilled by the detour, but Ellie had been less than impressed, especially when told that she couldn't fly her kite there, for fear of downing the nice men's expensive toys. The word 'toys' had been overheard by one of the pilots and word soon spread that they had an unbeliever in their midst. Rebecca, who had to that point, shared Ellie's irritation, had found great hilarity in their retreat from the scene. She had ribbed Steve mercilessly about his hidden secret of wanting to join the big boys' little planes club. Back above Firle they had had a wonderful time with the kites, albeit Steve's homemade example, which he boasted was a match for the kids' expensive shop bought affairs, lay in a crumpled heap within two minutes of them launching. More ribbing and this time Ellie and Liam joined in. Days like that stood out in his memory as islands of successful family life, but they were few and far between. Most of the time, the ocean of work stretched uninterrupted as far as the eye could see.

He'd only been there about ten minutes when Owen's vehicle, a predictably smart and sporty Peugeot, swung into the car park and came to a halt alongside his ageing Audi.

As she stepped from her car, he followed suit and walked round to greet her.

"Nice morning for it," he noted dryly.

She ignored the edge to his comment, "Yes, I love it up here. Pity I don't have more time to enjoy the Downs."

"Looking on the bright side," Reason smirked, "when you're eligible for your pension, you'll still be young enough to cope with the terrain."

"Are you happy to walk and talk, Steve?"

"Why not?" he replied, "Kill two birds with one stone, eh?"

As they started their ascent, Harriet picked up the threads of the briefing that had been aborted at her cottage three days earlier.

While she couldn't deny Reason's assertion that there was nothing unusual about Gilligan, a successful importer and exporter, making copious trips to the Continent, she directed his attention to some of the people he had met there. Europol had been following the web that radiated out from Vladamir Karpov, one of the business oligarchs who

48

Driven To Murder

had emerged smelling of roses from the dung heap of the former Soviet Union's economy.

"Our colleagues in four European countries are involved," Owen explained. "They've been trying to develop a number of cases against Karpov. You know, the usual, money laundering, drugs, human trafficking and corrupt payments to government officials. Then, a few months back Conrad Gilligan showed up in the net, when he met with one of Karpov's financial fixers, a Swiss banker called Weber."

"Nothing unusual in that. Rich guys buy expensive antiques," Reason said slightly dismissively.

Owen was not to be deflected, "Europol took the same view ... at first, but when Gilligan kept reappearing on their radar, for meetings with other members of Karpov's circle of acquaintances, they were convinced that he wasn't there simply to sell the odd Ming vase."

"Did they find any hard evidence that he was doing anything illegal?"

"Not exactly, but some of the transactions were decidedly odd."

She proceeded to tell Reason how sizeable amounts of money had been transferred into Gilligan's accounts.

"As I said before, payment for antiques," Steve was growing impatient and being buffeted by the wind on Firle Beacon wasn't helping his mood.

"On the face of it, yes. It's taken Europol a long time to be able to access records for his Swiss account, but once they got that information we could check deposits against the items that we know, from Customs documentation, Gilligan had sold."

"But not those that bypassed the tax authorities," Reason raised his voice in what he supposed was a 'Eureka'.

Owen disappointed him, "On the contrary, there was a perfect match between payments and shipments."

"So, Gilligan was squeaky clean after all?"

"Hardly, you see, the fishing around I've done at this end, suggests that some of the antiques that he is supposed to have shipped to Karpov never existed."

"How do you know?"

"It's not rocket science, just old fashioned logic and detective work. The rarer the artefact, the more expensive it is and a man like Karpov is only interested in accumulating the very best. Let's suppose the records show that he buys an early eighteenth century cabinet, of which only ten were made. It's not that difficult to construct a map of who owns them. If none of these owners is selling, the one that shows up on Gilligan's customs docket is the non-existent eleventh."

"Unless it's the real deal and the seller wants to keep it quiet to avoid capital gains or inheritance tax," Reason responded keenly.

"Granted, if we were talking about just one shipment that is plausible, but at the last count, this has happened on at least ten occasions."

"What?!" Reason exclaimed. "You mean he was stupid enough to cross people like this? Take their money but give them nothing in return?"

"That's how it seems. It would certainly be reason enough for Gilligan to end up dead."

They walked along the ridge in silence for a few paces, Owen breathing in the fresh air and the amazing views, Reason deep in thought.

"If it's already that clear cut, why the hell are you interested in my views? If I'd known you already had it sewn up, I'd've stayed in bed."

"Because I don't share my colleagues' acceptance of that explanation," Harriet frowned." It's too convenient and, I think, deeply flawed. I need your help in challenging the consensus."

"How much is he supposed to have screwed Karpov over for?"

"About eight million ... dollars not euros."

Reason whistled, "Then he's either got balls and/or no brains to keep going back to Malaga. I assume that's where the rendezvous are with Karpov's foot soldiers."

"Yes, he's got a villa overlooking the city. It's not clear that Gilligan ever met Karpov in person, but there's no doubt that his visits were linked with the Russian's business and collecting interests. What do you make of it Steve?"

Reason stopped and rubbed his chin, shook his head and broke the silence.

"Whatever other motives you can come up with, I'm sure Gilligan wasn't ripping off Karpov or anyone else. He'd only have one shot at pulling a stunt like that and he'd have to know which people to buy off into the bargain. Even then the risks would be sky high. Unless Karpov is happy for his loot to remain in packing crates and, as my fantasy is that he likes to spend time drooling over his treasure, that's extremely unlikely, Gilligan wouldn't have a cat in hell's chance of getting away with the scam ten times or more. This suggests that some other valuable commodity was in the consignments."

"That would tie in with the suspicions about drug trafficking," the DCI affirmed.

"Except that the UK isn't exactly renowned as an exporter of the stuff! No, if there really was something of value in the shipments, it's more likely to be weapons. Now that is something we're good at selling abroad, legally and illegally."

"Shit!" Harriet gasped, "This is going from bad to worse."

"Only if that explanation is correct. As far as you know, has Gilligan's business ever been in trouble?

"No, he seems to have had the Midas touch, gone from strength to strength ever since he left university more than fifteen years ago."

"So, it's highly unlikely that Karpov and his cronies had anything on him that might help lever him into involvement with gun running. All of which bring you back to the consensus that several of the exports from Gilligan were things of little or no value masquerading as highly prized antiques. Now, all you have to do is come up with an explanation for Karpov being complicit in the scam. If I can borrow a well-used phrase, it's not rocket science."

Harriet responded immediately, "It points to money laundering."

"Bingo!" Reason cried.

"It undermines the hypothesis that Karpov had Gilligan killed."

"It certainly does," Reason concurred. "If his death was a professional hit, it's almost certainly from the British end of the chain. Once you know where the money was being washed, you might come across a disgruntled punter who's been short changed by a few thousand."

"Thanks for the loan of your grey matter, Steve."

"It's a bit early for thanks, in both senses of the word 'early'. Gilligan was a rich businessman who would've been making plenty more if he was importing dirty money from Karpov. Not the sort of bloke who'd risk killing the Faberge goose and losing his own life as a result."

Harriet was crest-fallen, "Where does that leave us?"

"Where I've been all along, open to the possibility that Gilligan's death was *not* linked to the dodgier among his clientele."

"You really want this back as your case, don't you Steve?" Harriet sounded angry.

"Of course, but I'm resigned to not always getting what I want. Besides, as things stand, you may have a bigger problem on your hands than me being a bit pissed off."

"Namely?"

"If we're right that Karpov and Gilligan were in cahoots over the bogus shipments, they've been lucky to get away with the scam so often, unless ...." he gave Harriet the privilege of finishing off his chain of thought.

"They've been receiving a helping hand from someone with influence in Customs," she said gloomily.

"Or Europol," Reason added. He glanced at his watch. "I don't know about you but this fresh air is making me distinctly peckish. By way of thanks for the lovely dinner you cooked me the other night, how about

I reciprocate with a bacon butty? If we're lucky that van in the lay-by on the A27, not far from the Newmarket Inn, opens on Sundays."

12

As usual, Danny Young had felt twitchy in the run up to the deal. The adrenaline rush was fuelled in equal measure by the money he'd make and the risks involved. Not that this transaction seemed very risky, given the choice of venue, a pull in on the road that runs from the A22 to Arlington Reservoir and Mickleham Priory. Reflecting his confidence in the arrangements, he had decided against taking something to boost his bravado and had driven with more control than was usually the case.

He normally kept his customers waiting, to show them that he was the boss, but on this occasion calculated that the buyer might not hang around in the secluded spot for long, so he made sure that he was at the rendezvous with a few minutes to spare.

Right on time, the second car turned into the appointed space and the driver stepped out to join Danny who was waiting by a five bar gate.

"Have you got the merchandise?"

"Eh?"

"The gear."

Danny nodded and took a packet from inside his bomber jacket, "Come on, let's get this over with."

"Fine by me, Danny."

To the drug dealer's astonishment, the driver's hand was not holding a wad of notes, but a gun, complete with silencer.

Before he could take a step towards safety or utter a single expletive, Danny Young lay dead next to his car.

13

With the Gilligan case officially off limits, Reason went into a dip where he had little relish for work. As expected, Shaw was on his back to complete the paperwork for a couple of his recent successes. Other than when engrossed in a discussion of possible outcomes to unsolved crimes, he hated being at his desk. He hadn't become a detective to push a bloody pen.

"Can't Peter wrap things up while I attend to other more serious matters?" His rear-guard action was in vain.

"Dawson's 'phoned in sick," Superintendent Shaw said, barely unable to suppress a smirk, "so this is a perfect opportunity for you to complete those reports."

Reason's day dragged. For every sentence he wrote, he broke off to give further thought to the ramifications of Conrad Gilligan's murder. He longed to hear how Detective Chief Inspector Owen was getting on and more than once started to call on his mobile, before checking his frustration and returning to the even more frustrating task in front of him. The only thing missing from the agony was Shaw standing over him like an invigilating teacher, swishing a cane threateningly as he passed Reason's desk.

Although it wasn't quite midsummer, it felt like the longest day to him. As he at last staggered over the finishing line of his written exam, the day was about to get even longer.

His desk 'phone rang. "Reason." he snapped. "Oh, it's you, Frank. If you're calling to hound me about some poxy requisition I didn't fill in properly, forget it. I've already had a bellyful today."

"Nothing like that," Sergeant Graham reassured him, "I've just taken a call from a farmer out Hailsham way. He's found a dead body and I thought you might want to take the first look at it."

Reason looked at the clock, fifteen minutes to go to the end of his shift and in the light of the recent circular on budget cuts no certainty of securing overtime

"How did he die? Hit by a tractor?"

"No, shot in the head."

"A hunting accident, perhaps," Reason was trying hard to balance curiosity with the desire to go home.

Frank Graham was starting to get impatient, "Look, Steve, either you want this one or you don't. I can wait a few minutes and give it to Roger and his team when they come on duty if you prefer."

"Sorry, Frank. Didn't mean to be awkward. I've had a shitty day, but there's no reason to take it out on you."

"I forgive you and you'll take it?"

"Yes, I'll be down in a minute to pick up details."

With Dawson indisposed and everyone else in CID about to knock off, Reason negotiated a couple of uniformed officers to follow him out to the Arlington road in a squad car. In the meantime, he got Frank to summon up the SOCOs.

"Delay your call by fifteen minutes, Frank," he had said on the way out to his car, "That way, I'll get a chance to take a good look for myself before the boys and girls from forensics convert the scene into their own professional playground."

As the two cars approached the turning off the A22, Reason saw a large, ruddy-faced man, whom he correctly assumed to be the farmer who had called it in, standing waving to them. "OK, Farmer Giles," Reason muttered, "We know where the turning is." He decided to let uniform conduct the initial interview.

If the farmer had expected a lift the few hundred yards to the murder scene, he was to be disappointed as first Reason and then the patrol car sped past him.

The couple of minutes that elapsed before the farmer arrived back at Danny's car gave Reason precious time to gain control and deploy his resources.

"Barry, take whatever you've got in the boot to seal off the A22 end. While you're there request another car to get over here and close the road from the West at the Arlington/Mickleham fork. Geoff, I want you to get underway with the interview with the farmer. I'll join you when I've taken a good look around here."

He broke off to meet the farmer as he came panting up to the pull-in.

"Couldn't you have given me a lift?" he puffed.

"Sorry, sir, we had to secure the scene without delay. And you are?"

"Derek Mayfield. I found the body."

"Well, Mister Mayfield, I'd like you to go with PC McDonald and tell him all about your gruesome discovery."

Geoff McDonald led the farmer away to the car and Reason commenced his scrutiny. A tractor was parked on the other side of the hedge, close to the five bar gate. As the constable was to confirm later, Reason hazarded a guess that Mayfield had been planning to leave the field by the gate, only to find his route blocked by a car. In vain, he had tried to get the driver's attention and, climbing down from his cab, had found Danny Young's body.

"What have we got here?" Reason said to himself, "A single shot to the head, small calibre weapon I should think." He donned rubber gloves and carefully slid into the driver's seat and started to explore the glove compartment. He pulled about a handful of old petrol receipts, a packet of rolling tobacco, a few boiled sweets and a scrunched ball of tin foil.

Throwing the rubbish back into the compartment, he sniffed at the shiny package and his nostrils acknowledged the familiar aroma of its contents. Reason extended his search to under the front seats and in the crevices that surrounded him and his exploration was rewarded with two further quantities of drugs. "This suggests small scale dealing," he mused, "but hardly enough to die for."

Sliding back out of Young's car, he left the three packets on the driver's seat and looked around the pull-in. Apart from a couple of long since discarded condoms, nothing caught his eye. The ground was firm and dusty after a protracted spell of good weather and it wasn't possible for Reason to spot any recent tyre marks, either from the parked car or any other vehicle. "Perhaps forensics will come up with something," he thought, more out of hope than expectation.

On cue, the SOC team arrived and took over.

Reason joined McDonald and Mayfield.

"I've just finishing taking Mister Mayfield's statement," McDonald reported.

"I'm sorry I couldn't be more helpful," the farmer said, "If only I'd called you when I first saw the car."

"When was that?" Reason probed.

"When I first entered the field," Mayfield replied.

"At what time?"

"Three thirty," McDonald spoke on the witness's behalf.

"I take it that you didn't go in from this side," Reason noted, "or you'd've seen the body."

"That's right," Mayfield said, "I'd been working the next field over from this one. There's an opening in the hedge that connects the two. I didn't really take much notice of the car at first. It's not uncommon for people to pull off the road there."

McDonald looked bemused.

"You know, for a quickie," the farmer explained. "It's usually all over inside ten minutes, 'cause they don't want to be caught, but this one stayed there all the time I was working in the field."

"You didn't think to take a look sooner?" Reason asked gently, not wishing to seem ungrateful.

"No," Mayfield said ruefully, "I reckoned he wasn't here for sex." His expression changed into a broad grin, "Unless he was a super stud or something."

Reason smiled uncomfortably. Mayfield continued, "I assumed he'd parked up and gone for a stroll. Not very likely I admit, but these days 'live and let live' is the best policy."

Having checked that McDonald had got a sufficiently detailed statement, Reason thanked the farmer again, "You've been most helpful, Mister Mayfield. I may be back in touch if I think of anything that isn't clear."

Once Mayfield had gone, Reason checked in with the scene of crime team, "I've done as much as I can here for now and my shift ended a while ago," he said, "so I'll leave it to the experts and head off home. Can I have your preliminary findings first thing tomorrow?"

"Yes, apart from the ballistics report," Laura Hooper, the senior SOCO, replied.

As he lived a few minutes' drive from the murder scene, Reason had little time to mull over his initial thoughts and on arrival home he sat thinking for a while in the car port. He had never been formally trained in ballistics analysis, but the sharpness of perception that he had acquired during years of experience as a detective had given him a working knowledge. He didn't need to be a brain surgeon to realise that both Gilligan and Young had been killed with a hand gun, but his visual recollection of both bodies suggested a more significant degree of similarity. "What if they were killed with the same gun?" he wondered, before reining himself in, "Mustn't get too excited, the chances of a match are slim."

"But it doesn't hurt to speculate," was his parting shot as he locked the car and headed to his front door.

14

With the force's top brass worried that Danny Young's death marked the start of a wave of drug gang violence, the lab pulled out all the stops to turn around its analysis of the bullet that killed him. Less than twenty four hours after his call-out, Reason perused the ballistics report. Danny's miserable existence had been cut short by a SIG Sauer. As if anticipating the detective's curiosity, the guys at the lab had appended some handy technical information about the Swiss-made weapon. Reason's eyes flicked past the series of numbers and fell on the piece of information he was most interested to find. "Recommended Silencer option: Evolution 40," he read out loud.

Reason looked across his desk at DC Dawson, "That's a serious piece of kit, Peter. I know we don't see much gun crime in any event, but a SIG Sauer really is a new kid on the block."

Dawson did not seem unduly impressed, "If you've got the money and the connections, you can get hold of any hardware these days."

"You're right, of course," Reason conceded, "but without wishing to speak ill of the dead, I'm surprised to see such extravagance being lavished on a small time operator like Young."

"I never had you down as a snob, guv'" Dawson quipped, "Who'd have thought that even murder isn't immune from the class system?"

Reason briefly joined in the humour of the moment before picking up his mobile and calling DCI Owen's number. Her 'phone was on voicemail and he decided against leaving a message, instead opting for a simple text, 'Ring me when you can'.

When she called about an hour later, Owen talked breathlessly, "I haven't got long, Steve. It's all kicking off here. We've really put the cat among the pigeons by suggesting that Karpov, Gilligan et al must've received some inside help to carry out their business with so little impediment."

Reason didn't like her reference to 'we'. She and Shaw had made it clear that this was her case and even though he'd contributed some ideas, Reason felt that she ought to take responsibility for what was hers. However, he decided against pulling her up over this, as he had more pressing matters to cram into the little time available.

"I've got another murder on my hands," he said.

"I had heard. Some low life druggy, wasn't it?"

"Yes, shot at close range in what appears to have been a deal that went wrong," Reason said, neither believing this hypothesis nor wanting to share too much information about *his* current case with someone who had stolen his last one. "By the way," he changed tack, "what was Gilligan killed with?"

Owen was intrigued, "Do I detect another Reason hunch?"

"Maybe," he answered coyly.

"As you're such a clever dick, perhaps *you* can tell *me*?"

"A SIG Sauer, maybe."

There was silence from the other end as Owen assimilated his answer, "Are you saying that your man and Gilligan were taken out with the same weapon?"

"Not for certain, but what's the chance of two SIG's turning up on the Sunshine Coast within a few days of each other?"

"I'll get straight onto the lab," Owen said.

"I was thinking of doing the same, but wanted to run it past you first."

"I appreciate that," the senior officer responded assertively, "but the Gilligan case takes precedence."

"And I'm left out in the cold again, is that it?"

"No need to act like a disappointed child, Steve," she mocked him. "I'll bring you up to speed over dinner tonight. My place at seven thirty?"

Reason's irritation quickly abated. Not only would he find out more about whether or not the two murders were linked, he'd have the considerable pleasure of her company again.

Having grown tired of the lack of intelligence or, for that matter, intelligible information being gleaned from their audiences with Superintendent Shaw, several of the media circus packed up their tents and drifted back to the metropolis, leaving a couple of freelance colleagues to act as their runners. The few who remained were predominantly from the tabloids, especially the red tops, whose foot soldiers were under orders to fish around for any titivating stories while waiting to see if there were any developments with the businessman's murder. With the exception of some young women, who were impressed by the flow of drinks that accompanied the newshounds on their visits to the town's night clubs and bars, no-one found their company at all pleasant and gave them an increasingly wide berth. They weren't bothered, having grown accustomed to being seen as lepers or pariahs. So long as the expenses accounts held up and the local girls remained interested, they could imagine worse places to be and, if any news did break, they'd be in pole position.

15

From the outset of their second evening meeting, Owen insisted on a pact to limit themselves to two glasses of wine. Once bitten, twice shy, she wanted Reason to have a clear head throughout proceedings on this occasion. Besides, she didn't plan for him to stay the night and needed him to be in a fit state to drive home.

"Well, what have you got for me?" Steve asked agitatedly as he helped carry the food through from the kitchen.

"Gilligan and Young were killed with the same gun, Steve."

"I thought as much," Reason said, a triumphant edge to his voice, "and that pretty much blows the professional hit theory out of the water. There's no way that Danny Young was tied up with a big-hitter like Conrad Gilligan."

Owen wasn't in a hurry to embrace his conclusion, "Young was involved in drugs," she remarked.

"Just small scale stuff, not the same league as organised crime. Anyway, I thought we had established that Gilligan's link with Karpov was probably through money laundering."

"But the money's from an illicit source and drugs are one of the more logical ones."

"Even allowing for the fact that drugs are cascaded from the big boys and some will eventually find their way to the smallest of dealers, it's one hell of a leap to conclude that Young and Gilligan knew each other."

"They both lived in Eastbourne."

"Is that the best you can do, Harriet?" Reason derided, "If that's all you've got to go on, why don't we just say that the entire population of the town is working for Karpov?"

"I'm surprised you're not giving the possibility of a connection more serious thought. If Gilligan's death was a professional hit, then Young's probably was too," Owen riposted.

"That's nonsense," Reason said with his frustration becoming more transparent by the minute, "If Gilligan's was a contract killing, can you really imagine that the quality of assassin that would be brought in for that job, would demean himself by accepting a tuppeny hapenny hit on the likes of Danny Young? Sorry, Harriet, it stacks up about as well as Jenga being played by two guys with the DTs."

"Well, like it or not, that's the view back at Serious Crime."

"You've told them about the link, already? Before telling me?" "Of course, Steve. You know that's not the sort of information I could sit on."

"And that's all the thanks I get from giving you the lead?"

"Oh, grow up, Steve. Forensics would've made the link today. What do you think you gave me? An hour's start at most."

The junior officer disconsolately pushed the food around his plate as he took stock.

After a brief silence, Owen was the next to say anything. Her tone was more conciliatory now, her voice softer, "I am grateful for your help, Steve. I really am and I can't begin to imagine how tough this is for you."

Reason shrugged, "It's not that big a deal if we don't see eye to eye on a case. Hypothesis, antithesis and resolution, eh? No-one can stop me holding onto my views, until they are categorically proved to be wrong."

"That's true," Owen said, "but you can't hang onto the second murder."

Reason abruptly dropped his cutlery onto his plate, "What?!" he cried, "You're joking aren't you?"

"I wish I was," Owen tried to sound supportive, but knew that she couldn't veil the reality of the situation, "but now we've got a theory based on the two murders having a weapon in common, we've got to integrate the Young investigation into the Gilligan case."

Reason had heard enough. Dramatically, he pushed his chair back from the table, sprung to his feet and hurled his napkin at Owen.

"If you think I'm going to help you after this," he shouted as he turned to leave, "you can forget it!"

As the slamming of the front door reverberated through the cottage, Owen tried to rationalise the latest regrettable twist in their relationship. She knew it would be a bitter pill for him to swallow, but she'd hoped that he wouldn't take it so personally.

Minutes later, Reason's car screeched into his driveway, prompting a few of the neighbourhood curtains to twitch. It was good for him and all the other road users between Glynde and Hailsham that his journey was short, because throughout the Audi had been driven as much by anger as by its own engine.

"How dare she?!" Reason ranted once inside. He made a beeline for the sideboard in the lounge and dragged out a bottle of single malt whisky, the occasional dram of which he permitted within his healthy living regime, before stomping off to the kitchen for a tumbler. He slumped onto his sofa and drank as manically as he had driven. By the time he tumbled into bed the revulsion he had felt when Owen had announced her latest takeover had been joined by a burning sickness in his half empty stomach.

16

Uncharacteristically for a working day, he overslept the next morning, but by limiting breakfast to a large mug of coffee, which was all he could face, he arrived at the station less than five minutes late.

"The Super wants to see you," Dawson greeted him.

"Well, he knows what it means to want," Reason spat out his response.

"He said he wants to see you as soon as you come in. Sounds urgent, guv'."

"Give me a break, Peter. You know what Shaw's like, he thinks the bloody world revolves around him and everyone has to drop anything whenever he indulges in his most dangerous pursuit."

"What's that?"

"Thinking!"

Both men laughed, but there merriment was cut short by Shaw's appearance at the door.

"Reason," he said with an air of impatient authority.

"Just coming, sir," Reason replied as he followed the superintendent to his office, pausing to wink at Dawson on the way out.

"There've been some developments with the Gilligan murder," Shaw declared once they were both sat down in his den. "It seems that the young man who was found dead near Arlington Reservoir was killed with the same gun as Gilligan."

"I know," Reason said sullenly.

"What? How do you know? I've only just been informed by the Serious Crime Team."

"I've got a nose for these things," Reason said.

"I dare say you have," Shaw said in a tone that was not meant to sound complementary, "This means that DCI Owen and her colleagues will be assuming responsibility for both murders."

"There was me thinking that the killings were committed by the criminal fraternity," Reason said flippantly, but his joke was lost on his po-faced superior.

"Make sure that any information you have is collated by midday. I'll personally deliver it to Headquarters."

Whether it was accurate or not, Reason held firmly to a vision of Shaw and other senior officers whiling away a couple of hours at the trough and he didn't doubt that the Super intended to milk as much credit as he could out of the situation. As Reason had had hardly any time to delve into either murder, it would serve Shaw right if he found the udder dry. And if the top brass colleagues in Lewes started to pepper him with questions on things he knew next to nothing about, that would add another helping of natural justice to their lunch.

"Did you hear me, Reason?"

"Yes, midday. No problem."

Shaw dismissed him and he made his way back to his own office where Dawson was waiting like a faithful dog.

"Bad news?" he enquired.

"The usual," Reason replied, "losing one murder case is unfortunate, losing two is downright careless."

72

"On what grounds?" demanded Dawson, his righteous indignation bouncing around the room.

"The SIG Sauer that Gilligan was killed with also put paid to Danny Young. So, our friends in Serious Crime want to merge the two cases. It's bloody annoying, but only natural."

"You're taking it very philosophically, guv'," Dawson observed.

"On the surface, maybe," Reason responded, "but underneath I want DCI Owen and her crew to get nowhere and come begging for us to take the investigation back."

Dawson wondered whether that was the only thing Reason wanted the DCI to beg for, but this time, he wisely kept his thought to himself.

"And in the meantime, we just sit around twiddling our thumbs do we?" Intentionally or not, Dawson's question had a reverse psychological effect on Reason. "Certainly not," he said, browsing at a note on his desk. "It seems we've got an aggravated burglary in Old Town to deal with. Not as sexy as a double murder, I'll admit, but the living are as entitled to a slice of our brilliance as the dead."

17

Despite immersing himself in other cases, Reason remained curious about developments in the Gilligan and Young murders, but unable to do anything to satisfy his curiosity. He hadn't expected Owen to brief him and couldn't bring himself to make the first move. Not only would she probably tell him that it was no longer his business, but also she might expect him to apologise for his outburst the last time they had met and he was in no hurry on that front. The extensive network that he had built up over his long service in the force was unable to shed any light on the Senior Crime Team's on-going investigation. "They're keeping this one very close to their chests," one usually reliable source at HQ reported, "Probably operating within the constraints of some stupid EU policing directive."

As the days passed, Reason's interest in the demise of Conrad Gilligan and Danny Young began to wane. He had plenty on his plate and took some satisfaction in the continuing lack of news emanating from police headquarters. With a degree of justification, he guessed that this was not just down to the secrecy in which the case was shrouded. "If they'd made real progress, they'd have wanted to put out a bulletin to reassure the public that they were doing a great job in keeping them safe" he explained to Dawson, who noted that the DI's comments lacked the desperation that infected his every word in the immediate aftermath of Owen's second raid on their cases.

"Fancy a curry this evening, guv'?" Dawson asked cheerily as they strode towards their cars at the end of another day's toil.

"I've not tried your cooking before, Peter," Reason replied suspiciously, "Is it safe?"

Dawson ignored the dig, "I was thinking of going to one of the Indians on Seaside. Heather's gran is very poorly, so she's gone up to the family home near Birmingham for a few days. Cooking for one is no fun, even when you're as good in the kitchen as I am, so I thought I'd treat myself tonight."

"And me?" Reason asked mischievously.

"You've got to be kidding. No, if you're up for it, we're going Dutch."

18

The old man walked along the pathway to Whitbread Hollow. Six thirty - same time every morning, regular as clockwork. The watcher smiled. The small dog trotted happily alongside his master, a man thought by almost all who knew him as a 'regular good guy' 'Almost all' because the watcher knew; knew that they were oblivious to the man's filthy dark secret. "Now," the watcher thought, "Mister Good Guy would have to pay." The watcher was about to move forward when a runner appeared, puffing up the hill. The watcher darted behind a bush and waited patiently.

The runner said something in passing to the old man and set off round the corner. As the man continued on his way, the watcher moved towards him nonchalantly, asked for directions to Holywell, patted the dog and reached for the gun.

19

Reason hadn't intended to overindulge at the restaurant, but the food had been top notch and the helpings large. He didn't usually baulk at leaving food on his plate, but noting that it seemed to matter a lot to Dawson that he had agreed to the meal, he had ploughed on beyond his normal limit, rather than cause offence. The Kingfisher beer, which initially helped smooth the way for his curry, had become part of the problem by the end of the evening.

While he couldn't fault the quality of the previous night's meal, he was still in a lot of discomfort on his drive into work the next day. His stomach was griping badly and only eased momentarily when he farted. "Heaven help the rest of the team if Peter and I are stuck in the office all day," he said to himself.

By carefully timed visits to the washrooms, Reason was able to avoid major embarrassment. He marvelled that Dawson didn't appear to have the same need for evasive action. "You must have a cast iron stomach, Peter," he remarked after returning from his fourth comfort break.

"When I first joined the team, you said I'd need one," Dawson chuckled, "and like a good subordinate I took you at your word."

The phone rang and Reason picked it up.

"Shaw" he mouthed silently and deliberately as Dawson watched on.

"I see," he said to the Superintendent, "and presumably DCI Owen will pick this one up from the word 'go'?"

Reason waited for Shaw's response, "I see" he repeated, "Definitely no connection?"

Another pause then, "OK, DC Dawson and I will drop everything and get straight over there."

Dawson fought to contain his laughter as he thought about his boss's struggle to avoid dropping everything of the previous evening's excesses.

"Another shooting," Reason recounted when he'd put the 'phone down.

"What sort of weapon?"

"Small arms again."

"The same gun as before?"

"That was my first thought, but it seems unlikely. The victim's a retired teacher, Alan Morrissey, lives in one of the flats in that new development by Holywell. They found him above Whitbread Hollow, where he'd been taking his dog for a walk."

"Did they shoot the dog too?" Dawson asked anxiously.

"I don't know, I didn't ask. I must be slipping," Reason said.

"Either that or I'm continuing my unstoppable climb to the top," said Dawson.

The climb from the cafe at the start of the Holywell spur of the South Downs Way is very steep and Reason had broken out into a profuse sweat by the time he had joined Dawson at the summit, where his colleague greeted him cheekily, "Not as fit as you thought, guv'."

"Shut up!" Reason snapped, "I'd've been fine if you hadn't ordered so much food."

"I didn't order you to eat it all, though."

"All right, let's forget it. Now where's this body?"

They turned left towards the sea and descended to the murder scene, which was already demarcated by a tent and several lengths of blue and white incident tape. The SOCOs hadn't wasted anytime in securing the site and a uniformed officer had already taken statements from the couple who had discovered the body at the start of their ramble to the Cuckmere estuary and Exceat. They were both badly shaken by the experience and Reason decided not to stress them further with a second wave of questions.

"At least they didn't harm the dog," Dawson said as he spotted one of the uniforms hanging onto an agitated collie.

"I owe you an apology, Peter. I've always assumed that your interest in animals was confined to the greyhound track at Hove or the racecourse at Plumpton."

"We always had dogs when I was growing up. I love them. Heather won't have one, she says neither of us would have enough time to look after it properly. She's probably right."

As they closed in on the hive of activity, they were met by a woman, who was wearing a familiar blue plastic over-garment but whose face was unfamiliar.

"Isobel Perry" she extended her right hand to Reason, "I'm the duty pathologist."

"DI Reason and this is DC Dawson. Where's Erickson? Not slipped off into retirement without buying his mates a round or two of drinks?" Reason had worked with Jon Erickson for as long as he'd been in CID. The son of an English mother and Swedish father, who'd deserted them in Gotheborg when he was ten, Erickson had lived most of his life in the UK. Reason reckoned he was about sixty years old, so retirement wasn't a bad hunch.

"No, he's taken some overdue leave, visiting long lost relatives in the States, I think."

"I've not seen you at his side, learning the ropes off the old bugger."

"No, I've been drafted in from Surrey to provide your force with some cover. And for the record, I am both fully qualified and experienced."

"No offence meant. It's just that you look so much younger than any of the other pathologists I've dealt with to date."

"Flattery will get you absolutely nowhere," the pathologist sighed, "No, you'll have to work harder than that if you want to get back into my good books."

"There's a thought," the DI thought. There had been some talk way back of merging the Surrey and Sussex constabularies, and, faced with opposition from both counties, the Home Office had abandoned the idea although the two forces had collaborated effectively in a number of regional initiatives. Reason tried to form a visual impression of Perry through the distorting features of her body suit. Whatever else, she had beautiful, azure eyes and a warm smile. Thoughts of extending the collaboration with Surrey flitted around inside his skull.

82

"What have we got here, Doctor Perry?" Dawson's question snapped Reason out of his reverie.

"A white male, late sixties..."

"Yes, we know the identity of the victim," Reason said clumsily trying to mask embarrassment with impatient efficiency, "What do you make of what happened?"

"If you'd like me to like you," the pathologist thought, "you're going about it in a very strange way."

"I don't respond well to rudeness," she said out loud.

"I'm sorry," Reason backed down, "Tell us what you've found out ... please."

"Death was by a single shot to the front of the head. You'll have the usual wait for ballistics, but for what it's worth I'd say that it was 9 millimetre ammunition. If I was a betting woman, I'd probably go for either Glock or SIG, those two against the field."

Reason had expected a reference to the SIG and her last three words made a stronger impression on him, "For someone who's not a gambler, you seem to know your betting terms, Doctor Perry."

"It's a long story," she responded, her expression clearly becoming sadder. "And not one I'll be sharing with you in a hurry," she added inwardly.

Briefly cross with herself for opening one of the windows onto her private world, Isobel quickly regained her professional composure, "He was found at seven forty five by which time I would estimate he had been dead for between one and two hours," she said authoritatively.

Reason rubbed his chin, "I wonder why he was up here that early."

Dawson was incredulous at the DI's apparent lack of grasp of the situation.

"He was walking his dog, sir," he offered gently, to minimise his boss's embarrassment.

Without turning away from the pathologist, Reason reacted sharply, "I am fully aware of that, DC Dawson, but I am interested in knowing if Mister Morrissey regularly came up here at that hour."

"In my experience," Dawson replied, "dog owners are as much creatures of habit as their pets. My hunch is that today was no different from any other."

"I'm not interested in your hunches. Make a point of checking it out with his neighbours when we interview them for background information on him."

Isobel's initial dislike of Reason deepened, "How can anyone bear working with you?" she said to herself. She felt sorry for Peter and directed her next comment to him.

"Do you know this area well, DC Dawson?"

"Yes, Heather, that's my wife, and I often walk up here."

"I guess it's a popular place for people to bring their dogs," Doctor Perry continued.

"Yes, but not as much as inland," Peter pointed as he spoke, "over by the Downs golf course, but living so close this would be the obvious spot for Morrissey."

"He'd be up here every day, then?"

"Of course."

Reason could see what she was up to and had had enough of it, "OK you two, thanks for establishing that. I didn't doubt that while alive the deceased exercised his dog on a daily basis, but I want to know for sure whether today fitted a pattern."

The pathologist caught his eye with a strange expression and the slightest of nods in Dawson's directions.

"I didn't mean to have a go at you, Peter," Reason found himself saying, "just want to make sure we take nothing for granted."

"Me included?" Dawson replied a smile spreading across his face.

"You included," Reason said with a similar comradely grin.

Isobel Perry smiled too, but hers was one of self-satisfaction in having some influence over the man who had so recently blundered into her life.

"Everything's been photographed," she reported, "and we've got the private ambulance standing by once you've taken a look around. I'll carry out the post mortem this afternoon. I'll call you when I've finished."

"Thank you, Doctor Perry," Reason said, having at last deduced the need for civility with this colleague.

"You can call me Isobel," the pathologist felt another wave of smugness as she headed back towards her car.

Apart from the difference in location, Reason found the murder scene very similar to the other two and he had no doubt that the wound in Morrissey's head had been caused by the same Sauer P226. In Reason's opinion, Shaw wasn't right about much, but he concurred with the Super's guess that this murder wasn't connected to the other two. However, once it was established that the SIG was the common factor in all three, Shaw would doubtless yield to pressure from Serious Crime for the Morrissey case to be annexed by their growing empire. He and Dawson would have to build up a compelling argument if he was going to hold onto this piece of detective real estate and perhaps reclaim part of his earlier losses.

"Time for the good old fashioned leg work," he directed his constable, "Let's go and see what Mister Morrissey's neighbours have got to say."

They tried to keep an open mind, but neither detective was surprised by the responses they got. Without exception, the other residents of the apartment buildings gave the ex-teacher glowing posthumous references. He was variously courteous, helpful, sociable, kind and considerate. Of all these qualities, the last mentioned seemed to get most votes, as he never failed to clear up his dog's shit or 'excrement' as it was more precisely and genteelly reported. Morrissey had retired to Eastbourne seven years earlier, after what one informant thought to have been a successful career in education 'somewhere up North'. Technically correct this turned out to be in Guildford and subsequent enquiries confirmed beyond a shadow of doubt that he had lived an exemplary and blameless life.

Reason had no counter to Dawson when at the end of their series of door step and living room interviews his junior remarked that they were up a well-known creek without a paddle as far as motive was concerned. "That won't help our cause," he agreed, "though it won't do Owen much good either. Unless she and her chums in Europol

86

have got some pictures of Mister Morrissey cosying up to Gilligan or Karpov's associates, they'll be hard put to stake a claim for this investigation. The nearest thing we have to him having European connections is the annual trip to France of the local wine appreciation society of which he was a member."

"Back to the station then?" DC Dawson said sensing that they had finished.

"Yes," Reason concurred, before coming to an abrupt halt after a few steps. "Wait, I've just had a thought. Did you ask any of Morrissey's closest neighbours if they held spare keys for his apartment? My hunch is that they do a lot of looking out for each other round here."

"No, I didn't."

"Me neither. Let's go back and check. If we strike lucky we might find something of interest."

Dawson wasn't convinced and more to the point was feeling hungry, "I hardly think we'll find that despite everyone's rave reviews he was really Public Enemy Number One."

Reason didn't disagree but if they could search the dead man's home, they might be able to steal a march on Shaw, Owen and the others.

Now alerted to their friend's tragic end, the residents were in no hurry to answer their bells when the detectives returned. In the event, Mrs Tovey, who lived three doors away, turned out to be the keeper of the keys and while she didn't hesitate to let the police officers in again, she was reluctant to part with them, "I made a solemn pledge to Mister Morrissey not to give his keys to anyone without his prior authorisation."

The two colleagues said they understood and patiently chipped away at Mrs Tovey's resistance, gently impressing upon her the urgency of the situation and surmising that the deceased man would have expected those around him to assist him in death as he had always helped them when alive. This appeal to Morrissey's and her own public spirited qualities worked and she fetched the keys.

"Shouldn't you make out a receipt for them?" she enquired before handing them over.

"I promise we'll return them as soon as we've had a look around the apartment. I expect it will be within the hour," Reason coaxed her.

Mrs Tovey hesitated a little longer.

"Our word is our bond, madam," Dawson added in his most earnest tone he could muster.

The keys safely in their possession, they walked the short distance to the Morrissey apartment, where, once inside Reason let out the most explosive laugh, "Priceless, Peter. 'Our word is our bond, madam'!"

"It worked didn't it."

"It worked," Reason quickly regained his composure, "now let's see if anything here throws light on the killing."

Like many older people's homes, Morrissey's apartment was cluttered. Not untidy, but full of all sorts of objects d'art, bookcases bursting at the scenes and several pieces of furniture most of which didn't complement each other. Without knowing what they were looking for and in spite of Reason's reputation for efficiency, the search took them longer than they had intended. Not that they were conscious of the time. Their quest was interrupted by the ring of the telephone in the hall.

Reason gestured to Dawson to answer it and the DC again put on his exaggerated voice, "Mister Morrissey's residence. How can I help you?"

On the other end of the line, Mrs Tovey said that they'd been gone for over an hour and the other officer had assured her that they'd return the keys within the hour. She had to go out in ten minutes and expected them back without further delay.

"Oh well," Reason sighed, "We'd better not upset her any more than we already have. I can put up with Shaw having a go off his own bat, but I'd rather he didn't have ammo from a disgruntled member of the public."

Dawson had already opened the front door when the inspector noticed a drawer in the telephone table. They hadn't had time to look through all the furniture, so it didn't matter if they overlooked this piece, but he decided to take a quick look. Next to the telephone directories was a small bundle of papers held together with a bulldog clip. "Only old receipts," he said as he flicked through them.

"Come on, guv'" Dawson said, more concerned about his empty stomach than Mrs Tovey's irritation.

Reason ignored him, "Well, what do you know? A couple of the receipts are for items purchased from one Conrad Gilligan." He stuffed the papers into his pocket. "Not a word to anyone about this, Peter. Right?"

"About what?" Dawson pulled an innocent face.

"That's my boy," Reason beamed before slapping his colleague firmly on the back and carefully pulling shut the door to the apartment.

20

Their early start had meant that Reason had neither heard nor read the morning's news. On arrival back at the station he was brought up to speed by the desk sergeant.

"What do you make of this, Steve?" he said, waving a tabloid around vigorously.

"Not a lot if you can't keep the bloody thing still, John," Reason retorted. He snatched the newspaper from the uniformed hand and looked at the headline, 'Exclusive – New Lead on Eastbourne Murder' and noted the invitation to find out more on pages 5, 6, 12, 13 and 14.

He didn't usually have time for these rags, but his interest in the case over-ruled his disdain. According to 'our man on the spot, Ed Warren' Gemma Gilligan was alleged to have had an affair with one of her husband's business associates. The claims were backed up with grainy pictures of a couple relaxing in swimwear on a yacht and in a warm embrace on the quayside. Crystal clear images of Mrs Gilligan and Oliver Appleton were presented as insets in the corner of the damning pictures. As he flicked through the pages, Reason was not surprised to find Warren's account littered with innuendo and supposition and almost completely bereft of useful facts. On one of the two page spreads another headline screamed, "Is this why Conrad Gilligan died?"

"No," Reason flung the paper onto the desk.

"So, you don't think there's anything in it, then," the sergeant teased.

"How perceptive of you, John."

"Thanks, any jobs going in CID, 'cause I think I'm outgrowing my role here?"

"Even if Gemma Gilligan was having an affair and this rubbish doesn't prove anything, it's not a very plausible reason for her husband's murder."

As they climbed the stairs to their office, Peter Dawson was keen to explore the possibility, despite Reason's assertion.

"What if Appleton knew of Gilligan's links with organised crime? He could get rid of him and make it look like a hit by his criminal partners."

Reason shook his head, "And where do Young and Morrissey fit in with this theory?"

Dawson looked blankly, so Reason answered for him, "Appleton would gain nothing from killing two other people or having them killed. On the contrary, the second and third murders with the same weapon increases the risk of detection. I expected better of you than that, Peter."

This stung the younger detective, but he wasn't finished, "Unless the person he contracted to kill Gilligan carried out the other two off his own bat, or for a different employer."

"Less likely than the motive being linked to an affair and in any event a contract killer worth his salt would use different weapons."

"Which brings us back to your other point, guv'" Dawson concluded the conversation in the corridor outside their office, "with three murders and maybe only one weapon, solving this just got a whole lot easier and we should have this case cracked by teatime."

Reason knew his colleague's enthusiasm and optimism were assets that needed to be cultivated, but they could leave him exposed to exaggeration and disappointment. "I hope you're right, Peter. Let's see what ballistics come up with. In the meantime, I'd like you to make sensitive contact with Mister Appleton to see if he's able to help us scotch the rumours about him and Mrs Gilligan."

21

As Reason had feared, the following day's confirmation that the same gun had accounted for three of the local population, prompted another wave of interest by Serious Crime.

When Shaw and Owen entered his office, he noticed that the DCI was unusually sheepish. "DCI Owen has something to ask you," Shaw announced, unnecessarily in Reason's opinion, as he knew she was capable of talking for herself without introduction.

"Really," Reason sneered, "I've become accustomed to being told not asked when I'm about to be pressured into relinquishing a line of enquiry."

Owen tried to dismiss his soreness, but she didn't have to go deep down to know that he had every reason to be pissed off. She would have been just the same, no, much worse, in his shoes.

"I'll be honest with you, DI Reason," she opened.

"That will be a first," he muttered under his breath.

"My team is already stretched and this latest killing pushes us over the limit. In short, I don't have sufficient resources at my disposal to incorporate the Morrissey murder into our on-going investigation."

Reason smiled, "I see, so you want me to deal with that one and report back any useful leads?"

"Not exactly, I've asked Superintendent Shaw to second you to Serious Crime until we've put this mess to bed."

Reason didn't react, but feigned careful consideration of Owen's proposition. "I'll make her sweat a little," he said to himself.

"Well, Reason?" Shaw interrupted his game, "Having bemoaned your previous exclusion, you can hardly refuse, can you?"

"Of course I can," the DI snapped, "I've already noted that you are not instructing me to make the move, which is very wise. You know that if you try to force me across to DCI Owen's squad against my will I'll be straight onto the Police Federation. But don't worry, I will accept the secondment..."

"Good!" the two senior ranks spoke in unison.

"..on two conditions."

"I don't think you're in a position to make demands, Reason," Shaw broke off from his celebrations.

"Then you think wrong, sir. I'll only agree to the move if 'a' DC Dawson comes with me and 'b' the case, by which I mean all three murders, passes back to me if it becomes clear that this is not about organised crime."

Shaw stood open-mouthed, stunned by Reason's bare-faced cheek.

"Agreed," Owen said, knowing that at this precise moment she needed Reason more than she needed to be in control of every aspect of the investigation.

The taste of victory coursed through Reason's veins. He was on a roll. "I'd like to suggest that you and your team relocate to Eastbourne, DCI Owen. After all, this is clearly where the main action is."

"Don't push your luck," she smiled, "HQ is better equipped as the communications hub for a complex case like this."

"That's a shame," Reason responded, "because we have much better fishmongers here than in Lewes."

"What the hell are you blathering about, Reason?" Shaw roared.

The DI ignored him, "Your reference to communications does raise another issue, DCI Owen. With some of the press already off the leash and news of Morrissey's death breaking, we'll need a stronger, more effective media strategy."

"You're right," Owen acknowledged, "I suggest we discuss it on the drive over to Lewes. Can you be ready to go in half an hour?"

"Twenty minutes should be plenty."

"Good, I'll be waiting in Superintendent Shaw's office," Owen announced. She shook hands with Reason and Dawson, "Welcome aboard gentlemen" before leaving with a speechless Shaw at her side.

22

After the relatively cramped conditions in which he'd been operating, Reason was impressed by the scale of accommodation that had been made available to the team at police headquarters on the outskirts of Lewes. "More like an incident suite than an incident room," he whispered to Dawson as they were introduced.

Owen's decision to entrust subsequent media conferences to Reason did not go down well with established members of her team and their mood worsened when Reason insisted on these being held back in Eastbourne, "As well as making sense in terms of the location of the murders, it will help delay the media's progress up the organised crime path."

One of his new team mates sighed and looked to the ceiling. Saying each word slowly to emphasise his belief in Reason's stupidity, he said that the involvement of the Serious Crime team would certainly give that particular game away.

Reason was having none of it, "I don't think many members of the press or public have a precise grasp of your, I mean *our* role. The general perception will be that three murders in and around a sleepy seaside town is a serious matter and the team's involvement will be viewed both as logical and as a source of reassurance."

Despite his length of service, Reason only recognised one of the team. Evidently, local experience didn't often count for a great deal when it came to breaking into Serious Crime. For whatever reason, perhaps a concern about officers becoming too set in their parochial ways, most of the team had arrived from service in other forces, especially the Met.

The awkward preliminaries out of the way, Owen briefed the new team members, who didn't think that the investigation had progressed very far. The Karpov connections were still being explored from a distance by Europol, though no different patterns of activity had been detected post-Gilligan. The origins of the murder weapon were still unknown, although one theory was that it had gone absent without leave from a military base.

"How likely is that, boss?" Dawson said, testing the water of how to address DCI Owen.

"It's not as uncommon as you might think and we might like. The army misplaces a small arsenal of equipment every year but the Americans are much worse," Owen replied.

Dawson continued his enquiry, "Could this one have come from the US Army?"

"Yes, the Yanks use them but so do we and any number of other countries' armed forces."

"So we could be looking for an American hit man?"

"In theory, but it's likely to have been sold on a few times since it was discharged from the armed forces. We must keep an open mind about the nationality of the killer."

"What about a link between Young and Gilligan?" Reason asked.

"Nothing yet," Owen said with an air of dejection, "there's nothing to suggest that they knew each other."

Reason resisted the temptation to say 'I told you so' and tried not to sound condescending when checking through possibilities, "No suggestion that Gilligan bought drugs locally then?"

100

"Nor anywhere else," Owen confirmed, "every indication is that he was as clean living as he was successful."

"Any unexpectedly large amounts of money passing through Young's account?"

Owen shook her head.

"And I assume that Gilligan didn't take his Merc to Danny for a service," Reason smiled.

"You assume correctly, St... DI Reason," Owen corrected herself. She would need to be careful in the way she spoke to Reason, "I don't think we've left any stone unturned. I'm beginning to worry that you might have been right when you hypothesised that the murders weren't linked to a major criminal enterprise. The latest killing seems to point away from that link too?"

"But we..." Dawson started.

"Shit," thought Reason, "he's going to spill the beans about the receipts we found at Morrissey's." He acted swiftly to cut his colleague off, "We need to check that we've not exhausted every possibility. That's what you were going to say wasn't it DC Dawson?" He scowled as he spoke.

"Er, yes, sort of," Dawson stumbled, getting the message.

Owen wondered why Reason had been unwilling to let his junior finish. Perhaps he didn't like other people having ideas. "So, what have I overlooked, Dawson?" she held a hand up in Reason's direction, indicating that she expected the constable to share his own thoughts uninterrupted.

Dawson paused. Reason squirmed, then his colleague spoke, "What if Danny Young had seen something, the hit on Gilligan, for instance? Perhaps the killer or an accomplice saw his car, traced him and silenced him."

"He had plenty of time in which to come to us during the time that elapsed between Gilligan's murder and his own," Owen noted.

"Danny Young wasn't exactly the sort to take his civic responsibilities seriously," Reason laughed, "and in any case I can't imagine him being out of bed at the time of day when Conrad Gilligan was killed."

"Unless he was on his way home after a night out," Dawson said hopefully.

Owen came to his assistance, "It's a possibility, worth looking into."

"Except that in her statement Gemma Gilligan said she heard nothing, just her husband's car ticking over. If Danny was driving in the area, you can bet he'd have been in a noisy, souped up, old banger. Either Mrs Gilligan or one of her neighbours would've recalled something that loud."

"And if he was on foot?" Owen pursued Dawson's chain of thought a little further.

"The killer would've seen him and disposed of him there and then," Reason said confidently and neither of the others challenged his assertion.

When they had a chance to take a break, Reason suggested that he and Dawson familiarise themselves with he lay out of the building, "Let's check out where the canteen and gents are."

102

"Some host eh? I didn't think to show you around as soon as we got here. Let me give you the tour now" Owen intervened.

"No need, DCI Owen," Reason said, "After all, we are detectives and our street cred would be shattered if the others saw you taking us to the toilet like a nursery school welfare assistant."

Once inside the loos, Reason checked that they were the sole occupants before turning on his colleague. "Don't you ever pull a stunt like that again, Peter."

Dawson tried to act innocent but he knew he didn't have a leg to stand on.

"Didn't I make myself clear? Not a fucking word about the receipts!" Reason hissed.

"I thought things had changed what with us joining Serious Crime."

"Well, they haven't. We're not here to get into Detective Chief Inspector Owen's good books by sharing everything we've got on day one."

"What about getting into her bed? Isn't that part of your plan?" Dawson immediately regretted saying this, his regrets confirmed by Reason's grabbing hold of his jacket lapels and thrusting him against the wall.

"Watch your step, Peter," he growled, "Watch your fucking step!"

The door into the washroom started to open and Reason released his hold. Dawson knew he'd spoken out of turn and was swift to restore the status quo as they walked along the corridor. "Sorry, guv'. That was out of order, but you can't deny that I struck a raw nerve there," he whispered.

Before heading back to Eastbourne, Reason discussed the following day's press briefing with Owen, while Dawson got to know more about the team's other members and its methods.

"How can you be certain that Shaw won't want to run the show as usual?" Reason was sceptical about sharing the platform as Owen had directed.

"That's been addressed," she explained, "He's had an unequivocal order from upstairs to do the basic introduction and then hand over to you."

"He'll hate that," Reason remarked.

"Superintendent Shaw's feelings are irrelevant. While he can be relied upon to dull the edge of his audience's interest, the top brass want conferences to be more informative and reassuring. They're coming under some pressure from Borough and County councillors, who are freaking out about the damage being done to tourism in the area. You'll be expected to give a bit more substance in your responses than Shaw has in previous conferences."

"While still giving little or nothing away?" Reason presumed.

Owen passed a folder across the table, "A few bullet points for you to build your briefing around. Try not to deviate far from these and put as much emphasis on appealing for information from the public."

Reason felt uncomfortable, "Sounds like a sure fire way of communicating that we're stuck."

"I've got every confidence that you can pull this off," Owen said placing a hand on his arm, which he immediately slid away from her.

This unnerved her, "Steve is there a problem between us? I thought ..."

"Yes, there is," Reason thought, but decided against giving her the full reason for his coldness, "Things have changed, DCI Owen. It's one thing for us to socialise when I was just a CID foot soldier in Eastbourne. Now we're part of the same team, we've got to play it cool."

Owen couldn't argue with him. She'd just have to bide her time until the case was over.

"I hope it doesn't drag on for too long," she said to herself.

23

Reason couldn't remember ever feeling as nervous as he was waiting for the media conference. He'd done a few of them in the past, but this one was for higher stakes. The third murder had prompted a hurried return to the coast by more of the crews from the capital and when he and Shaw walked onto the stage he was impressed by the turnout. The packed hall was abuzz. For a short while, cameras clicked and flashed until Shaw raised his hand to signal his intention to get under way.

"Good morning, ladies and gentlemen. Can I start by introducing Detective Inspector Reason, who is one of the lead officers in the murder investigation?"

Keeping a deadpan expression, which colleagues later said made him look like a startled rabbit in headlights, Reason could only imagine how it must have stuck in Shaw's throat to talk publicly of *his* importance.

"In a minute I will ask him to give you a brief update on developments, then I will allow some time for questions. I hope you will understand that DI Reason will only be able to give you limited feedback, such is the sensitivity of the case."

As he surveyed the throng before him, Reason could detect a wave of irritation. The media folk were growing tired of being fed crumbs by Shaw and were obviously hungry for something more substantial. He cleared his throat as he prepared to speak, but to his horror Shaw had not completed his handover.

"I can reveal that the name of the dead man discovered above Holywell was Alan Morrissey, a former teacher in his late sixties. He moved to Eastbourne when he retired and there is no obvious motive behind his murder. There are currently no suggestions that his death is linked to that of Conrad Gilligan."

"Are you saying this is linked to the death of Danny Young, then?" a voice called out from the middle of the pack.

"No, of course not," Shaw fended off the suggestion, but realised that he was better handing over without further ado to Reason, who breathed a sigh of relief. The nerves about his own performance had been supplanted by far greater anxiety about Shaw's inability to withdraw from the limelight.

He cleared his throat a second time.

"As Superintendent Shaw has just indicated, we now have three murders to solve, the victims being Mister Conrad Gilligan, Mister Daniel Young and Mister Alan Morrissey. All three men were shot and there are strong indications that each death was instantaneous.

We are exploring a number of possible theories in each case. At this stage it does not appear that the victims knew each other, which points to these attacks being unconnected. However, given some similarities, which may or may not be significant, we are keeping open minds over this.

On the other hand, the profiles of the three men are so divergent that it is highly unlikely that their deaths were linked by a common motive.

One of the concerning aspects of the situation is the lack of witnesses to any of the shootings. This probably reflects the times at which they took place and, in the case of Messrs Young and Morrissey, the locations too. In cases like this, it is almost unheard of for people close to the assailants, a partner, family member or friend, to know nothing of what they have done. I would appeal to those people to look into their hearts and do the right thing by getting in touch with

108

us. They should not hold back out of misplaced loyalty to the perpetrators of these terrible crimes, nor should they be concerned about their own safety. Anyone assisting us with our enquiries will be afforded the highest level of protection."

Reason continued to pick his way through the bullet points, using his margin notes to convert them into recognisable language. He didn't enjoy working to a script, but at least he was happy that he had neither omitted nor embellished anything that Owen had instructed him to say.

Shaw invited questions as the DI sipped on some water. Several hands shot into the air.

"Mmm," Reason said to himself, "I didn't expect their hunger to be satisfied by that."

"When I indicate that it is your turn," Shaw was saying, "please say who you are and who you represent."

For openers, Shaw pointed to someone he knew personally, having briefed Reason that this would mean they would have a tame start.

"Another Shaw misjudgement," Reason thought, moments after the selected journalist had got to her feet, "Carole Burke, Daily Telegraph. Detective Inspector Reason, you said that all three murders involved firearms. Can you confirm that the same weapon was used on each occasion?"

Reason's senses and sensitivity were thrown into turmoil and for a beat he felt rattled. Was it just the custom and practice to ask for confirmation? Why hadn't she been more direct and asked 'Was the same weapon used?' Perhaps her quest for confirmation indicated that someone had already told her something. Shaw, maybe? No, however much he might want to discomfort Reason, the Super wouldn't take this level of risk.

After a fragment of time that had seemed to him like an age, he responded, "No."

Carole Burke sought clarification, "Does 'No' mean that you cannot confirm this or that the same weapon was definitely not involved in all three murders?"

"I cannot confirm it," Reason said calmly. He didn't like lying, but he had shared Owen's view that it was too soon to let the SIG Sauer cat out of the bag.

"Or, presumably, deny it," Burke thrust again.

"No," Reason responded without hesitation.

Shaw winced. When Burke came back for more, his fear that his colleague had left himself exposed, proved well founded.

"So the same gun was used on all three occasions?" the journalist hurled her rhetorical question at the stage.

Reason remained calm, "You know that is not what I am saying. It's a matter of simple logic. If I cannot confirm something because I don't have all the facts at my disposal, it follows that I can't deny it either."

Shaw sighed inwardly, "Next question." He pointed to someone whom he vaguely recognised from television.

The latest interrogator got to his feet, "Jonah Standish, BBC News. DI Reason, when you *do* have all the facts," he spoke with a hint of a sneer, "and you then find that a single weapon *was* used, what conclusion will you be able to draw?"

Reason patiently explained that a single piece of information, however significant, would not alter the overall shape of the investigation. Until any case was solved, they had to be open-minded, keep a range of theories in focus.

"So three murders with one weapon might equate with organised crime, contract killings that sort of thing," Standish noted.

"We would have to remain alert to any possible explanations, however unlikely," Reason affirmed, while playing down the probability of the TV newsman's suggestion.

"Including wanton attacks by a psycho?" a voice rang out.

"Name?" the Superintendent said, sternly reminding Reason of his childhood encounters with teachers.

"George Smith, Daily Express."

"Can I remind you all that to make this conference both fair and manageable, we can do without people calling out?"

"Those who can't teach become police superintendents," Reason muttered.

Smith offered a theatrical apology to the podium and the hall, eliciting giggles from some of his colleagues in the press corps, before returning to his question.

"I wouldn't embrace or dismiss that possibility any more than all the others," the DI explained.

The next contributor was the author of the scandal mongering piece about Gemma Gilligan's supposed affair that had surfaced from the gutter a few hours earlier.

"As far as Conrad Gilligan's death is concerned, could there have been sexual connotations?"

"I don't think so," Reason answered, for once abandoning the 'keep open all possibilities' line.

The journalist asked him if he had read today's edition, which had carried some pretty convincing evidence, or, as many might say, ugly unconvincing garbage.

"I have to admit, it's not my paper of choice," Reason swatted the question aside, much to the mirth of the representatives from the broad sheets.

"Perhaps it should be," the tabloid man quipped, "then you might progress this case quicker."

Secure in the knowledge that Oliver Appleton's solicitors would soon be launching a suit against the tabloid, Reason made no comment. The little shit had already had enough of his time and attention.

From where Shaw was sitting it looked as if Reason was floundering. The Superintendent squirmed. He wanted to call time on proceedings, but had the sense not to activate the guillotine too swiftly, "We can take one more question." He peered out to the sea of faces and invited one of the local newshounds.

"Tom Redfern from the Gazette. With respect, people in Eastbourne aren't bothered about the number of guns and gunmen or even the reasons these shocking crimes have been committed. No, their main concern is their safety. We're on the verge of mass panic, with people scared to take their dogs for a walk, set foot into their own driveways or go for a ride in the surrounding countryside. They need to know that you will solve these cases soon, bring an end to the killing spree and restore order to the town. Can you give us something, anything, concrete to reassure us that you've got this under control?"

Reason knew he couldn't, not yet. They might only need one lucky break, an unexpected lead, a courageous witness and the case would fall into place. But that hardly constituted the substance that Redfern, the rest of the media circus and the general public craved.

For one of the few occasions in the years they'd known each other, Reason had reason to be grateful to Shaw, as the Superintendent stepped in. "As DI Reason has made clear throughout the conference, we are continuing to pursue several lines of enquiry. We understand and share the public unease and are deploying additional resources in order to expedite the investigation. I appreciate that most of you are motivated to support our efforts. I am committed to rewarding that support with as much information as we can share, but, you will need to be patient. We will not share intelligence just to satisfy your readers' and viewers' curiosity and in the process risk the investigation. Now, ladies and gentlemen, that brings to an end today's conference."

"One swallow doesn't make a summer," Reason said to himself, but it was good to know that Shaw could occasionally be more useful than a chocolate teapot.

As the technicians packed away their equipment and the hall emptied, Tom Redfern swam against the tide towards the podium. He reached its hem just in time to catch Reason before he disappeared from view.

"Detective Inspector," he called.

Reason and Shaw both turned around. "It'll have to wait," the Super snapped, "DI Reason needs to get away."

Reason overruled his senior colleague. He intuited that remaining on good terms with the local press mattered more than ingratiating himself with the nationals. He gestured Redfern to join him.

"I'll see you back at the station for debriefing," Shaw said.

"OK, sir," the DI replied with genuine and novel deference, "I won't be long."

During their brief conversation, Reason formed a positive impression of Redfern. He appeared younger than his twenty three years, almost baby-faced, but what stood out from this rather podgy countenance was the sharpness in his eyes. Until you got to know him, you might think you were in the presence of someone who was either crazy or consumed an alarming amount of stimulant drugs. Even when standing as still as stone, Redfern's eyes sparkled and darted incessantly. Although this feature was undeniably remarkable, the greater impact on Reason was the reporter's genuine concern for his fellow man and woman. The DI didn't doubt that Redfern was ambitious, but it was evident that in the current climate he was driven solely by a concern to see tranquillity returned to the town, where he had been born and bred, leaving it only for three years at university.

"If I can assist in anyway, Detective Inspector, don't hesitate to get in touch." He handed over his card, then added modestly, "I know you'll go straight to the editor if there's an angle that you want the paper to emphasise, but she's not your best bet if you need some extra spade work for which you lack the resources."

Reason kept his doubts to himself and thanked Redfern politely.

114

24

By their standards the debriefing was akin to a mutual appreciation society between Shaw and Reason. The former pointed out a couple of points at which his junior colleague could have been more guarded but, on the whole, thought that he handled the trickiest moments with aplomb. "Until Redfern's soliloquy," Reason conceded, "which I found impossible to refute and was more than a little relieved when you intervened. You managed the ending very skilfully."

"Years of experience at bullshit, eh?" Shaw winked.

"That wasn't bullshit and you know it."

Shaw felt pleased that Reason knew it too and had acknowledged it.

"What did Tom Redfern have to say after I left?"

"Not much. He offered to help us if he could. Of course, he's got very little clout at The Gazette, but he's very much on our side. I like him and he may be useful, although it's not yet clear how."

"Be careful, Steve," Shaw counselled, breaking new ground in terms of familiarity.

"I will."

"You know where I am if you want to run any concerns about him past me."

Reason was genuinely touched by the offer, "Thanks, I may well take you up on that."

25

The salient points of Reason's press conference appeared on both national and regional television news that evening. The killer watched and fumed.

"Well, Detective Inspector Plod. That was quite a performance. Keeping an open mind are you? Not ruling out anything at this stage? How wise that sounds but what does it really mean? Absolutely nothing. You know nothing so embracing everything is your only scant consolation. You're clutching at straws, tilting at windmills and pissing against the wind all at the same time. Multi-tasking on a grand scale!

Do you even know that the same gun killed all three miserable bastards? You couldn't confirm or deny it. Very clever. Clever that is when confronted by some imbecile journalist, but I'm not fooled. You must at least know about the weapon by now, but how much does that really help you? No witnesses? I could see in your eyes that that was no lie. No motive? Perhaps it's time you stepped up your checks on dangerous inmates of prison or psychiatric institutions. In the hands of private contractors, many of those places are sieves. And you mustn't rule out those who have done their time, apparently reformed their ways or been cured. You've got quite a reservoir of human excrement to wade through there. Good hunting, Defective Inspector Plod and be patient, for you'll have to wait a while before you receive any help from me."

26

In the absence of anything meatier to get their teeth into, newspaper editors hastily filled the space that they had reserved for a detailed update on the Eastbourne murders. For the broadsheets this meant lengthy analyses by a parade of criminologists, psychologists, weapons experts and retired senior police officers turned security consultants. Inevitably, the tabloids went for a more lurid, less thoroughly researched approach.

"PSYCHO ON THE LOOSE!" screamed one headline, developing that particular shard of speculation from the previous day's media conference. Somehow the policy of keeping all avenues open had become translated into a string of spurious claims and in this particular rag, police were almost certainly looking for a homicidal maniac who had escaped custody on his way to a secure psychiatric hospital. Warning its readers not to approach anyone they suspected of being dangerous, the paper took them on a trip down memory lane with recollections of past cases, the Yorkshire Ripper, Hungerford and Columbine included.

A rival tabloid took its readership off in a similar direction to that followed by Dawson as he tried to cover the tracks of his near indiscretion. Under the banner "KILLED FOR KNOWING TOO MUCH!" the most likely explanation for the deaths of Young and Morrissey was that, independent of each other, they had discovered something about Conrad Gilligan or his murder that had put them in mortal danger. Any reader wishing to donate one pound fifty pence to a premium phone number could vote for their favourite from a list of possible things that the second and third victims had found out about the first.

Not to be outdone, Ed Warren, who had penned the exclusive on Gemma Gilligan's alleged but unsubstantiated sex romps in the sun, made sure that his paper remained in the gutter press category with an exposé of the growth of perversion in modern Britain, the inference being that the three deceased men may have been known to each other through a network of sado-masochists or paedophiles.

27

Isobel Perry had inherited two corpses from the resident pathologist, but decided to work backwards from Morrissey's, the one she had owned from the outset of her involvement. In her line of work, there were three distinct phases to her examination, firstly finding and stating the obvious, then a more detailed search for more obscure pieces of data, then generating some plausible explanations for these to enable the police to move forward with *their* part in the unfolding drama.

She had spent the last two days locked in on phase two, carefully and repeatedly going over the victim's body, the clothes he was wearing and any possessions he had about his person. This was painstaking labour, but the stage of the process she enjoyed the most, in anticipation of some hitherto unnoticed jigsaw shape leaping out at her. Today that excitement still seemed far off as she re-examined the dead man's navy blue fleece. Her intense focus hadn't wavered since she had commenced her scrutiny shortly after six a.m. Of course, this was not her contracted start time, but, driven by the concern she felt for the people of Eastbourne and in almost equal measure for Reason, she had committed herself to hours of unpaid and unnoticed overtime. Isobel's eyes were beginning to hurt with the sustained level of concentration that she had demanded of them, "You must take a breather and get some breakfast," she told herself aloud. Her stomach rumbled gently in agreement, but its sound was drowned out, "Hello, what have we here?"

Without taking her eyes from the microscope, she fumbled around on the desk until her right hand came upon a small pair of tweezers, which she brought to rest next to her discovery, gently poking it like a suspicious child might an unfamiliar type of food on its plate. Very carefully, she picked the find up and dropped it into her left palm. She peered closely at it, before securing it once more in the grip of the tweezers and placing it into a small, clear plastic bag. A black strand floating on the sea of connected navy fibres, possibly a hair. If so, not Morrissey's; his was a consistent silver grey. Isobel's stomach protested again. Torn between the need to eat and the desire to carry on her investigation of the specimen, she gave into the former, "I'll work better on a full stomach," she told herself as she locked the tiny evidence bag into her desk drawer.

Doctor Perry was not the only interested party to arrive early for work. Reason decided to be in the office before any of his colleagues arrived. A swift perusal of the morning's papers vindicated his decision. Several of the newspapers, and not just the tabloids, had given his media conference a rough ride and none had awarded a rave review. By being in situ when the rest of the team clocked on, he could be ready to field their responses which he anticipated would be a cocktail of anger, disappointment, sarcasm and resilience and he was in little doubt about which of these ingredients would be in greatest supply.

For once he was glad to have misread the situation. He did come in for a little ribbing including one wry observation that his performance had even made Shaw look good, but on the whole the other detectives were supportive of the line he had taken and the way in which he had dealt with 'those arseholes from the press' who didn't have a clue. "I expected that little tosser from the local rag to be more helpful," Dawson chipped in with his backing.

"I thought Tom Redfern was one of the very few among them who had an honourable motive for being there," Reason contradicted him, "He seemed genuinely bothered by what residents are feeling."

"From what I saw," another colleague said, lending his backing to Dawson, "he was as determined to give you a hard time as the others, more so, come to think of it."

122

Reason stood his ground, "Well whatever we think of our friends in the media, we mustn't let that deflect us. If we don't make some headway soon, we can expect a whole lot more grief and it won't only come from the press."

DCI Owen concurred with him before launching into her daily briefing, "We've had a development overnight that is probably significant."

The background noise that had greeted her moments earlier suddenly evaporated and the entire room fell completely silent.

"The Border Agency has advised us that one of Karpov's entourage has visited the UK recently."

The gathering emitted a collective sigh of disappointment. How was this significant? Karpov's associates regularly cropped up here.

"Not one of the usual suspects, the white collar crew," Owen continued, "but one of his personal bodyguards, a particularly unpleasant character, called Valery Boronin." She clicked the device that she was holding in her hand and Boronin's image was instantly projected onto the screen behind her.

Staring out into the room, Boronin's face dripped menace. Although not au fait with anything but the most basic computer techniques, Reason wondered whether someone had airbrushed an extra dose of malice into the photograph. The Russian's face, which filled the frame, was built on square jaws, pronounced cheekbones and a flat forehead, the depth of which was accentuated by his fair hair being crew cut. This was what Reason called a 'lived in' face and the profuse scar tissue was a window on what sort of life it had been. The overall impression of danger and violence was capped by Boronin's battleship grey eyes which looked as if they could pierce the armour plating of any vessel.

"He acquired a criminal record in his youth and served time for assorted acts of violence. Europol believe he is behind a few unsolved instances of people being threatened and or hurt following disagreement with Karpov, or when about to give evidence against him, but nothing's stuck so far."

"When did he enter the UK? Before the hit on Gilligan?" Dawson asked hopefully.

Owen was sorry to disappoint him, "Boronin arrived on the day that Danny Young's body was discovered and left the day after Alan Morrissey's murder."

Dawson's was not the only astonished face in the room when he interjected, "Left? He's got away, just like that?"

"And the wankers at the Border Agency have only decided to tell us now?" another Detective Constable, Vinnie Stockbridge piped up, " Why the hell didn't they give us the heads up when the bastard entered the country so we could keep tabs on him?"

To the accompaniment of mutinous murmurs, the Detective Chief Inspector explained that there had been a breakdown in communication between Europol, themselves and the UKBA. When there was a hiatus in their tracking of Boronin, colleagues on the continent had not predicted that he would surface this side of the channel and it was only when he was back on their radar at the end of a Eurostar journey from London to Paris that they had confirmed his recent whereabouts.

"So much for cross border co-operation!" Stockbridge said angrily, "We're going to have a lot of egg on our faces when it turns out that he was Morrissey's killer."

Reason, who had stood calmly and quietly to one side of the room during this exchange, now spoke, "What odds are you offering, Vinnie?"

Stockbridge looked bemused.

"You seem very confident that Boronin's in the frame for one of the killings. As you're so sure, it must be worth two to one on. Shall we say your two hundred pounds against my hundred?" He held five twenty pound notes up.

No response.

Reason put his money away, "I thought so. None of you has properly assessed the likely value to our investigation of the snippet about Boronin."

"Quite," Owen said.

"I'm afraid I'm including you in that, DCI Owen," Reason responded, "Talking about this as probably significant has raised expectations that have backfired. Why? Because you haven't calculated the probability before giving your opinion. In that respect you and DC Stockbridge are as bad or as good as most of the media people I met yesterday."

Owen's face reddened with angry embarrassment. Damned man was right, of course, but she would have something to say about his attempt to publically humiliate her.

A ripple of excitement spread through the team, a couple of whom smiled. One whistled audibly.

"Cut the crap, boys," Reason snapped, "I'm not doing this as some form of early morning entertainment for you, so don't wet yourselves in expectation of a display of DCI baiting. What I'm trying to get across is that jumping to conclusions about Boronin's appearance is the lazy option. Let's take a step back and see if we can come up with a rational judgment of the latest piece of information."

Reason proceeded to throw out questions and observations.

Who thought Boronin killed Gilligan or Young?

No-one.

Why not?
Because he hadn't been in the country.

Correction. We know that he hadn't entered the country through official channels. What if he had arrived somewhere obscure, by helicopter or boat?

Wasn't Reason trying to rule the Russian out of one murder rather than pinning all three on him?
Laughter.

Reason reminded them that they couldn't afford to remain pre-occupied with the obvious.

And if Boronin *had* killed Alan Morrissey but not been in the country days earlier, how could they explain the gun as the common link?

There was a suggestion that someone known to Boronin had committed the first two murders and passed the gun on to him.

Was it more or less likely that Boronin had been involved than that the killer of the Gilligan and Young had also murdered Morrissey?

126

Driven To Murder

The consensus was 'less likely', but Karpov's man had the right sort of profile.

And as for motives?

Silence and head scratching.

And the continuing lack of connection between the three victims?

Reason had made a mental note to pursue the question of the receipts when he could next break free from the incident room.

In the meantime he was happy to have re-engaged their curiosity and to have weaned them off merely being pulled along by simplistic explanations. He had just challenged them to suspend the absurdity of Boronin's entering the country illegally to commit two murders while coming and going through customs for the execution of Morrissey ('As he couldn't have taken the gun out with him, where might it be?'), when a phone rang at one of the desks towards the back of the room. Dawson, who was standing nearest to the desk, answered it, while Reason waited for resumption of his think tank.

"That was the pathologist, Doctor Perry," Dawson said. "She wants you to call her back as soon as the briefing's over. Sounds urgent, guv.'"

Owen was uncomfortable that Perry saw fit to bring her findings to Reason, but this wasn't the time and place to pull rank.

Reason let the briefing run its course, but his level of concentration dropped as he wondered what Perry had for him. "Don't you ever talk to me like that in front of the team," Owen hissed him once they had retired to her office to telephone the pathologist.

Reason's apology was tempered by his claim to credit for re-energising the team, but Owen was having none of it, "Don't waste your time trying to justifying your behaviour. You were out of order and you know it."

She gestured with her head towards the phone to bring their 'discussion' to a close.

"Thanks for 'phoning back' Isobel Perry's voice boomed through the speaker phone."

"DCI Owen's here with me," Reason advised, "it's more efficient that way."

"And I do happen to be the officer in charge of this investigation," Owen added with a knowing glance towards Steve, "What have you got for us Doctor Perry?"

The pathologist took them through the discovery of the black fibre.

"How unusual is that, though?" Reason was still in his challenging vein, "Surely we've all got little bits of alien material on our clothing?"

Perry could not dispute that, "But Mister Morrissey's fleece had been washed recently, possibly in the twenty four hours leading up to his death. I cannot be precise, but the presence of microscopic soapy deposits points that way. And as there's no trace of detergent on the fibre that's the odd one out, it must have found its way onto the fleece later on within the same time period."

 Owen was the next to speak, "Can you tell us more about the fibre? What sort of garment did it come from?"

"It's not from another piece of clothing, it's a hair."

"From his dog, maybe?" Reason conjectured.

"No, that's the first thing I ruled out. I did find a few of those, but this strand is no match for them. No, it's human hair."

"The killer's?!" Owen reacted excitedly.

"That's for you to find out," Perry answered, "I'm afraid my expertise doesn't extend that far yet, but, of course, the hair could be his."

"Thank you Doctor Perry," Owen gushed, "you may have just handed us our first crucial lead."

"You said 'his'" Reason interjected.

"Sorry?"

"When talking of the killer, you said the hair could be his."
"Did I?" Perry seemed a little flustered, "Yes, I suppose I did."

"So, you've been able to determine the gender of the owner of the hair?"

"Oh, I see what you mean now. No, we are not yet able to determine the gender from a single human hair. I just assumed that the killer was male. If there had been a follicle attached, I could run some tests to help determine gender, but all I have here is a piece of hair, not a complete strand."

"What about DNA testing?" Owen enquired.

"Again, we'd need some root cells and there are none present on this sample. I could try, but it's likely to be an expensive way of finding nothing new."

"I agree," Reason came in, "Our best bet is to re-interview those people closest to Mister Morrissey and appeal for anyone else to come forward who had been in contact with him forty eight hours before his death. We can ask for a hair sample from each of them. My hunch is that in the current climate anyone with nothing to hide will help us and if we can't match your sample to any of them, it increases the probability that the hair is the killer's."

28

With *real* detective work back on his agenda, Reason was reluctant to host another media conference that afternoon in order to broadcast the appeal.

"It's OK," Owen had reassured him, "I'll contact the television and radio stations in person and ask them to get some help. Do you think you can reach Morrissey's known contacts by the end of today?"

"With Dawson and two others, we'll soon have that part turned around. I'll take the samples straight to Isobel Perry and I'd expect her to establish whether or not we have a match before close of play."

Owen noticed his use of the pathologist's forename, but made no comment.

Once back in Eastbourne, Reason despatched Dawson, Stockbridge and a third DC, Tony Edgar, to talk to Alan Morrissey's neighbours again and obtain permission for samples of hair.

"I want to take another look round Mister Morrissey's apartment," he said heading towards Mrs Tovey's. Dawson caught his eye and winked surreptitiously.

"I'm assuming that collecting hair's beneath you, guv'," he smiled, "so do you want me to come with you to Mrs Tovey's and deal with the menial task, while you go to the Morrissey apartment?"

Reason thanked his junior and a couple of minutes later he was back inside the dead man's flat, where he retrieved the bundle of receipts from his jacket. Having already rearranged them so that the Gilligan bills of sale were on top of the pile, he started a slow trawl of all the rooms, seeing if we could identify the objects that were recorded on the sheets of paper in his hand. His search was complicated by both the extent of Morrissey's collecting bug and his own lack of knowledge of antiques. He adopted a strategy of starting with the painting, working on the premise that he knew what a painting was and, so long as it wasn't too abstract, he'd be able to figure out the subject matter. This approach yielded almost instant success as the 'post-impressionist painting, The Water Meadow, oil on canvas, after Seurat' had pride of place on largest expanse of wall in the lounge. Reason looked from painting to the receipt and back again. "So that's what four thousand quid buys you, is it?" Was this a realistic price, or was there a major discrepancy between price and value? As the transaction had actually taken place he didn't hold out a great deal of hope about Morrissey's collecting being a cover for something illicit.

The other three items proved harder to track down. Among a cabinet dedicated to silver objects, Reason found three goblets and lacked the expertise to distinguish which was 'hallmarked London 1778, Bateman'. Taking care not to put his finger prints on them, he took each out in turn and photographed it with his mobile phone. "Just in case none of them is the listed item," he said to himself.

He assumed that the extensive display of silhouettes included the one referred to on the paperwork, but without taking pictures of them all, he settled for a hunch that the one depicting the man with a wig and long, pointy nose was 'English aristocrat by Beetham'.

Each stage of the search had left Reason more perplexed and the final item 'A pair of early Kangxi vase, famille verte' priced at twenty thousand pounds was no exception. Of all his collecting interests, Alan Morrissey had evidently been most passionate about oriental vases, which occupied every available space on shelves, in cabinets and on the floor. The DI decided to call it a day. He was confident that the Kangxi examples were somewhere among the treasures and, as with the other items, he would have its receipt checked against its proper market value. Even if there were no discrepancies, he was left with an impression of wealth that was out of kilter with Morrissey's former profession. "If the Gilligan receipts are anything to go by the old boy's collection must be worth hundreds of thousands," he told Dawson when they caught up with each other.

The three constables' efforts had been as productive as Reason's. Between them they had gathered hair samples from the sixteen residents and a gardener who claimed to have had close contact with Alan Morrissey a day or two before he had met his untimely end. They stood before him holding up their clutches of clear evidence bags like a party of proud anglers. "The woman at number five gave me such a hard time," Stockbridge moaned, "kept banging on about this being an infringement of her civil liberties and the world being a better place if we concentrated on tracking down Morrissey's killer. There's no way she did him in, but *I* came close to adding *her* to the death toll. It was only when I explained for the third time that the penny dropped that this was a request for voluntary help, but I reckon the Chief Constable will be hearing from her."

"You deserve a medal for your perseverance," Reason smiled, "But I don't doubt that among the other sixteen, there'll be some who hadn't seen Morrissey for days, but want to feel they're involved in the action.

He relieved them of their trophies, making sure that each was labelled with the name and address of the donor. "Good job," he said in a pathetic American accent. He looked at his watch and sent his colleagues off for a late lunch with an instruction to head back to Lewes for further orders from DCI Owen once they'd eaten. "I'll run these round to the pathology lab and may catch up with you later. If not, I'll see you all at tomorrow's briefing."

Reason was relieved to find that Isobel Perry's work station was in a side room, away from the main space in which the pathologists examined the dead. He wasn't queasy about corpses; he'd seen a few over the years, albeit not with the recent frequency. But he was happier, if that was the correct word, looking at them in the context where they had been discovered. At the scene there was still an odd sense of life in and around them, probably associated with the fresh excitement at the start of the investigation. Here in the lab, on the slab, they were what a character in a Monty Python sketch had once described as 'completely dead', stripped of any lingering sense of their humanity. That was it; he wasn't spooked by the cadavers in this setting, but disinterested because he was unable to make much of them in here, which is why he had always admired the pathologists' skill in unlocking new clues.

In Perry's case it wasn't only her work that he admired. As she welcomed him, he again noted her attractive features, which he had appreciated even when he had encountered her in a blue plastic cocoon. She looked even better in a crisp white lab coat. "Shit," Reason said to himself, "am I starting to get a thing about women in uniforms."

"Have you got the samples?" Perry broke into his thoughts. He handed the seventeen bags over.

"Quite a haul," she remarked.

"Yes, but I hope there'll be several more once the DCI's appeal has gone out on the early evening news shows. How long do you think it will take to analyse this lot?"

Perry quickly scanned the bags, "Not very long. I'll have completed my checks by the end of the afternoon."

"Great. I'm going to follow up a couple of other things, then I'll come back to see if you've found anything."

Stopping en route to buy a chocolate bar for lunch, Reason parked the car in the police station yard and made the short walk along Grove Road to Eastbourne library where he bought some time on a computer. He could have had internet access for free at the station, but at this stage wanted to keep the antique cards close to his chest. He'd come clean once he was sure about the significance of the receipts.

One by one, his hopes of finding something untoward, particularly Gilligan substantially undercharging, were dashed. Whatever his own view of the amounts of money Morrissey had parted with for things that Reason wouldn't give house room to, it was clear that he had paid the going rate. That still left the unanswered question of where the former teacher's wealth had come from. To be certain that he had not been involved in criminal activity, they would have to delve into his financial history. It had to be done though Reason had a hunch that the paper trail would only confirm what everyone had said, namely that Alan Morrissey was a thoroughly decent man.

29

Doctor Isobel Perry was nearing completion of her analysis of hair samples when Reason arrived back at the lab. She gestured for him to sit down while she continued to scrutinise the strands. It was clear that she wanted to work without interruption. This suited Reason, who took advantage of this brief down time to observe the pathologist more closely. While he was fascinated by her intense level of concentration, his thoughts and eyes soon turned to her physical attributes.

After a few minutes she lifted her gaze from the microscope, stretched and started to massage her stiff neck muscles.

"And the winner is ..." Reason said expectantly.

"Sorry," Perry responded, turning to face him, "None of these matches the stray hair on Alan Morrissey's clothing."

The DI was disappointed but not surprised, "Perhaps we'll have more luck tomorrow."

Perry pulled a disapproving face, "So, this is about luck, not my professional expertise, is it?"

"I didn't mean to suggest..."
She cut him off, "I'm only teasing you, but if you do need evidence that I will do a thorough job, I've been here since the early hours of this morning double checking Gilligan's and Young's clothes to see if there are any of these hairs on them."

"And as you'd've told me the moment I walked in the door if you'd found some, I am quietly confident that you drew a blank."

"Despite what people say," Perry continued to tease, "you're actually very good at your job, Inspector Reason."

"You too," Reason replied.

He decided to strike while the iron was staring to warm up. "I don't know about you, but I haven't had much to eat today."

"I rarely do."

"Then how about we celebrate today's lack of success with an early evening meal?" he probed, "Unless you already have something lined up."

"As it happens, I do."
His face dropped.

"Home delivery pizza and a beer," she continued, "You can join me if you want."

"I'd like that."

She told him her address in case their vehicles became separated in the drive across town.

With his superior knowledge of the area, Reason stopped following her after a couple of minutes and took his own route to her flat which was in a block a stone's throw from the sea front towards the Grand Hotel.

He was waiting smugly by the steps up to the front door when she pulled into the kerb side.

They had mounted the steps when Isobel turned to him, keys in hand. He suspected that she was going to issue an injunction about physical contact when she announced that she wanted to make something clear,

"I am not responsible for what you're going to find in here. It's a holiday let, arranged by your force for the duration of Erickson's absence. I don't want you jumping to wrong conclusions about my sense of design."

Isobel hadn't exaggerated how awful the flat was. The furniture seemed to have been determined by a random number generator and the colour scheme appeared to be the work of a gang of blind painters.

"I told you it was grim," she said, tuning into his thoughts, "but for the time being it's home." She didn't wait for a response but headed for the bedroom. "While I take a shower, can you ring for the pizzas?"

She continued to throw her order back towards the lounge, "The leaflet is on the coffee table. I'll have the nine inch vegetarian with a side of coleslaw. There's no landline here, so you'll need to phone on your mobile. Beer's in the fridge."

Reason perused the leaflet to the sound of Isobel's shower running.

"Thin crust?" he called to her, but his voice was drowned by the water jet.

He followed his instinct and ordered thin crust vegetarian for them both. 'When in Rome ...'

Reason sat on the sofa nursing his beer and mulling over the day's findings. Hardly ground-breaking but he knew that ruling things out was an integral part of finding the answer to criminal puzzles.

Up to this moment, he hadn't realised that from his current vantage point he could see into Isobel's bedroom through the door which she had left ajar. Aware of a movement he looked up to catch a glimpse of her as she let her bath sheet fall to the ground. The favourable impression he had formed of her in her various working clothes was instantly superseded by the sight of her naked body.

A moment later and she had disappeared from view to get dressed, but the image remained branded on Reason's visual memory.

"You got me a beer too?"

"Of course. You said you were looking forward to one."

"How considerate."

"A quality that is only matched by my brilliance," Reason boasted jokingly.

"And your modesty," she added, before picking up the bottle, chinking it against his and sliding to the floor where she propped her back against the sofa.

"I haven't got any contagious diseases," Reason said, wondering why she had chosen not to sit next to him.

"That's a relief, but I am not so sure about the sofa. I haven't run detailed tests yet, but it doesn't look very healthy. Judging from the stains, it's probably harbouring myriad nasty germs."

Reason launched himself forward and immediately regretted the manoeuvre as his coccyx met the hard floor and a geyser of beer shot from his bottle and hit him in the face, "Shit that hurts!"

Isobel laughed, "Well, don't expect anyone in here to kiss it better! I'll fetch you a towel."

When the pizzas arrived, Reason insisted on paying.

"I guess I'll have to defer to the hunter gatherer in you," she said, giving up her protest, "especially as you know how to spoil a girl."

They returned to the floor and ate in silence for a while, their lack of words a reflection of their ravenous hunger.

"When I first met you ..." Isobel said as they neared completion of their meal.

"You couldn't believe what an amazing person I was," Reason chimed.

"I thought you were a complete shit," she corrected him "which is a pity because you're not bad-looking."

"From your intonation, I'm hoping that there's a 'but' clause on its way."

"And...," Isobel emphasised the word to demonstrate that she might not be as transparent as he thought and paused, "the more I see of you the more I'm growing to like you."

Reason thought of the momentary vision of her naked body, "Me you too."

"And what do you intend to do about it?"

Reason hesitated. He was out of practice with women. He doubted whether he had ever been able to read them well and since his divorce he had lurched towards illiteracy. Then, a thought: what had he got to lose?

He put his pizza box down, twisted towards her, and leaned forward to kiss her. Her lips parted and their tongues engaged.

30

"Come on, lazy bones," Isobel poked the still fast asleep Reason and blew the steam from the freshly ground coffee towards his nostrils.

They had gone to bed early but gone to sleep late and, unused to such a demanding partner, a night of passion with Isobel had left Reason shattered.

"What time is it?" he asked drowsily.

"Eight," she said, "I assume that you've got to be in Lewes for nine."

"Shit!" Reason was suddenly back in the land of the living, "I'm supposed to be there for eight thirty."

"Oops. I've got to get going too. It doesn't look as if you'll have time for breakfast, but grab anything you fancy."

"Again?" Reason smiled, "You're insatiable Doctor Perry!"

"Just make sure that the door shuts properly. It can be a bit stiff .. and don't even think of that as another innuendo."

She kissed him lightly on the lips, "I enjoyed last night."

"Then we must do it again sometime soon," he grinned.

"Steady, let's not run before we can walk."

"Bloody hell, Isobel, if that was walking, even a jog could kill me."

As soon as she had left, Reason swung into action. A quick swig of coffee, a burnt mouth, clothes on in a flash, a perfunctory brush of his teeth ('I'm sure she won't mind me using her brush') and out to his car.

Once inside, he consulted his mobile. Two messages on his voicemail, both from DCI Owen. "Message one, seven nineteen p.m. yesterday: Hello Steve, just calling to see how you got on with Doctor Perry. If you get this before ten give me a ring, otherwise I'll catch up with you in the morning."

Bleep.

"Message two, eight a.m. today: In the middle of an investigation like this it would be helpful if I could contact you twenty four/seven. I assume that you're on divert because you're driving. Don't you have a hands-free set?"

Reason took a deep breath, collected his thoughts then dialled headquarters. Moments later he was through to the DCI.

"Sorry about missing your call last night. I'd switched my phone off while I was with Doctor Perry and forgot to put it back on again afterwards." The truth, of sorts.

"What about this morning?" he echoed her irritated question, "Same problem, didn't take it off divert when I went to bed."

"It isn't good enough," Owen reiterated.

"Mea culpa," Reason responded humbly, "Do you want me to fall on my sword or will you just kick me off the case?"

"Don't be stupid as well as careless, Steve. How long before you get here?"

Thinking on his feet, Reason came up with a plausible response, "Change of plan. I'm going to swing into the Eastbourne station to see if there's been a response to the appeal. Whether or not there's anything to report, I'll call you before setting out for Lewes."

"You should have consulted me."

"Sorry, again. It's no excuse but what Doc Perry came up with has left me distracted." Also true.

"Which brings me back to the message I left yesterday," Owen snapped, "How did things go with her?"

"Marvellously, bloody marvellously," he said to himself.

"No match from yesterday's collection," he said to her.

"From Stockbridge's feedback, I didn't think an elderly neighbour was responsible for Morrissey's death."

"We've ruled out the gardener as well, "Reason tried to put a positive spin on Perry's work "and although I agree that anything else would've been a shock, a process of elimination is our best bet at present."

Owen grudgingly conceded the point and said that she wanted a more detailed debrief as soon as he reached the incident suite.

Reason let out a huge sigh of relief and stretched. His unshaven face stared at him out of the driver's mirror. He didn't have time to do anything about that or his rather dishevelled appearance. "I'll get away with it at the local nick," he said to himself, "but I'll have to take a detour home before I next see Harriet Owen."

He hadn't factored in that Shaw might see him at the Eastbourne station, but the superintendent was in reception talking to the officer on desk duty when he walked in.

"Good God, Reason!" he exclaimed, "You look a state. I hope you haven't been drinking heavily."

"No sir, I was up till early this morning, going over and over a few things." Another version of the truth. "I fell asleep fully clothed, overslept and dashed straight here." A little more economical with the truth this time.

"Shouldn't you be in Lewes?"
"I've squared it with the DCI. She agreed that I should call in here to see if anyone's come forward in response to the appeal."

Shaw confirmed that three shopkeepers had been in touch with fairly accurate timings of Morrissey's visits to their establishments. "I've got a uniformed officer on his way to take more details and collect hair samples and I was just about to speak to someone who's called in person. But now you're here you had better take over." He turned to the constable at the desk, "What was the young lady's name?"

"Emma Partridge, she's in Interview Room Two."

Reason entered the room to find a very slim, blonde woman in her mid-twenties, dressed in a tee shirt and cut off white jeans. She was shaking like a leaf. "Good morning, Miss Partridge. I am Detective Inspector Reason. Can I get you a hot drink? You look cold."

"No, er, no thanks. I'm not cold, just ... just frightened. That's why I didn't get in touch straight after the man was murdered up at Holywell. I was worried that if I said something I could be next."

Reason joined her at the table and took out a note book, which appeared to startle her more. "Just so I don't forget key points," he said, "nothing formal, nothing for you to sign. Now Miss Partridge, I understand that you're here in response to the appeal on radio and TV for people who saw Mister Morrissey during the day or two before he died."

"I saw him on the day he died," Emma Partridge blurted, "I was probably the last person to see him alive."

"The penultimate person," Reason corrected her, "assuming that you're not our murderer."

"What, oh, er, yes, I see what you mean. I was nearing the end of a training run and I saw this man and his dog walking towards me."
"Mister Morrissey?"
"Yes, but I didn't know his name at the time. Then, as I got closer, I caught sight of someone else off to my right."

"Can you describe the person?" Reason was at pains not to attribute a gender in case he planted ideas into the woman's head.

"He was thirty yards away, maybe more and I was running downhill, avoiding rabbit holes so I didn't get a long look. When I passed the man with the dog he'd disappeared."

"So you're sure it was a man?"

"Yes, well, I'm fairly certain. He was wearing a light grey hoody and jogging bottoms."

"Old, middle aged, young?"

"I'd say he was young."
"Because he was wearing a hoody?" Reason was concerned that the witness was building up a picture based on resemblance to previously formed views rather than on what she saw.

She promptly disavowed him, "No, because he moved so nimbly. I don't know if it was because I'd seen him, but he moved very quickly out of sight."

"That's very good, Miss Partridge. Can you estimate the age of the person you saw?"

"As I've already said, he was some distance away, but he was definitely younger than.." she bit her lip.

Reason smiled, "You were going to say younger than me, weren't you? OK, so we have someone well under thirty years old, then." His smile turned to laughter and she joined in.

"That's it," his inner voice was speaking, "help her relax and she'll be more focused, more able to recall things accurately."

"You've been very helpful and I don't want you to think that I disbelieve what you've said, but I need to ask some more questions that may feel as if I'm challenging you. It's to help make sure you've not missed anything and that I've got the right picture through my thick copper's skull." More smiles. "OK?"

"Fine."

"You made a link between youth and nimble movement, but the two aren't mutually exclusive. What's to say that you weren't looking at a very fit person of my age or older?"

"Nothing I suppose," Emma said, "it's just that my overall impression was of a younger person. There was something about his stature as well as his movement."

"Go on."

"I know what you're saying about older people who work out and keep themselves in trim. I see plenty of them at the gym, but they don't look like this person did. I almost want to say he was petite but that's an adjective for women."

"Yes, the feminine of the French adjective for 'little'. I know it's unusual, but I suppose there's nothing to stop us saying a man is petit. That's if you're sure it was a man."

"As sure as I can be from that distance and moving at that pace."

"Can you put a percentage on that?"

"Seventy, maybe seventy five per cent. That's pretty sure isn't it?"

"Yes," Reason agreed although in his heart of hearts he knew that this equated with uncertainty and inaccuracy.

Reason thanked her again and pushed his chair back from the table and stood up.

"Wait," Emma blurted out, "Aren't you going to make arrangements for my protection?"

Reason sat down again, "You're still afraid?"

"Wouldn't you be?" she cried.

"Honestly, no I wouldn't be."
Emma Partridge couldn't believe her ears, "What?! I saw a killer shortly before he struck and he almost certainly saw me, so how does that not put be in danger?!"

Reason maintained a supreme calmness in his response, trusting that the anxious woman would be infected by it, "At times like this, it's difficult to remain rational, we can even end up convincing ourselves that emotional reactions are rational. The time when we're least able

to take a step back, is the time when we really need to do so.. Will you let me try to ease your anxiety?"
Emma nodded.

"The first point is that we can't jump to conclusions that you saw the killer. It's no less pleasant, but the person you saw might have been a flasher, who was about to expose himself to you, when he saw Mister Morrissey and ran away."
"Ugh, that's gross," Emma grimaced.

"I agree, but not entirely unlikely. Over the years, we've had more reports of perverted behaviour in that area than we've had murders. In fact, Mister Morrissey was the first in *that* category."

Secondly, how many female joggers are there in the town?"
Emma looked bemused, "I don't know. Tens, a hundred, a few hundred maybe."

"You got a short look at the person from some distance. As he was in the act of running away, it's safe to conclude that he didn't get such a good look back. How confident are you that you could pick this person out from our collection of photographs?"

"Not very, I suppose."

"So, the person you saw is even less likely to pick you out from the small army of women runners that we have in the town."

"Unless he plans to kill us all, to make sure he's got me."

Reason raised his eyebrows as he looked her full in the face, "Now you really are letting your imagination get the better of you. However, I intend to take your concern seriously." He wrote something in his note pad and tore out the page.

"If you have the slightest concern that you are in danger, don't hesitate to ring 999 and quote this case number. We'll get someone round to you without delay."

Emma thanked him and apologised for being so silly.

"Don't be too hard on yourself," Reason said as he opened the door for her, "I really don't think you're at risk, but you've every right to be rocked by what's been happening recently, just like the rest of us."

It was after ten when Reason at last stepped into DCI Owen's office. She had a face like thunder.

"Can we get one thing straight, DI Reason?" she hissed, "I will not tolerate mavericks on my team. You may be the best detective on the planet, but you won't need to make a habit of doing your own thing before I kick you off this squad. There's no 'I' in team. Is that clear?"

Reason nodded. His temporary boss had every right to be displeased by the lack of consultation but the vehemence of her reaction had taken him aback. Had she sussed that something might be going on between him and Isobel? Although unlikely, he knew that the combination of excellent detective skills with feminine intuition was likely to be explosive.

"Anyway, now you have condescended to join us, have you got anything new to report?"

Reason fed back on the response to the appeal and Emma Partridge's contribution in particular.

"How do you rate her as a witness?"

"If I'm honest..." he immediately regretted using the expression which suggested, with some justification, that he might not be, "not very highly. I encouraged her to talk through what she saw but didn't take it down as a formal statement."

Owen frowned and Reason explained, "It's not yet clear what she was a witness to, other than Morrissey taking his dog for a walk and someone moving away from them."

"But her description of a young man in a hoody might point to an acquaintance of Danny Young's."

"Mmm," Reason briefly pondered how to put her down gently but drew a blank, "I don't blame you for clutching at straws. We're overdue a real breakthrough, but it's too big a leap to assume that the person Emma Partridge saw had any social connection with Young."

Owen ignored him, "You got a hair sample?"

"Yes and uniform have taken it round to the lab, but as Miss Partridge is blonde it's only going to be another case of elimination." "Hardly worth the detour, then," Owen sighed signalling the end of the debriefing as far as she was concerned.

Reason had other ideas on that score and held his ground, "There is something else."

"Oh yes?" Owen was curious.

"I found a link between Morrissey and Gilligan...."

Owen's demeanour immediately changed from sullen to animated, "Great, and it is ....?"

"..not significant in itself, at least, not yet."

He talked her through the discovery of the receipts and the accurate match between them and the value of the items they covered. She concurred that this indicated an above board commercial relationship between the two men and also shared his intrigue over the scale of Alan Morrissey's wealth.

"You think the bona fide purchases were a smoke screen and that Morrissey was holding valuable antiques for Gilligan as a medium for laundering Karpov's dirty money?"

"No, I don't," Reason disappointed her, "because we don't have enough to go on yet, but I may well do if we can't come up with another explanation for Morrissey's treasure trove."

Owen picked up the phone and dialled through to the main incident room, instructing whoever picked up to investigate Morrissey's finances.

"As far back as you have to until you find sizeable sums of money!" she snapped before putting the receiver down and turning back to Reason.

"If you think I'm going to thank you for this new angle, you've got another think coming. It may be an important piece of the jigsaw, which would be much needed good news, but the way you went about getting it is decidedly bad news. That's two examples of maverick behaviour, DI Reason, two too many. Watch your step or it will be three strikes and out."

For Reason, the rest of the day involved yet another tortuous office-bound re-examination of what the team had thus far. Not much, but he knew that without retracing every tiny step they ran the risk of leaving something important overlooked. Some of his colleagues were keen to get the process over and done with as swiftly as possible but Reason insisted that their deliberations were punctuated by coffee breaks and lunch, "We'll be sharper immediately after those breaks."

"In that case," Stockbridge had piped up, "why don't we spend the rest of the day at a nice curry house and get bladdered? According to your theory, we'll be shit hot detectives tomorrow morning." This interjection helped lighten the mood and they were all soon back on board.

31

Shortly after lunch, Isobel Perry phoned with the latest on the hair sampling. Reason had advised her to ask for the DCI whenever she called, but with Owen tied up with a series of lengthy calls of her own Dawson passed the receiver to Reason.

"Good afternoon, Doctor Perry."
"Not half as good as last night," she whispered huskily, then hoped to hell that he didn't have his end on speaker phone. As her comment wasn't greeted with loud cheers and laughter, she guessed she hadn't just made a huge mistake.

"What have you got for us?"

The pathologist reported that a further eight people had come forward with accounts of contacts with Morrissey but none of the donations provided a match. Having examined the control sample again and again, she was convinced that it had been cut, which might explain the lack of root, although she added the rider that of the hundred or so hairs that most people lose each day a proportion are fragments.

Reason thanked her for the additional information but had no intention of launching a salon-to-salon enquiry.

"Let me know if I can do anything else for you," she said reverting to her sexy voice.

When DC Edgar returned from his pursuit of Alan Morrissey's financial affairs, his body language communicated dejection.

Reason had learned not to hope for outcomes, so he had kept an open mind about Morrissey's wealth, but that didn't stop him sharing in the disappointment at Edgar's news.

"The bulk of his fortune came from inheritances," he flipped over his notepad, "a wealthy maiden aunt left him half of her estate about twenty years ago, then he received a smaller but still substantial sum on his father's death twelve years ago. Finally, having worked for nearly forty years, he got a six figure lump sum from his pension fund when he retired."

"Bloody teachers get a good deal, don't they?" moaned Stockbridge.

"Yes," Reason responded wryly, "theirs is almost as good as our pension scheme." He turned back to Edgar, "Thanks for your spadework, Tony."

"It's a pity I didn't find anything useful."
"On the contrary, you have significantly reduced the probability that Morrissey was tied up with Gilligan in fraudulent activity."

"But I thought that we were desperate to find that link."

"Only if it actually exists. If we're not open to the possibility that Morrissey's only relationship with Gilligan was legit, we'll end up deluding ourselves."

Unlike Reason, who was pleased that Edgar had helped challenge Owen's default position of a Gilligan-Morrissey axis of criminality, the rest of the team continued their review under a gloomy cloud.

When the sun at lost broke through, it came from an unexpected direction. After her lengthy absence in her office, DCI Owen came into the main office unnoticed. "Gentlemen," she called out over the hum of their activity, "I have some news for you."

Everyone stopped work and gave her their undivided attention.

"I have just been advised that, in response to lobbying by the Chief Constable and colleagues at the National Serious Crime Agency, Europol have arrested Valery Boronin on suspicion of the murder of Alan Morrissey."

The room erupted with excited cheers.

Owen stood silently with her right hand held up, but it was some time before she regained control over the room.

"I will be travelling to Paris tonight to join in the questioning of Boronin." She flourished some banknotes, "In my absence I entrust tonight's beer kitty to DC Stockbridge." She handed him the cash before continuing, "and DI Reason will take temporary charge of the investigation on this side of the channel."

She dismissed the squad early and they tumbled out of the office, making arrangements for car parking, taxis and sleepovers as they went. "Not joining us, guv'?" Dawson asked as he noticed Reason lingering. "I'll join you in a while, just text to say which pub you're in."

When all was quiet, Reason made his way along the corridor to the Owen's office. She looked up from hastily gathering papers into her briefcase, "Steve, I don't want to seem rude, but I've got to dash."

"I know, but it would be remiss if I didn't tell you about today's other development."

"Be quick then."

"We've established that Alan Morrissey acquired all his wealth from legacies and pension funds. There's nothing suspicious about his finances, ergo nothing to indicate a criminal link with Gilligan or anyone else."

"But that doesn't mean for certain that he wasn't involved in something fraudulent, does it," Owen snapped.

"No, but the probability..."

"Listen, Steve," Owen placed her hands firmly on the desk and leaned forward menacingly, "since you joined us, no, since before then, I feel that you've been determined to undermine this operation and my authority. You've constantly questioned the connection between the three murders, despite the common factor of the gun used. If Boronin *did* kill Morrissey and the others, perhaps you'll have the humility to apologise for your behaviour." With that she picked up her jacket and briefcase and swept out of the office.

Reason watched Owen disappear from view and shrugged, "If Boronin *wasn't* involved I wonder if she will apologise." It seemed extremely unlikely as he recalled, not for the first time, the expression 'Hell hath no fury like a woman scorned'.

Although he was keen to see more of Isobel, not that there was much he hadn't already seen, Reason decided that it would be bad for team morale if he didn't catch up with his colleagues in their chosen watering hole. En route he called Isobel to explain that he wouldn't be seeing her.

"I don't remember us making an arrangement," she said in mock anger, then in a more reasoned tone, "I don't want either of us to be too keen or demanding. It will only spoil things."

Reason quipped that he recalled her being very demanding the last time they'd met, but appreciated where she was coming from. "OK if I give you a call tomorrow, though?"

"More likely I'll call you..."

"Great!"

".. with the latest hair report."

"Oh, I see, of course."

"Now, run along and have some fun with your chums. It sounds as if you've got reasons to celebrate."

"I'm not so sure," he frowned, "it's early days."

"Which is exactly what I said."

The night with the team went much as Reason had predicted. Too much beer followed by too much whisky and an awful takeaway on his way to the railway station, where he caught the train to Eastbourne shortly before midnight, then a cab back to Hailsham. To his sober embarrassment the next day he recalled having to ask the taxi driver to pull over twice, so he could throw up.

32

Exercising his new authority over the team, he had agreed to a later than normal start. "With Boronin under arrest, it's likely to be quiet at our end," Dawson had suggested. Reason did not divulge his thoughts on that matter but had no doubt that after a night on the sauce they would all need a quieter day, but not an inactive one.

"The fact that DCI Owen is following up on the Boronin angle doesn't mean we can just sit around twiddling our thumbs and nursing our hangovers," he announced at the briefing, his words thumping inside his skull.

"Any volunteers for fresh air?"

Everyone's hand shot up.

"I thought so. Well, we need to check out Danny Young's associates. I know this wasn't deemed necessary earlier, because the weapon used provided a connection to Conrad Gilligan, but we've got a new angle to look at."

He provided a description of the slight, dark-haired young man whom Emma Partridge had recalled.

"I know we wouldn't usually expect co-operation from Danny's family and friends but they will be keen to see his killer brought to justice and that might swing them onto our side a little."

Stockbridge questioned the point of checking this out, "If the DCI comes back with a result, we'll have been wasting our time."

"There are too many 'ifs' at the moment," Reason countered, "but if you would prefer to be cooped up in this stuffy office doing paperwork all day...?"

Stockbridge waved submission and was sent on his way as part of the three-man group.

The shift ended with Reason still clinging onto his belief that ruling several things out could be as helpful as ruling one thing in. He would have preferred to have secured some sort of result ahead of Owen's return, but his colleagues' pursuit of the Danny Young network was taking longer than he had expected. He rationalised that a 'nil' return from that line of enquiry would confirm his doubts about the strength of Emma Partridge's account. Besides, there was always tomorrow.

His thoughts were interrupted by the ring tone of his mobile on the passenger seat beside him. He hoped it would be Isobel. Checking in his mirrors that it was safe to stop, he turned on his hazard warning lights, pulled in and picked up.

"Hello, Steve."

Owen! She was clearly agitated. "Is it OK to talk?"

"Yes."

"Things have hit the buffers over here and I'm on the way back to the airport. I'll need us to meet early tomorrow to figure out next steps."

Although he wanted to know what exactly had gone wrong, Reason knew that she wouldn't say anything more over the phone, "What time?"

"I'll be in the office at six thirty so let's make it seven, at the latest. That will give us enough time to draw up a plan before the troops arrive."

162

33

To say that Reason wasn't exactly thrilled at the idea of getting up at five thirty was an understatement, but DCI Owen's call didn't take much reading between the lines, so this was going be a vital and extremely difficult meeting. He wondered when the last time was that he'd gone to bed early, then realised it was only forty eight hours ago. "Pity Isobel isn't with me tonight," he thought as he pulled the duvet over his shoulders, "although I'd probably not make it in before ten if she was!"

Owen was showing all the signs of her manic trip to France. Had she been able to sleep in what little time was available, she would've been very tired. As it was, she had spent a sleepless night, endlessly torturing herself with replays of the day's events and what now lay ahead.

"Thanks for coming in like this. I really appreciate it."

"You look done in," Reason said sympathetically, "can I get you a strong coffee?"

"In a while, maybe, thanks," she smiled wanly, "once we've started the ball rolling."

"It's in your court and my racket is at the ready."

She gestured to the more comfortable chairs in the corner of her office and when he was settled, she quickly put him in the picture.

"The long and short of it was that Boronin had a full hand of alibis. We were ready for that of course and confident that they wouldn't hold water. My equivalent in France was sure that with the amount of time we'd been granted by the magistrate, we'd be able to chip away at the wall of bullshit that Boronin had built around himself. Our first knock-back was over his official entry into and departure from the UK, either side of Morrissey's murder. He claimed to have had an appointment with a consultant oncologist in Harley Street to examine a possible tumour, all paid for by Karpov, in recognition for his years of loyal service. The words had hardly left his lips and we were onto the Met to check it out. Not without difficulty, because the consultant wanted to hide behind patient confidentiality. The threat of being charged for obstructing the police in such a high profile case was enough to break his resolve. It seems he was more concerned about his own reputation than anything else. If that was the good news, the bad was that he confirmed Boronin's appointment and advised that the security camera at the clinic would remove any remaining shadow of doubt. It was physically impossible for him to have killed Morrissey and been thirty minutes early for his appointment.

While this was being verified, we had a go at Boronin over the other two killings. This looked more promising, because he was reluctant to say where he was on those days. He appealed to the French investigators as men of the world to understand that in certain circumstances you had to defend the honour of a lady even if it didn't look good for you.

She noticed Reason's expression.

"You heard me right, Steve. There we were interviewing a Russian oligarch's nasty Neanderthal henchman and he tried to delicately cover his tracks with a sensitive tale of illicit love. It was weird, almost amusing. I didn't believe a word though our continental cousins played along with it. If he expected them to understand his situation, he could trust them to be discreet in pursuing the matter. All he had to do was give them the woman's name.

Boronin expressed disappointment at their lack of empathy. As a matter of principle, he would not divulge her name. Carpentier, the senior of the two French officers, seized on this, accusing him of inventing this woman in the absence of a real alibi. As Boronin was not forthcoming, we would figure it out for ourselves. He didn't expect Mister Karpov to be too happy to be informed anonymously that his most treasured employee had been screwing his wife.

Boronin went crazy and had to be restrained. If they told Karpov this, *he* was a dead man and the French and British police would have his blood on their hands. Carpentier said he would sleep better knowing that the world was rid of scum like Boronin at which point the Russian's lawyer protested. And then it went from odd to completely surreal. Boronin instructed his lawyer to calm down, whispered something to her and she promptly got up and left. Once she had gone, Boronin dropped his bombshell. His affair had been with Karpov's daughter, Katarina. Evidently, she was bored with the succession of eligible and smooth young men that he father wanted to pair her with and decided that the best form of rebellion was to have a bit of rough on the side. Boronin implored Carpentier to follow this up with the utmost discretion, which he did. Three hours later, his alibis all stacked up, Boronin slipped through our fingers like sand."

"I'm really sorry," Reason said softly when she had finished her account.

He had not expected her reaction to his genuine empathy for a fellow detective whose main lead had gone cold, "Are you, Steve?" she asked sceptically. "I thought you'd be quite happy that I've returned empty handed from my little shopping trip to France."

Reason was bemused, "I don't get you."

"Oh, come off it, Steve. Playing Mister Innocent doesn't really suit you. You know damned well that you'll be getting the case back."

"Woah!" Reason raised a calming hand, "I can understand that you're pissed off about Boronin and you're also knackered, but you're wide of the mark if you think I'm revelling in the case stalling. I want *us* to nail the killer and I don't care who leads the investigation."

The DCI was apologetic, "I'm sorry, Steve. I had no right to have a go at you, but, if I can set my frustration to one side, it will probably make sense if the top brass do separate the murders from the joint operation with Europol."

"We'll cross that bridge when we get to it," Reason responded thoughtfully, "In the meantime, we need to decide what direction we're going to travel in next. And, no, Harriet, that wasn't a jibe about your trip to Paris," he added before Owen had a chance to react.

At the ensuing briefing, Owen received much needed support from the rest of her regular squad, who both shared her dismay and appreciated the effort she'd made to progress the case. Watching Dawson's facial expression, Reason could see that his side kick was far less impressed. "When you've make it up to the top of the greasy pole, Peter, perhaps you'll know how she feels," he said to himself.

For the rest of the day the team was in a state of suspended animation. The collapse of the path towards Boronin as the likely murderer had left uncertainty about the future focus of the permanent Serious Crime squad detectives, for whom the three murders now seemed of diminished importance. In Owen's absence, summoned along with the Assistant Chief Constable to London, for an urgent review of the Karpov enquiry, Reason did his best to keep his colleagues engaged, but only Dawson remained at his usual level of keenness.

Driven To Murder

The mood wasn't helped by the fact that Stockbridge's team had returned empty handed from the previous day's reluctant engagements with Danny Young's associates.

"Either they know nothing or they aren't prepared to share what they know," Stockbridge complained, "It amounts to the same thing. Zilch!"

"God, being around this lot is getting me down," Dawson confided in Reason.

"I'm pleased to see that you have such abundant empathy for your fellow officers, DC Dawson," Reason said sarcastically.

Dawson said he knew that it was no fun to have an investigation knocked back, but in his view they ought to pick themselves up and get back on the horse.

"Don't overlook how much there is at stake for the DCI and her team. Oh, they'll soon get over losing the murder cases if that's how it pans out, but going for Boronin at this stage was a high risk gamble, which may have set back the wider operation on the Karpov network. In similar circumstances, even you might be feeling down, Peter."

With some reluctance the junior detective accepted the need for sensitivity around the other members of the team and was greatly relieved when two telephone calls in quick succession liberated him from the office's depressing stranglehold.

Firstly, DCI Owen, ringing to confirm her prediction that the Eastbourne murders were to be disconnected from the organised crime investigation.

Secondly, Doctor Perry advising that she had found a match for the stray hair on Morrissey's clothing. His heart pounding with excitement, Reason forewarned her that he was setting the handset to speakerphone to enable Dawson to listen in. "Don't get carried away too quickly," the pathologist advised, "The hair belonged to Danny Young."

Reason groaned, "A cock-up in the lab?"

Perry was very displeased, "Certainly not. I won't have you questioning the competence of the team here."

"Then are you trying to tell us that one of Young's hairs ended up on his killer and it was passed on when he killed Morrissey? That's a bit far-fetched," Dawson responded more loudly than was necessary.

"You're the detectives. It's for you to come up with a more plausible explanation, but just because the transfer I've described is statistically unlikely, it is far from impossible given the amount of hair loss that everyone experiences daily," Perry explained.

Reason thanked her, put the phone down and checked his watch. "I suggest you knock off a little early today, Peter. I'll need you back here at sparrow fart tomorrow, so we can take everything back to Eastbourne without putting Serious Crime's backs up."

Dawson was happy to be released. As soon as he had departed Reason was back on the phone to Perry, "I wondered if you were doing anything this evening."

"What have you got in mind?"

"Dinner. Italian again, maybe, but in a restaurant this time?" he responded, holding back a sizeable proportion of his thoughts.

"And afterwards?"

"A nightcap at yours?"

168

"No," she replied, briefly dashing his hopes before adding, "this time we'll go back to yours."

"Shit," Reason thought, "I'll have to tidy up," but he managed to keep his composure.

"In that case, it probably makes sense to eat in Hailsham. You might want to get a taxi, then you can have a drink."

Isobel Perry laughed, "How considerate, but I'll come over in my own car and, in case you're wondering, I intend to have a few drinks but not to drive home."

34

Reason was keen to find out more about the pathologist's latest discovery and she briefed him during the stroll from his house to the restaurant, "On the strict understanding that from the moment we get there, this visit is entirely social," she had insisted.

"Not unnaturally, we'd all assumed that the single strand of hair on Morrissey's clothing belonged to someone who was alive. Given my line of work, I'm professionally embarrassed that I didn't consider the possibility that it came from a dead person. All the time you and your colleagues were bringing in samples, I had the match lying on a slab just feet away. I hope the delay hasn't thrown things out for you."

Reason was quick to reassure her on that count, "Not at all. We weren't getting anywhere fast and knowing that the hair was Danny Young's helps confirm that the same person killed Young and Morrissey."

"I thought you already knew that."

"We knew that the same gun was used. Although logical to assume so, we couldn't be certain that it was the same killer. I suppose we still can't but your discovery has weakened any lingering doubts. Also given me some fresh ideas for the next news briefing, perhaps I can rehearse them with you."

"Sadly, no," Isobel shook her head as they stood by the restaurant entrance.

"Over a drink before we eat maybe?" Reason asked meekly.

"N-O," Isobel responded forcefully. "You'd better not be one of those awful men who pretends not to understand what 'No' means."

Much as he wanted to pursue his own and her thoughts on the implications of her finding, Reason found it easy to slip into the relaxed social conditions that Isobel had imposed. Isobel's ultimatum that she would get up and leave if he tried to talk shop created an opportunity for them to exchange pieces of their respective life histories, a transaction for which their last encounter had left no time or energy. She was a little annoyed to find that Reason had such a good memory when he brought up the subject of her apparent knowledge of gambling.

"I don't want to go into the gory details, Steve, but a few years ago I was living with someone for whom betting was a way of life. He liked to see himself as a professional gambler, you know, able to make a living out of it. For a while he had me fooled as well as deluding himself. Unless you count the City, there aren't many people who can make a successful career of betting. Anyway, to cut a long story short, he ended up owing a great deal of money to a great many firms, some of whom were willing to resort to unorthodox methods to get their money back. Although I wasn't threatened myself, I grew as concerned about my own safety as I was for his. I was on the verge of leaving him when he gave me a push by removing a sizeable sum of money from my bank."

"You didn't take it to the police?" Steve asked in amazement.

"No, he was well connected, from a so-called good family and I'm pretty certain they'd've taken his word against mine."

"What became of him?"

"I neither know nor care, although I bumped into his air-headed sister a few months later and she said she thought he'd gone to live in China."

Reason hadn't intended to tell Isobel about Rebecca and the children so early in their relationship, but taking a lead from her openness, he ended up giving a reasonably unbiased account of his slide into divorce.

Reason was in a mellow mood as they started out on their walk home, which Isobel had suggested when he had mentioned getting a taxi "It's not often this warm this late in the evening."

"I've missed you," Reason said both recalling the last time and in anticipation of what lay ahead.

"That sounds a bit too heavy for my liking," Isobel countered unexpectedly. "Let's just enjoy each other's company and not read too much into it."

Reason didn't know how to respond. Isobel filled the space, "And while we're on the subject of keeping things in proportion, I'm not in the mood for sex tonight. It's nothing to do with you, I'm just exhausted by the crazy hours I've been working and what I really crave is a good night's sleep cuddled up against you. You don't mind do you, Steve?"

"No," Reason lied, "I've been working flat out too and not sleeping well when I do get to bed."

"Good," Isobel smiled, "as long as we know where we stand."

They walked a few more paces, then she added, "And please don't spoil a lovely evening by trying it on when we go to bed. I need sleep more than anything else."

Within minutes of walking through his front door, Reason's famed skill at predicting outcomes lay in tatters. He had poured them both a whisky and joined Isobel on the sofa. Barely had the first sip slithered down his throat and her hand was stroking him through his jeans.

"I thought.." he spluttered.

"Wrong," she finished the sentence for him. "You know, Steve, I'm beginning to worry about you. If you're regularly as gullible as you've been this evening, I can't see you ever catching the killer."

"I thought we said no more talk about work," he smiled.

"It's a fair cop," she replied, squeezing his erection through the denim. She manoeuvred an ice cube into her mouth from her glass which she set down on the coffee table before deftly unbuttoning his fly.

35

Reason hadn't forgotten his agreement with Dawson to get over to Lewes early the next morning, but didn't expect the detective constable to appear on his doorstep. "I thought it made sense for us to go in one car, guv'" he explained, "I'm happy to drive."

Reason instructed Dawson to help himself to a coffee, while he got a few things ready, which was a euphemism for picking up Isobel's underwear from the lounge and quietly telling her to stay put in bed until he'd left.

"Are you ashamed of me?" she asked pretending to be hurt.

For once, he did read her correctly. He smiled, leaned onto the bed and gave her a long deep kiss.

"Or are you gallantly protecting a junior officer? That's it, you're worried that DC Dawson will be corrupted beyond redemption if he were to see me here like *this*" Isobel continued, throwing the duvet back to reveal herself.

"You're incorrigible," Reason whispered. He kissed her nipples and headed for the door.

"You can uncross your fingers," she said softly, "I'm not going to follow you downstairs."

After they had driven a mile, Reason noticed an inane, know-all grin on his colleague's face.

"What is it, Peter?"

"Nothing."

"Oh, I see. Aren't you going to share this particular 'nothing' with me?"

Dawson's grin grew bigger until he could no longer contain it, "Wasn't that Doctor Perry's car in front of your place?"

Reason tried to deflect the question, "God, you're in a suspicious frame of mind this morning. Do you know how many Volkswagen produced of that model?"

"Not a clue," Dawson responded, "but I think it's the only one with that particular number plate!"

"Bloody hell, Peter," Reason choked, "Have you ever thought about a career in CID?"

"I thought I already had one."
"And if you want to keep it, I strongly advise you to keep your observations to yourself."

"Isn't that going to make our brilliant teamwork difficult to sustain. If I can't share information with you..."

"Cut the crap, Peter. You know exactly what I mean."

"Your secret's safe with me, guv'. No-one else would ever suspect that you could pull someone that attractive."

"Watch your step," Reason chided, but he was unable to conceal his enjoyment of Dawson's back-handed compliment.

For the remainder of the journey, they reviewed the revelation about Danny Young's hair.

"Doesn't really get us anywhere," Dawson had started, before heading off Reason's impending correction, "unless you subscribe to the view that ruling possibilities out is the most important aspect of detection."

"Which I do," Reason said proudly.

"And don't we know it!" Dawson laughed.

With very little early traffic and the detective constable more or less staying within the speed limit, they were able to make Lewes in good time and, as planned, were ready to escape back to Eastbourne before nearly all their Serious Crime counterparts had arrived for work.

DCI Owen was the notable and, in the circumstances, unwelcomed exception.

"Slipping away like thieves in the night," she remarked as Reason and Dawson gathered the last of their files.

"I thought it would be better this way," Reason said uneasily, "given the rawness of feelings that some of the team might be experiencing."

Owen smiled unconvincingly, "Don't worry yourself on our account, DI Reason. I've got a team of hardened professionals here. They won't be crying into their cornflakes over the loss of one part of the investigation."

Reason directed Dawson to take the first consignment of documents to his car, "I'll be down with the rest in a couple of minutes," then shut the door.

"I appreciate the way you've gone about this, Steve," Owen admitted. "And you're quite correct that we're feeling a bit fragile, but passing the murder investigation back to you is the least of my worries. Of far greater concern is the damage that may have been done to the major operation over Karpov."

"But that's not down to you."

"It's not a question of responsibility, it's the agony of seeing months of work starting to unravel."

"Well, for what it's worth, if you think I can be of assistance, you know where I am," Reason said.

"I think you've got enough on your plate with a triple murder investigation," Owen nodded towards the box of documents, "but now we're not part of the same team, perhaps we can socialise again." She took a couple of steps towards Reason and smiled, but he didn't reciprocate.

"We'll see."

36

It felt good to be back in Eastbourne and once more in control of the murder investigation. Although the short spell with Serious Crime had opened Reason's eyes to the sort of resources that the big hitters at headquarters could command, he thought he would happily swap those material advantages for the greater freedom he enjoyed in his home nick any day. It hadn't helped that from the outset he had been at loggerheads with Owen's hypotheses, which too neatly fitted the views of those in higher command in London and on the Continent. He had her down as cleverer than that, so perhaps her motivation was to avoid rocking the boat in order to protect her career prospects. Reason terminated his own musings. What did it matter what he made of Owen's wider investigation? Now that he had regained ownership of his cases, it was all water under the bridge. As was his fledgling personal relationship with Owen, thanks to Isobel Perry's timely and beautiful appearance.

DC Dawson appeared at the door with the results of the search of Conrad Gilligan's luxury cruiser in Sovereign Harbour. "Clean as a whistle, I'm afraid, guv'" he said, having reeled off the list of substances that forensics had been asked to test for.

"And what do you deduce from that nothing?" Reason enquired in a manner that reminded Dawson of an inscrutable, oriental martial arts master in a B-list movie.

"That Gilligan had no involvement in anything shady?"

"Or?" Reason pressed him.

"That he avoided using his boat for dodgy cargo," Dawson added hopefully.

"Another possibility?"

"That he took great care to clean up after himself whenever he had carried something illicit."

"Good," Reason said, pleased that the junior detective had his thinking cap on.

"Whichever explanation is correct, nothing is still nothing," Dawson concluded.

"Don't forget, Peter that ..."
Dawson interrupted him, "Confucius, him say that the absence of one thing can carry more significance than the presence of a thousand others."

Reason grinned, "Confucius also say that if you don't piss off home right now, you will be leaving this building in a coffin!"

"I've still got some of my shift left," the DC protested.

"You've been putting in extra hours without pay, so you're due a break," Reason said, "and in your current mood if you stay here the only break you'll get will be of your neck. Apart from my command appearance in the court of the fourth estate, I'm finished for the day too."

37

"Good, another news conference. Up to the usual standard of entertainment, I hope, because there's nothing else worth turning on for. The Reason and Shaw Show. Watching the detectives.

I see you're still fumbling around for the light switch in an unfamiliar, darkened room, Detective Inspector. I know I have the benefit of inside knowledge, but I don't think the most ignorant of the general public really swallow this. So, you're looking for a Caucasian man aged twenty to twenty five, slightly built, five feet six to five feet eight, straight black hair and pale complexion. Priceless, a description of that little scumbag, Danny Young. Last seen wearing a grey hoody and matching tracksuit bottoms. So the bitch saw that much. Well, it won't do them any good. Those clothes are long since gone, but you and your colleagues remain as incompetent as ever, Reason. You couldn't catch a cold!

The Super's turn to speak. They've identified the gun. No, really?! That's hardly news, Superintendent Plod. Reason to believe it was stolen from a military armoury. Mmm, I was going to award you no points again, but perhaps you deserve a measly one out of ten for that snippet.

Not another Shaw reassurance. The world and his wife know you're doing everything you can. What they are having trouble with is how piss poor you are at it!"

38

Friday evening at last and with his next shift not until Monday, Reason sat on his sofa, whisky tumbler in hand, Isobel Perry's head resting on his lap. "Ready for bed?" she muttered seductively.

He looked down at her and smiled, "I just want to catch the news headlines, then your wish is my command."

The top story concerned the discovery of the bodies of a married couple in Derby. "Police have confirmed that the couple, believed to be in their forties, were shot, but at this stage are unable to say whether or not they are looking for anyone else in connection with the shooting," the newsreader advised. Her words struggled to break into Steve's consciousness, which was already filling with thoughts of more sex with Isobel.

"Oh what a night" Steve sang what little he could recall of the Four Seasons hit from 1963 while he rustled up breakfast.

Isobel groaned at his tuneless rendition, "No thanks, Steve," she pleaded.

"Too early in the morning, eh?"

"Too dreadful for words!" she retorted.

He playfully flicked at her backside with a tea towel as she turned the radio on, "It'll be good to hear someone singing in tune," she laughed.

Instead of music, she found the set tuned to a news channel.

"For more on the deaths in Derby, over to our correspondent, Jackie Upton."

"Can I switch programmes?" Isobel asked.

"In a minute," Steve replied.

"Police have just this moment issued an update," the reporter waved a piece of paper as she spoke, "confirming that they are looking for a third person in connection with the deaths of the couple, who have been named as Geoff and Marion Allen. The couple were both killed with a single shot from a hand gun."

Reason felt a shiver run down his spine. Was it just that the Derby murders had shaken him out of the sheer pleasure of Isobel's company and back into the reality of his own unsolved killings, or did he have a horrible sense that the same gun had done for the Allens as had despatched the three victims in Eastbourne?

Isobel immediately tuned into his mood shift, "Try to switch off," she said throwing her arms around him from behind, "you need this weekend to be one of wall to wall chilling, we both do," she soothed.

Reason sighed. "Same as it ever was," he said to himself, fleetingly remembering the impact of his work on his marriage and fearing that his first meaningful relationship in ages was under a similar threat.

In her heart of hearts, Isobel knew that he couldn't simply park up his work, especially a major case like this one, but she was determined to do all she could to take his mind off it.

She let one of her hands drop a few inches and started to fondle him, "Why don't we put breakfast on hold for a little while and go back to bed?"

"I thought you said you're hungry."

"I did and I still am, but not for bran flakes and toast."

184

As Isobel enjoyed a post-coital shower, Reason took the opportunity to make a sneaky phone call to Peter Dawson. Could he ask Derbyshire Police to let him know as soon as they had identified the weapon used in the Allen case?

"Yes, I know it's a big ask, but if I could do it myself I would, Peter.....Yeah, it's your weekend off, too. ... Great, I owe you..... Don't push your luck..... If there's anything before Monday text me."

Reason wished he could be frozen in the time of that weekend. Sure, his thoughts occasionally turned to the case; after all, he was a fallible human being, but for the most part he lost himself in Isobel. He couldn't recall such an enjoyable interlude. Those two days seemed to have everything: a walk in the country, lunch at a delightful pub, sex in the afternoon, a band at Hailsham Pavilion, Sunday papers with breakfast in bed, more sex, another walk, another pub lunch, sport on the box, inevitably interrupted by Isobel's hand and tongue. "I don't like football and I'm not going to let you ignore me for two whole hours!"

39

Despite his craving for more of the same, Reason's return to work didn't feel like a drag. In fact, he felt energised by his weekend, sharper than he had done for some time. Peter Dawson arrived at the station moments behind him. "Derbyshire got back to me yesterday evening. They've done well to turn this round at a weekend. I thought we wouldn't hear anything until today."

Reason was about to ask why the hell he hadn't passed the information on, but, whether or not his junior had intuited that he needed to be left alone, he was actually grateful that his pleasure had not been interrupted.

"Come on, Peter," anticipation coursed through Reason's voice, "What did they come up with?"

"A Browning."

Reason puffed his cheeks out, "For one dreadful moment I thought it was our old friend, the SIG."

"No, that's a small crumb of comfort for us."

The DI frowned, "A Browning? Isn't that a service weapon too?"

They hadn't been in the office for long enough for their coffee to cool to a drinkable temperature when the 'phone rang.

"Redfern, that reporter from the Gazette is downstairs," Dawson said holding his hand over the speaker, "he wants to see you. Shall I fetch him up?"

"Thanks, Peter."

"I'll be right down," Dawson advised the front desk.

He returned with Tom Redfern who was carrying a slim folder under his right arm. When Reason extended a welcome him, the reporter awkwardly shifted the folder to his other arm pit and shook the DI's hand.

Dawson offered him a coffee, "It's only from a machine, but it's drinkable."

Tom ordered a Cappuccino. Dawson pulled a face behind his back and walked out of the office in a camp fashion, making sure to resume normal service as soon as he hit the corridor.

"You seem very excited," Reason noted, "What have you got there?"

Redfern spoke while continuing to clutch the unopened folder.

"It's about the murders at the weekend... you know, in Derby," he spoke rapidly.

"Yes, I did catch the news, but I don't see what that's got to do with us."

"Well, when the identity of the couple was announced the names seemed vaguely familiar."

"Allen," Reason said, "isn't an uncommon name."

"I know but I recognised their Christian names too. I'd seen them in print some time ago, but I couldn't recollect exactly where and when, so I got onto our intranet to see what I could dig up."

He paused as Dawson re-entered the room, "One Cappuccino," he said placing the cup on the table with a laugh. "I know you'll think I'm stating the obvious but most drinks from that machine are indistinguishable from each other."

"Mister Redfern was just telling me about a possible lead on the Derby murders," Reason said.

"But..."

The DI cut him off with a hand gesture and Dawson sat down.

Reason turned back to the journalist, "Carry on."

"I *knew* I had seen the names before. Right there in my own newspaper, a few months back."

He placed the folder on the table and took out a newspaper cutting, which he handed to Reason.

Under the heading "CYCLIST DIES IN BLIZZARD" the DI skim read the account of a driver losing control on an icy patch and ploughing into a cyclist on Victoria Drive. The dead man ... local resident, Leonard Skinner. The couple in the car ... Christmas visit to relatives ... from Derby ... Geoff and Marion Allen. Pending outcome of inquest, police confident ... dreadful and unavoidable accident."

"Shit!" Dawson gasped, "So there *is* an Eastbourne connection."

"Excuse the pun," Reason said, "but we must be careful not to jump the gun. The weapon used in Derby was different and this may just be a coincidence."

Dawson was shocked by his boss's apparent loss of the power of deduction, "Yes, but ..."

Reason cut him off, "We'll certainly have to look into this further, DC Dawson, but we mustn't be blown off course by every puff of wind."

Without giving Redfern time to touch his coffee, he thanked him for his assistance and encouraged him to get back in touch if he came up with anything else. "I'd prefer you not to publish what you've found yet," he said as he saw him out of the station, "I don't want mass hysteria to take hold all the way from here to the Midlands. Of course, when it is OK to go ahead with the story, it will be your exclusive."

The reporter agreed to sit on his findings for a while and not proceed without consulting Reason but he issued a parting warning, "So far, it's only the three of us who know about the link, but if I can unearth it, it won't be long before other newshounds sniff it out. I don't want to hold this back indefinitely."

"Before you say anything, Peter, my performance was for Redfern's benefit. I'm on the same page as you over the Allens. I can feel in my water that it's no coincidence."

Dawson decided to play Devil's advocate, "Surely the different gun outweighs the fact that the deceased visited Eastbourne?"

"Maybe, but it's not uncommon for multiple murderers to have more than one weapon at their disposal."

Dawson picked up the press cutting that Redfern had left them, "So, you think we should start with Mister Skinner's family? Perhaps they didn't accept that it was an accident and wanted an eye for an eye."

Reason concurred that they had to be checked out, but wasn't optimistic. "If we thought we had trouble connecting Gilligan with Young with Morrissey, it's nothing compared to the puzzle we've now got."

190

His pessimism was well founded. Leonard Skinner's parents, who were his only relatives, were living out their retirement in a beachside chalet bungalow at Pevensey. They had adopted him as a baby when they were in their late thirties. Forty years of happy family life had been brought to a crushing end on that dreadful December day. There was not a hint of anger in their recollection, only a disabling hollowness.

40

"Given your miserable performance to date, DI Reason, I think you are due some assistance. But what does one give to someone who is floundering in a sea of his own ineptitude? A life belt? That would be fitting, but posting it would be a problem. St Jude on a silver chain? The patron saint of lost causes! That would be splendid; however, if I could find one, the risk of being traced would be unacceptably high.

No, this will have to do. Just need to come up with an appropriate mode of delivery.

Ah yes, let the train take the strain!"

41

The unattended package was noticed as the westbound coastal service neared Hampden Park. Within minutes of it coming to a halt at the platform, a major crisis plan had swung into action. Under the watchful eye of a police helicopter, a cordon sanitaire was thrown around the area either side of the tracks causing widespread confusion. With the exclusion zone stretching beyond the post office in one direction and to the empty pub on the roundabout in the other, the impact on local life could hardly have been greater. Residents, travellers, traders and shoppers were torn from their customary activity. Anxious parents and carers frantically tried to figure out how they would collect their children from school with their cars impounded. Within a quarter of an hour the road and rail networks had ground to a halt. A local church threw its doors open to any displaced persons, but there were few takers, the twin attractions of fine weather and unprecedented excitement winning most votes. Despite the scale of the potential threat, some people refused to be evicted from the area. Things turned particularly nasty at a bookie's where a group of punters became angry and abusive at being deprived of their right to lose money. The threat of removal by force did the trick, but the incident left a sour taste that would for some time adversely affect relationships between the police and sections of the local community.

"A parcel about the size of a shoe box, wrapped in plain brown paper" the train guard explained to the police officer taking his statement. "Didn't touch it, of course, but I could read the label from a safe distance. Addressed to 'DI Reason, Sussex Police'.

Reason and Dawson were soon on the scene, where they were greeted by the uniformed inspector who was in charge of the scene, "We're in luck, 33 Engineer have been on a job over at Rye and are already on their way."

Dawson looked quizzical.

"They're the bomb disposal boys," Reason said, turning back to his uniformed colleague, "but I'd prefer not to have to sit tight until they get here."

"If you're thinking of doing anything *without* them, forget it," his uniformed colleague said firmly, "We may be of equivalent rank, but I'm leading on this so you're under my orders until we hand over to the military. Have you got that, Steve?"

"Yes, sir," Reason responded in an exaggerated, respectful tone.

The next hour passed agonisingly slowly and the two detectives busied themselves by assisting uniform with the essential but mundane task of securing the area and ensuring that no-one was trapped inside the cordon.

The convoy of army vehicles sped into sight to a chorus of cheering by the crowd that had gathered just outside the cordon. The officer in charge presented himself to the uniformed inspector who in turn introduced Reason as the intended recipient of the package.

"Captain Roger Bentham, 33 Engineer, E-O-D" the military man shook Reason's hand. "Couldn't have worked out better for you chaps really. We had just finished with dealing with some World War Two ordnance along the coast when we got your call."

Reason didn't quite share the captain's optimism; he couldn't see how a bomb threat could ever constitute things working out well, but he wasn't going to quibble. Despite his earlier show of bravado he was pleased that the experts were on the scene. "E-O-D?" was all he said.

"Explosive Ordnance Disposal," Bentham said as he surveyed the scene, "You've done a good job so far," he said in a tone that Reason thought sounded condescending. "I'll take over from here."

"If at all possible, Captain, can you recover this without blowing it up?" Reason asked, a trace of anxiety in his voice "It could contain vital evidence for a major investigation."

"Oh, yes, I've been following your little local difficulty on the news," the captain remarked nonchalantly. "We'll do what we can, but if it contains explosives I'll have no option but to take it out with a controlled explosion."

He broke off to bark orders to his colleagues, one of whom lead a dog over to where Bentham and Reason stood. "Let Jerry take a sniff around, lance corporal."

"Yes, sir," the NCO saluted with his free hand and set off with the dog.

Bentham turned to Reason, "Springer Spaniel, you know, hence the name."

"He didn't respond, sir," the lance corporal reported back two minutes later.

"So, it's all clear?" Reason asked hopefully.

"Not so fast, inspector," Bentham retorted, "In our game you don't leave anything to chance. I'm going to send in the Cutlass for a second look." He waved to two other members of his squad who were tinkering with a small, tracked vehicle.

"It's out latest bit of kit," the Captain spoke proudly as the robot bomb disposal device. "Of course, I miss the Dragon Runner but this fellow can do so much more."

Reason didn't know the full extent of the machine's capabilities but he had seen footage of similar devices in operation and his abiding memory was that their main purpose was to blow things up.

"Can I repeat that it would be helpful if the package didn't end up in a thousand tiny pieces?"

"Heard you the first time, old chap," Bentham said, "and I'll repeat that I'm doing nothing, neither handling the bloody thing nor disposing of it until we've completed a thorough assessment."

With the assistance of the station's wheelchair ramp, the robot slowly made its way to the package. Each passing second seemed to become stretched as the remotely controlled machine fed back initial intelligence.

"No ticking," the unit's sergeant announced, briefly removing his earphones which were connected to the monitor in one of the unit's vehicles.

"Not on a timer," the Captain advised Reason, who was becoming unbearably hot in the protective gear that the officer had insisted on him wearing as a condition of being able to remain at the epicentre of the activity by the level crossing gates.

"I'm still not convinced that our best bet isn't to detonate the bugger and be done with it," Bentham continued.

Reason was beginning to feel desperate. He had great admiration for the bomb disposal team, but didn't like Bentham's apparent preference for 'route one'.

"I appreciate the difficulty of your decision, Captain," he tried to be placatory, "but the solution to the killing of three people may be at stake here."

"And the body count could increase a notch or two if we act hastily and the situation goes belly up."

"How about letting me have a look? After all, technically it's my parcel," Reason heard his own words and immediately doubted the wisdom of attempting reverse psychology in such a dangerous context. "Couldn't you mike me up and talk me through things?"

"Totally out of the question," Bentham reacted angrily, "this isn't a scene from some bloody movie!" Then, as Reason had hoped, his professional pride got the better of him. "If anyone's going in, it'll be me."

"I'd be happy to keep you company," Reason added without a tinge of irony.

"Also out of the question, inspector. If I assess that it's safe for me to inspect the item, I'll do it without the distraction of you crapping yourself a couple of yards away."

"I understand. Can we at least be in radio contact so you can give me instant feedback?"

"Again, no can do. For starters you're not authorised to have anything to do with my operation and secondly, I don't even want to hear my own breathing when I'm taking a shifty at the parcel."

Bentham headed off to the carriage and reappeared much sooner than Reason had expected.

"Sorry," he said, "I can't be certain that it isn't a parcel bomb, there's too big a margin of doubt with this one."

Reason struggled to disguise his dejection, "You did try and I appreciate that, I just don't like the thought of crucial evidence going up in smoke."

Bentham rubbed his chin thoughtfully, "I may have one more ace up my sleeve which could reduce the scale of your loss. As an alternative to detonation, we could try using the Cutlass's steel arm to smash into the parcel. If that doesn't set it off, we can be pretty damned certain that we haven't got an IED in there."

Reason was grateful but couldn't help muttering something about it not being a very scientific or precise approach.

Bentham was furious, "Listen, my men risk their fucking necks on a daily basis for plebs like you. I can do without your snide ingratitude. I've a good mind to blow the bugger up just to teach you some bloody manners!"

Reason offered a fumbling apology. The frustration and strain of his faltering investigation had got to him. An explanation, but no excuse.

Bentham accepted the olive branch and insisted that Reason remain patient, "This will take a while. We'll need to tape up the windows and erect some heavy duty screens to minimise the amount of debris if the parcel explodes. Then the Cutlass will have to manoeuvre the item away from the seat in order to get a good swing at it.

The Captain suggested that they retire to the control vehicle, where they could watch the robot's progress on a monitor. "I am using the word 'progress' advisably," he laughed, "because this will not be the most riveting TV you've seen."

200

Driven To Murder

True to its master's description, the Cutlass worked painstakingly slowly until it had finally dislodged its target from under the seat and nudged it to its final resting place against the closed door of the train's toilet.

In response to the sergeant's promptings the device jerkily got into position before the hammer on its hydraulic arm was brought crashing down onto the box, which crumpled and split under the force of the assault. No explosion, a relief to everyone. The robot's camera zoomed in on its handiwork to show a large hole in the package. Reason leaned forward and peered at the screen. The image became more sharply focused and revealed the contents, a hand gun.

"Just one final check, please sergeant," Bentham said over the robot operator's shoulder.

"Yes, sir," the operator responded as he carefully and skilfully manoeuvred the camera into the opening.

"No wires, sir," he said after further perusal of the monitor.

"Safe then?" Reason asked.

Bentham relayed the enquiry, "Sergeant?"

"How many points are you allowing me on this one, sir?"

"Ninety eight or below and we detonate."

"Ninety nine per cent certain, sir," the sergeant said assuredly. Reason noticed his smile, reflected in the screen.

"Decent odds," the captain concluded.

Reason could only marvel at the relaxed and swift which way in which they had calculated the chances. He was sure that this was not just for his benefit.

"You'd make an excellent bookie, sergeant," he observed.

"My dad was one," came the reply, "As a kid I often went with him to weekend meetings. That's where I got my head for probability."

Bentham told Reason that he could accompany him to the train on the strict understanding that he would follow any instruction without question. "There is one exception to that rule, Detective Inspector. If I say jump you ask 'how high, sir?'"

Reason said nothing.

"Good," Bentham carried on, "I'm glad we understand each other."

While life in and around Hampden Park was returning to normal, Reason headed back to Grove Road with his prize, having profusely thanked Captain Bentham and his team. He arranged for one of the force's forensics and ballistics experts to be waiting for him at the police station. "Having gone to such trouble to get this," he said, nursing the battered box on his lap while Dawson drove, "I don't want to let it out of my sight."

Ray Miller, a chubby, jovial-looking man in his fifties, was hovering expectantly outside Reason's locked office when the two detectives turned up.

"You shouldn't have done, Steve. It's not even my birthday," he joked as he followed them inside. "What have you got for me?"

Reason carefully prized the cardboard apart, then lifted the Sauer out, using his handkerchief to avoid leaving his prints on the weapon.

"Don't they teach you anything in detective school these days?" Miller quipped. "If you want to do things properly, you'd better put these on." He fished inside his silver equipment case and tossed a pair of surgical gloves to each of the officers. "The slightest trace of your snot on the gun and you're either in the frame for murder or in deep shit for having screwed up the investigation."

He waved aside Reason's protests that the handkerchief was unused, relieved the DI of the hand gun and commenced his examination of the piece. After each stage of the process he paused to inspect the weapon through a large magnifying glass and scribbled some notes down on a pad.

Dawson was astonished that he was resorting to such basic methods.

"I'd have brought my GX microscope if I'd known you wanted hi-tec, although as it's bolted to my bench at the lab that would be a bit inconvenient," Miller chuckled and gave Reason a knowing look about inexperienced colleagues.

"Joking apart," a position that Miller was notoriously unable to sustain for long, "after the preliminaries, I'll take it away for a more detailed analysis."

"I'd like to hold onto it for a while, Ray," Reason protested. "I want to get to know it better."

"Well," Miller grinned, "if you're taking it to bed with you, make sure it's empty and the safety catch is on."

"What can you tell us so far?" Dawson demanded.

"A man in a hurry, I see," Miller responded, directing his comment to Reason. "Well, gentleman, the provisional score is as follows. No prints that I can see and I'd stake my reputation on nothing showing up under the GX when you do eventually allow this baby to leave home. Whoever's handled this has taken great care not to leave their mark, more care than you did, Steve. They also know that each gun's got its individual signature, as a result of minor imperfections and variations in the barrel. This has been worked on with a file, probably a rat's tail, for several hours to wipe out the distinguishing features and for good measure the serial numbers have also been removed."

Dawson was curious, "Why would anyone go to that sort of trouble? We can safely assume that this isn't registered to a legitimate owner, so it would be bloody difficult to trace its history."

"Not if it *was* stolen from a military base," Reason offered, "NATO forces may not be good at accounting for its weapons in the flesh, but you can bet your bottom dollar, they'll all be individually listed on some clerk's computer. I don't know how long it would take, but I'm sure we'd be able to discover its last known whereabouts if we had the serial number."

"At least this confirms our suspicion that the killer is ex-Army," Dawson concluded.

"Or had an army connection, or simply bought the weapon several steps removed from its origins," Reason added.

"If we could get hold of army records, we could narrow our search down to servicemen who've left in the last year, maybe two."

Miller laughed and shook his head, "Do you know what their turnover is? I'll tell you, over twenty thousand people leave the armed forces every year. It would be like looking for a needle in a haystack."

Dawson refused to be put down that easily, "What if we focused on those who had received a dishonourable discharge, or been in trouble during their service?"

"Not forgetting the thousands who go off the rails after leaving the service, because they can't cope with life on the outside. I'll grant that your haystack just got smaller but the needle's still the same size!"

Reason, who had continued to inspect the box, brought the war of words to a close, by drawing their attention to a slip of paper that he had fished out with a pair of tweezers.

"Retired from Active Service" he read out the computer-printed legend on the paper, "A reference to the gun, the killer or both?" he wondered.

"Do you think this means an end to the murders, guv'?"

"No, Peter, sadly, not. More likely it's an indication of a change of game plan."

42

"I hope you enjoyed your present, Inspector. How will you play it at your next briefing? No doubt you'll claim great credit and tell your gullible public that this represents a major breakthrough in your investigation. But behind your weasel words and lying eyes, you'll know that your operation has foundations of sand. Quick sand and you are drowning fast. You'll need more than an untraceable hand gun to get you out of this mess.

Unimpressed though I am by your miserable efforts, I almost feel sorry for you. So I've done my civic duty and lent a hand. Yes, I'm feeling very public spirited at the moment, in just the mood to give you another piece of the puzzle. If you're as clever as you obviously like to think, you may have a hunch about this one as soon as you take delivery. And you'll be positively ecstatic to have your guesswork confirmed. But where will it get you? If past experience is anything to go on, not very far.

Enough of this idle chatter, I must get back to the business in hand. Excellent, the coast is still clear. Any time now. Yes, here she comes, right on cue. How can she tolerate that bland existence? Never mind, today is just about to become extraordinarily exciting for a change and she's going to get a great deal more than she bargained for."

43

"Peter," Reason said cautiously after a visit to the washroom where he had given his appearance the once over, "I think I'm overdue a haircut. Can you recommend a good barber?"

"We call them hairdressers these days, guv'" Dawson smiled, "Even most of the short back and sides brigade with their red and white striped poles seem comfortable with that title."

"It's as broad as it's long," Reason said dismissively.

"A bit like your hair then," Dawson couldn't resist having some sport at his boss's expense, "Where do you usually get it cut?"

"Nowhere, anywhere," Reason answered vaguely, "I usually drop in on spec while passing."

"Which isn't very often!"

Reason was growing irritable "OK, Peter. Are you going to help me or not?"

"Well, there's a good one in Willingdon Village. A friend of Heather's put us onto her."

"Willingdon Village? Sounds a bit flashy for my liking."

"Not at all. I can guarantee that Anji, the owner, will have a strong opinion on what's going to suit you, but I can also guarantee that you won't be left penniless and with a Mohican! Anyway, so what if it costs you a few quid. You can afford it and Isobel Perry's worth it."

"Who said anything about Isobel Perry? I just thought I should smarten up a bit, you know, as the lead detective on a case of such major interest."

Dawson smiled. Reason had lead dozens of investigations and he had never shown the slightest interest in his appearance. The detective constable handed him a post-it note with the hairdresser's number on. "This isn't one of your 'turn up and hope for the best' establishments, guv'. Anji's very popular and very busy. You'll need an appointment."

44

"Nice haircut."

Steve Reason looked up from his newspaper. Today he had decided to take an early morning break at Fiesta, in the hope that he might find fresh inspiration there.

Isobel leaned over the table and kissed him lightly on the lips.

"What are you doing here?"

"I'm delighted to see you too, Steve. I've just dropped some reports off at the station. I could've emailed them, of course, but this way I get to see you. Peter Dawson said I'd find you here."

"Time for a coffee?" In what looked like a synchronised move, he got to his feet as she sat down.

"Hot chocolate, thanks."

"Chocolate sprinkled on top?" the proprietor asked as Reason handed over the money.

"Oh, er, yes, I guess so," Steve answered tentatively.

"A heart?" the proprietor waved a silver template, smiled and nodded in Isobel's direction and, before Steve could respond, embellished the drink with a perfectly formed shape.

"What a lovely touch, you think of everything," Isobel smiled as he placed the mug in front of her.

"It wasn't my idea," Steve said awkwardly.

"It sounds as if you're embarrassed about our romantic relationship," Isobel stared darkly at him.

"No I'm not, it takes some getting used to, that's all."

"I can always pick up with one of the numerous other men who are vying for my affection," Isobel threatened.

Steve's face dropped.

Isobel's expression turned from a frown to a beaming smile, "I had you going there. I didn't realise that you were *that* insecure."

Steve smiled back and offered his hands across the table. Isobel accepted.

"I really enjoy being with you," he said softly.

"And me you too. I thought we might go for a Thai tonight, if you're free. I've come across a nice little place not far from the flat, in Carlisle Road."

"The Siam Orchid?"

"Yes, that's the one."

"Parking's not too easy around there," Steve said pragmatically.

"You can park near my place and this time make sure you bring a change of clothes and your shaving kit."

Steve squeezed her hands affectionately, "I'm looking forward to dinner already."

"And not just dinner, I hope," Isobel responded huskily.

"You hope correctly."

212

His unexpectedly romantic break was brought to an end by the ringtone on his mobile.

"Hello, Peter. Can't a man enjoy a nice cup of coffee in peace?" ... "Shit" ... "I'll be back inside two minutes."

He quickly got to his feet.

"Is there a problem," Isobel wondered.

"You could say that. We've got another murder on our hands. It'll save time if you come with me."

45

Dawson, Reason and Perry picked their way over the shingle towards the temporary shelter that had been erected close to the shoreline not far from the entrance to Sovereign Harbour. Inside, lying where he had been found by a council worker as she picked up litter was the body, later to be confirmed as that of Mike Jarvis. Evidently, he had gone night fishing and chosen a spot well away from any other anglers. As expected, his death had been caused by a single shot to the head.

"Any sign of the bullet?" reappearing outside, Reason asked the uniformed officers guarding the site, neither of whom he knew by name.

"Not yet, sir."

"Well, now we're here, I'd like you to undertake a proper search of the immediate area with DC Dawson. On hands and knees, working out from the shelter for a radius of about three yards in the first instance within this sort of range," he defined an arc with his outstretched arms. "Turn each stone over one at a time. I'll check the ground inside."

"My initial judgment is that he died sometime between five and seven this morning," the pathologist noted during her examination of the body.

"I'd plump for the earlier end of the range," Reason said, "while it wasn't full daylight."

As Perry continued to take notes, Reason tried to reconstruct Jarvis's encounter with his killer. "Seated on his canvas stool," he muttered to himself, "facing out to sea, turning to look up, ... let's assume somewhere around six feet ... so the angle could be ..." He made a slow chopping motion with his hand as he imagined the line between the dead man's head and the gun. He dropped to his knees and explored the small area of shingle between the body and the rear of the wind break. Nothing.

"I've got it!" Reason heard one of the uniformed constables call out.

"Don't touch it!" Dawson commanded, stepping forward with an evidence bag and donning a pair of latex gloves.

He carefully removed the projectile from its resting place and put it in the bag. Reason hurried to his side, "Show me exactly where it was."

Dawson pointed to the spot and the DI took a felt tip marker from his pocket and drew a rough circle on the stones surrounding the site. "Keep away from this spot, I don't want it disturbed," he ordered and scurried back to the Perry's side.

"What's your assessment of the distance from which he was shot?" he asked the pathologist.

Perry looked at the entry wound. Quite close, a yard at most?"

After a few moments' contemplation, Reason marked a larger patch of shingle five to six feet from the canvas stool and re-joined Dawson.

"When the body and canvas have been removed, I might wish to take a closer look at the bullet's likely journey."

"Isn't it straightforward, sir?" One of the uniforms spoke. "I mean, the killer was standing, the victim was sitting, the bullet passed through his head and ended up here."

"You're not quite ready for a transfer, son," Reason smiled, "There's a bit more to being a detective than the obvious. For instance, would you be surprised to know that the killer was almost certainly five feet

216

six inches tall, give or take an inch either way? Of course you would, because it's not obvious from what you've looked at. Now, if you want to make yourself really useful, close your mouth, get some more incident tape and enlarge the perimeter of the sealed off area. There are already too many people skulking around for my liking. I don't want Joe Public to get within fifty yards of the tent."

Dawson and Reason examined the bullet through the clear plastic bag. "Fancy a bet on this being a match for the one used on that couple in Derby?" the younger detective asked.

Reason declined the offer as he shared his colleague's hunch on this one, but didn't want to miss the opportunity to test Dawson, "That's a colossal leap, Peter. Are you sure you're not getting carried away by events? Do you plan to link our murders to every other one in the country?"

To his boss's satisfaction, the DC didn't rise to the bait. Instead he simply answered calmly, "The similarities in the modus operandi are reason enough to consider the possibility, guv'. It's just a matter of keeping an open mind."

Reason liked that. It was always good to hear junior colleagues replaying his sagely advice to them without a hint of sarcasm.

Isobel Perry joined them, "I've done all I can pro tem so I'll head back to the lab and await delivery of the body. I'll catch up with you later."

The greater expanse of blue and white tape that Reason had commissioned had the effect of drawing even more people to the scene. "So long as none of them cross the line, I don't care how many people come to gawk" he told the constables. "I'll send for some CSOs to help you out."

217

From the gathering throng, a familiar voice rang out, "Inspector Reason!"

It was Tom Redfern, "Can I have a word with you? It's very important."

Dawson intervened, "We've got nothing to say at present. You'll get your story like everyone else, when we're in a position to tell you anything."

"It's not that," Redfern protested, "I've been giving further thought to the thing we spoke about last time."

Reason noted and inwardly praised the care with which the journalist had chosen his words so as not to let any of the people around him in on the act.

"As you can see, Tom, this isn't a great time for me. Why don't you give me a ring towards the end of the afternoon? I'll be back in my office."

"I'll drop round."

"No," Reason insisted, "things will be too hectic. Much easier if we catch up over the 'phone."

46

Although they were no nearer catching the perpetrator, the spate of killings had instilled a sense of urgency in all branches of the service that Reason had not always experienced.

The swift collaboration between the ballistics analysts in Sussex and Derbyshire had confirmed Dawson's conjecture that in death the beach angler had something in common with a couple from the East Midlands, whom he had certainly never met.

Superintendent Shaw entered the office, a grave expression on his face. "I've been pulling a few strings to get access to the army's records of missing weapons," he said handing a document to Reason. "It makes grim reading."

Reason glanced at the list of nearly two hundred hand guns that were unaccounted for, either misplaced or stolen in the last five years. 'SIG' and 'Browning' accounted for the vast majority.

Shaw pointed out that this was only the British tally, "I'm afraid the Americans haven't been forthcoming about their losses, but on the strength of what happened in Iraq, we can safely assume that they run into the thousands, maybe tens of thousands!"

Reason left the station feeling depressed. Although his hopes of there being a record of missing weapons had been endorsed, it had brought no obvious advantage.

"Sorry, you've just missed him," Dawson said when he picked up the phone to Tom Redfern.

"Yes, I know what he said, but as you may have noticed, he's a little busy at the moment."

"I can't promise anything, he may have it switched off. Failing that, yes, I promise to get him to call you back first thing tomorrow."

The discovery of a fourth victim in Eastbourne and the possible connection with the killings in Derby meant that Isobel had little chance of enforcing her usual taboo about talking shop over dinner that evening, not that she didn't do her best to distract Reason. Her first tactic was to eulogise over the food in order to restrict his talk time, but there was a limit to how long she could maintain her monologue on the vegetarian satay, however good it was. When this approach ran out of steam, she resorted to the more basic strategy of slowly rubbing her foot up and down his leg, moving higher with each stroke. Having elicited from him no more than a contented smile and the promise that he would respond with interest once back at her flat, Isobel gave up and went with the flow of Reason's reflections on the latest developments.

"There's no need to apologise," Isobel said gently from the other side of the restaurant table. "You wouldn't be human, if you weren't distracted by the case. I don't mind you talking it through over dinner. Besides, I'm confident I can take your mind off things later."

Respite came in the form of the *Siam Orchid* filling up, rendering continued discussion of a major crime investigation inappropriate. They left soon afterwards and, although Isobel permitted Steve some more air time on the short walk home, it was on the understanding that once inside the flat, his attention had to be totally committed to her sexual needs.

220

She was true to her word and against the odds he had predicted he was able to get to sleep quickly and with a satisfied smile on his face.

Isobel was woken at two o'clock by Reason writhing in the grip of an awful dream. He was walking in a forest, when he came upon a broad clearing, to one side of which was a high mound of freshly disturbed earth. Beyond the mound he could make out a long trench. He approached and peered into it. There side by side were several bodies, each with a single gunshot wound to the head. He wanted to run but was drawn to take a closer look. Each of the corpses was of someone close to him, Rebecca, the children, his parents, Isobel, Dawson, and Harriet. Feeling the earth crumbling at the side of the mass grave, he staggered backwards and was instantly aware of someone standing between him and the excavated soil. The figure was holding a gun which was smoking. Reason slowly raised his gaze from the gun to the stranger's face. To his abject horror, the face he saw was his own.

He woke with a start to find himself bathed in sweat.

Isobel wrapped her arms around him, "It's OK, you're safe," she whispered, "try to get back to sleep."

She was soon sleeping soundly again, but for Reason the die was cast and he spent the rest of the night agonising over the investigation.

47

Part way through the next morning, the front desk called up to advise that Tom Redfern wanted to see DI Reason.

"Shit," Dawson cursed, "I meant to tell you that he phoned yesterday and I promised that you'd call him back." To mask his discomfort, the DC continued, "He said he had something important to tell you, but, if you want my opinion, I think he's just getting off on being near to such a big story."

Reason made it clear that on this occasion he didn't want Dawson's opinion and he sent him away with a flea in his ear to collect the reporter. "And make sure you apologise to him on your way up!" he called after his assistant.

Redfern was once more in a state of excitement as he shared the fruits of his most recent labours.

"Taking what I found out about the Allens, I've carried on searching through the paper's archives. Predictably, their road accident was the only reference to them, so then I started to work my way through the other victims. I wish I hadn't started with Conrad Gilligan, 'cause there's a story or picture of him in most weeks' editions stretching back over years. But in the midst of all the adulation, I came across his court case for dangerous driving."

"We know about that," Dawson butted in, "he got off."

Taking no notice, Redfern picked up the thread again, "I knew it might be a coincidence, but now I had a possible link. Both the Allens and Gilligan had been involved in some sort of incident while driving. When I checked Danny Young against this variable, lo and behold, he had a conviction for ...

".. driving while under the influence of drugs and alcohol!" Reason completed his sentence emphatically, "I don't yet know its significance, but you could be onto something, Tom."

"What about Morrissey?" Dawson asked.

"That's where I've come unstuck," the reporter admitted, "All I have on him is sporadic references to talks to the historical society or Women's Institute, that sort of thing."

Dawson felt exonerated from blame for forgetting to relay Redfern's message, "So, what you're saying is that you haven't found a link between the victims. Not quite the earth-shattering news that I expected from the urgency you expressed yesterday."

Reason, who still hadn't completely forgiven Dawson for his laxness, was more tolerant of the gaping hole in the reporter's findings, "I am really grateful for your efforts, Tom. Don't beat yourself up if it doesn't quite all fall into place. In that respect, we're no better placed than you are and you've given us something to think about."

He turned to Dawson, "When Mister Redfern has gone, I want to run Mike Jarvis through the computer with RTAs or driving offences as the focus of the search."

Then back to Redfern, "It would be really helpful if you could also trawl for Mister Jarvis in your archives, Tom."

"I don't know why you asked him to look as well," Dawson complained, "We'll have a result before Redfern's got as far as logging onto his system."

224

Driven To Murder

"I'm well aware of that, Peter, but he's really committed to helping and I want to keep him onside."

"There we are!" Reason pointed triumphantly to the screen a few minutes later, "Driving without due care and attention. It looks as if young Redfern really could be onto something."

"With due respect, guv,'" said Dawson resorting to an expression that heralded an absence of respect, "We can't just leave Morrissey out, like a discarded score in Olympic gymnastics."

"I agree, Peter."

"The fact that we've got nothing on him here means that Redfern's theory doesn't hold water."

"Which is why you're going to revisit the late Mister Morrissey's neighbours," Reason asserted.

"And with what purpose?"

"To get their thoughts on his driving ability."

"You are kidding, aren't you guv'?"

"Never been more serious. If you leave now, I reckon you can have the job done by mid-afternoon. That's an order."

Peter Dawson was nearing the end of what was proving to be the wild goose chase that he had anticipated when one of Alan Morrissey's neighbours finally had been forthcoming. "It doesn't feel right to talk ill of the dead," Emily Peacock had said, "but it would be remiss if I didn't tell you that Mister Morrissey was a dreadful driver." When pressed, she described him as very anxious behind the wheel and with a tendency to overcompensate. "I accepted a lift to the shops once, but never again. I was a nervous wreck by the time I got home."

To her knowledge and astonishment, he had never been in any serious accidents, "A bump here, a scrape there, a miracle that there had been nothing worse than that."

Dawson thanked her and decided to double-back on his trail. When presented with a critical view of their late neighbour, the source of which he was careful not to divulge, a few of the others came out of the woodwork and he returned to the station with an emerging and reliable picture of Alan Morrissey as an utter menace on the road.

"Excellent work, Peter," Reason exclaimed, after Dawson had reported back, "The missing piece in Tom Redfern's hypothesis."

Dawson remained less than completely convinced, "It still doesn't quite hang together for me. There's one hell of a difference between being a bad driver and killing someone on the road, either accidentally or through recklessness, too much for us to be able to make any categorical claims."

Reason agreed, "But I don't want to lose sight of the possibilities. For the time being it occupies centre stage on the board," and with that he added a few words, arrows and question marks to the Perspex display.

"Where next with this line then?" Dawson sounded tired.

"The DVLA, but we probably won't catch anyone this late in the day. I'll get onto them when they open at eight tomorrow morning. What time are you due in?"

Dawson reminded his boss that he was on leave the next day. He'd cancel it if Reason wanted, but on condition that the DI took the flak from Heather.

226

"No need for that," Reason said. "I can pursue it on my own."

"Then text me if anything crops up. I don't want to miss out on the fun."

Given his experience of bureaucracy, Reason didn't expect there to be much to report, "You just enjoy your day off. I'll set aside time to brief you as soon as you're back in."

48

With the list of the murder victims' registration numbers at the ready, Reason explained to the DVLA switchboard operator the nature of his enquiry and the need for him to talk to the most senior manager possible.

"Barry Jones," the manager introduced himself, just in time to persuade Reason against attempting a recorded music loop induced suicide, "how can I help?"

What was it about large organisations that you had to explain everything afresh each time you were passed to someone else? Reason explained everything afresh.

"I hope you understand that I can't simply accede to your request. I'll need to clear it."

Reason said that he didn't want to hurt Mister Jones's feelings, but he had expressly asked to speak to someone in authority. The last thing he could do with was a long drawn out process of being bounced up the line or, worse, form-filling.

"Nothing like that. I just need to make sure I've got your name, rank and station correct, then I'll phone you back."

"The number is ..."

The DVLA man stepped in, "No, don't tell me."

"You're not thinking of playing a fucking guessing game are you?" Reason exploded.

"No," Jones parried, "I'll look it up. That way I can be sure that I am talking to a police officer. It'll only take me a few minutes and, for the record, I am a third tier manager here and calls may be recorded for fucking training purposes!"

The line went dead. Reason rued his impatience but was happy to see he hadn't lost his knack of ruffling feathers when he had to.

As promised, Barry Jones was soon back on the line.

"I seem to be making a habit of apologising to people recently," Reason thought as he put his rudeness towards the Welshman down to the pressure he was under.

"Don't talk to me about pressure, "Jones replied before listing the privations he had suffered as a result of recent cutbacks, leaving Reason wishing that he hadn't used the 'p' word.

With Anglo-Welsh relations restored to as amicable a state as possible, the detective dictated the vehicle registration details, which Jones repeated to ensure that there were no slip-ups.

"It would be really helpful if you could tell me whether any of these has been subject to an enquiry in the last.." he paused, "..three months."

Jones said he would hand the enquiry to an operative the moment he came off the phone. Stressing the importance of the investigation, Reason suggested that this was better handled by Jones in person. "There's too much riding on this," he said, "I want to know that it's in the safest, most experienced hands. And I don't want any delays as a result of the findings having to be fed up the line to you by some minion."

Despite the apparent difficulty in departing from normal procedure, the Reason magic worked and Jones was left feeling more important than ever with this high profile request entrusted to him.

"Do you know how many enquiries we get every day?" he asked.

"I haven't a clue," Reason confessed. "I imagine the number is astronomical, but this one takes precedence over all the millions of others, right?"

"Understood, Detective Inspector, I'll get back to you as soon as I have run the checks."

'Jones the Manager' may have acknowledged the need for urgency but that did not prevent the process dragging on for the rest of the day.

"I did forewarn you of the scale of the task," he said when he called back just after five that afternoon, "I can confirm that enquiries were received in respect of all the registration plates that you mentioned."

"Do you know who originated the enquiries?"

Jones, who appeared to have no knowledge of the Eastbourne and Derby murders, responded quizzically, "I assumed they were from you guys."

"So, you haven't checked?"

The DVLA man felt under attack, "You didn't ask for that, only whether or not requests had been received. The vast majority of submissions come from the police you know."

Reason bit his tongue. He wanted to scream abuse down the phone but not as much as he needed to keep the channel to the licensing agency open. Perhaps the bureaucratic culture of such institutions required slavish adherence to the letter of every procedure.

"Where else might enquiries come from?"

"Local authorities, car parking enforcement bodies, solicitors, finance companies and sometimes private individuals," Jones spoke assuredly.

"Private individuals?" Reason repeated.

"Yes, though only if they can provide evidence of reasonable cause. We don't dish out information willy-nilly."

Reason found that only mildly reassuring.

"I'd be grateful if you could undertake a further investigation into the source or sources of the applications."

"It'll have to be tomorrow morning."

Reason was resigned to this, "I assumed so." His preference that morning had been to have all the facts by the end of the afternoon, now he felt some relief that he would not have to engage with the DVLA any more until the next day.

"Perhaps I'll give Dawson that job," he smiled to himself as he left the office.

49

With Isobel committed to a social event back in Surrey, Reason went to bed early and although he slept fitfully, awoke refreshed and raring to go. He arrived well before his official start time and made contact with the South Wales Police. Having explained what he wanted to the switchboard operator and again to a uniformed sergeant, he found himself talking to another DI, Ieuan Griffith, in whom he found a soul mate. Like Reason, Griffith didn't suffer fools gladly, but sometimes felt he was surrounded by them.

"The rookie detectives can be a bit of a pain, but the senior ranks in uniform are worst. Like perpetual haemorrhoids!" the Welsh inspector laughed.

Reason explained his predicament. There was no way that he could travel down to Swansea, nor could he keep tabs on Mister Jones's work ethic from Eastbourne. Griffith was keen to help, "I'll go there in person to make sure he delivers with delay."

"Will you need the go ahead from upstairs?"

"I'm sorry," Griffith said, making a strange cracking noise, "I think the line's breaking up. I didn't catch that last bit."

"My kind of copper," Reason said approvingly.

"Steady on, Steve, I am happily married and if I were interested in an affair, which I am not, it wouldn't be with a man or, before you say it, a sheep."

Reason laughed, "When can you pay Mister Jones a visit?"

"Around ten I expect."

"I'll let him know."

"And deny me the pleasure of seeing his reaction when I call out of the blue? I don't like it when the villains get tipped off."

"He's not a suspect," Reason observed.

"But he *is* a bureaucrat," Griffith said, "next worse thing to criminals in my book, on a par with solicitors and estate agents."

"I knew you wouldn't get far without me, "DC Dawson crowed after Reason had finished briefing him on the limited development that had occurred in his absence. "Shaw wants us to hold another conference at eleven. If I haven't received the call I'm expecting from Swansea by ten forty five, I'll need you to wait here by the 'phone," Reason explained.

"Missing your latest love-in with the Super would be a bitter blow," Dawson joked.

50

The news that Barry Jones had called an impromptu staff meeting caused great consternation among his colleagues as they arrived for work. Geared up for bad news in the form of job losses, reduced overtime or yet another procedural review, they were relieved to find that his announcement, if not exactly positive, was at least non-threatening.

The manager puffed out his chest proudly, "I need to tell you all that I am currently assisting with the investigation of a major crime. You have probably seen news reports on the murders in Eastbourne and Derby. Well, the police are interested in a possible vehicular link between these crimes, something concerning the registration numbers of cars that may have been involved. I will try to minimise the disruption to your normal practice by personally taking on the extra work, but please bear with me if I need your assistance."

Reason's latest press briefing went as well or as badly as might be expected given the death toll in the town, the hostility in the journalists' questions mirroring the strength of the fearful vice in which Eastbourne was held.

The man from *The Mail* fired the opening salvo, "DI Reason, people are saying that you are not up to the job and are incapable of solving these crimes. What's your response?"

Reason grimaced. He didn't doubt that this *was* one of the opinions currently in circulation. "Which people?" he said defensively.

"People in general," the newsman clarified.

"A nice catch-all phrase, but lacking in accuracy. About as helpful as me saying that people think your newspaper isn't fit for wiping..." he paused and Shaw stepped in.

"DI Reason is an experienced and highly competent officer, whose ability and bravery have been acknowledged many times. I have every faith in him."

He immediately invited a new question in an effort to prevent the *Mail* reporter the chance for comeback. His tactic was in vain, for the representative of *The Independent* was no less conciliatory.

"I don't often find myself agreeing with *The Mail*," she opened to laughter from the rest of the pack, "but on this occasion, I endorse fully what my colleague has said. You have lost public confidence, both locally and nationally. I understand that the Home Secretary is very disturbed by the lack of progress and is likely to raise the issue with your Chief Constable, if she hasn't already done so."

Reason looked enquiringly at Shaw, who gave a slight shrug of his shoulders to indicate that he knew nothing about this. To his credit, the superintendent regained a measure of control, "With respect, Ms Lowe, we are here to answer questions to the best of our ability and, having given you the opportunity, I am still waiting for you to pose one."

A couple of reporters made mocking, "Ooooh" sounds which prompted more laughter. Eve Lowe apologised sarcastically for her oversight, "What are your thoughts on the Home Secretary raising doubts with the Chief Constable of Sussex Police about the ability of his detectives?"

"I am afraid I am not privy to the political contacts that you appear to have," Shaw responded coldly, "but I am in regular contact with the

236

Chief Constable and can assure you that he has not expressed any such concern to me."

"Perhaps you've lost his confidence too!" a voice called out.

Shaw thumped his fist on the table "Ladies and gentlemen, may I remind you that we are in the middle of a complex investigation of a very disturbing series of crimes. If you want me to continue to arrange for DI Reason to take time away from that investigation to keep you informed, in return I expect a greater degree of civility."

That seemed to do the trick. The room fell silent for a few seconds, before another hand was raised.

"Asif Mahmood, *The Times*. Is there any connection between the killings in Eastbourne and the murder of the couple in Derby?"

Reason, who had used Shaw's intervention to refocus, answered confidently, "Given the similarities between the murderers' M.O. in both towns, we are keeping open the possibility of a link. However, I can confirm that the gun that killed Mr and Mrs Allen in Derby was not the same as the one used on Mr Gilligan, Mr Young or Mr Morrissey, which could indicate a lack of connection."

"I note that you have omitted Mister Jarvis from your list. Was he killed with the same gun as the other three?"

"No."

Mahmood continued, "With the same gun as the Allens then?"

"I am not in a position to confirm that," Reason said assertively as he could.

Mahmood smiled, "Or, if my memory serves me correctly, deny it."

Reason didn't answer the question but turned his attention to the recovery of the SIG, which, he felt confident, tests would confirm as the weapon used in the first three killings.

He was well aware that this was old hat, merely a re-working of the two and two that the world and his wife had already pieced together, but right now, he'd use anything in reach that might help throw the newshounds off the scent, *his* scent.

"Would you care to comment on your relationship with the pathologist on the case?" the reporter from *The Star* consulted his notepad, "Doctor Perry, isn't it?"

Reason wondered if one day the Fates would smile on him and arrange for a chance meeting with this little shit in a dark alley.

"DI Reason and Doctor Perry are working closely on the case. She is an important and valued member of the investigation team," Shaw stated in a matter of fact way.

"Are you that close to *all* your colleagues?" the reported persisted, bypassing Shaw's contribution.

"What I do in my own time is not your concern," Reason growled, "and of no relevance to this investigation."

"You don't think that you're taking your eye off the ball because of your leisure pursuits?" the tabloid pressman countered.

"I did warn you," Shaw said firmly, getting to his feet. "That's it for today. I will be reviewing the question of who receives passes to future briefings. Good day!" He left the stage without Reason but waited for him by the rear exit from the hall.

"I think you've got some explaining to do, Steve," he said before they left the building, "not here and not now, but when we get back to the station."

"Didn't it occur to you to inform me of your affair with Doctor Perry?" Shaw fumed once they were back in the sanctuary of his office.

Reason indicated that it was not an affair and that his relationship with her was no more Shaw's business than it was the gutter press's.

"With the amount of media attention that the case has attracted, I'm surprised you weren't a little more circumspect. Didn't you foresee that the press would become interested in your private life?" Shaw riposted.

"I didn't give it a thought and with the benefit of hindsight I wouldn't do anything differently. Our private relationship has absolutely no bearing on my work."

"Mmm," Shaw remained sceptical, "Mixing one's professional life with the personal can be very distracting."

"You're beginning to sound worrying like those bloodsuckers from the tabloids," Reason hit back angrily. "Either you meant what you said about having confidence in me or you didn't. If it's the latter, then you can shove this job so far up yourself that you'll have a permanent lump in your throat!"

Shaw was on the verge of demonstrating that Reason had no monopoly over incandescent rage, when DC Dawson, who had caught the gist of their exchange from the corridor, interrupted.

"Sorry to disturb you, gentlemen," he said wryly, "I have DI Griffith from South Wales Police on the line. Shall I let him know you're on your way, DI Reason?"

"The follow up to our initial DVLA checks," Reason explained to Shaw who gave his permission to leave with a slight wave of his hand.

Reason pressed the speaker button on the handset for Dawson's benefit and greeted his opposite number.

"Hello again Steve."
Reason was pleased to hear Griffith's cheerful tones, a welcome antidote to the sort of morning he had experienced. His pleasure was short-lived.

"Do you want the good news, the bad new or the ugly news?" Griffith asked before correcting himself, "Obviously, you'll get all three but it's a question of order."

Reason didn't like the sound of the other two but he was in desperate need of hearing something positive, "Start with the best bits, Ieuan."

"OK, but I'd better start by saying that in this context 'best' is a relative term meaning not as grim as the rest of it," Griffith said by way of prologue, "From one point of view one of the worst bits might be the most useful."

"I hope our friendship can survive me telling you to stop beating about the fucking bush and tell me what you've come up with."

"Fair shout," Griffith replied, "probably best if I give you the information in a logical sequence and leave you to make the judgment call."

"Fine."

"Well, for starters, the searches for the number plates weren't conducted from the same computer."

"By different people then?" Dawson interrupted.

"Not necessarily," Griffith explained, "You're right that everyone at DVLA usually has his or her own console, but with the reduction in staff, there are always free computers and it seems that people have taken to plonking themselves in front of vacant ones. It helps break up the monotony of working there."

Dawson sighed, "I still don't see why you're not assuming that different computers probably equates with different personnel. Isn't that the obvious conclusion?"

"I'll come back to that in a minute, DC Dawson," Griffith replied. "No offence meant, but when you're as long in the tooth as Steve and me, you'll be much less inclined to follow the obvious."

Reason congratulated Ieuan on this observation, "So difficult to get staff! Carry on, Ieuan."

"Most unusually, there are no records of the source of requests for information on the said number plates."

"Do you mean that someone has forgotten to record that information or deliberately removed it?"

"Neither, Steve. Whenever a request is received, the operative has to complete an on screen form. It's like all the other infuriating online forms you ever come across, miss a field out or enter incorrect data and you can't progress to the next stage. And, once the information is in, it stays in."

Dawson, who had the IT edge over both DIs, explored the scenario further. "What if someone completed all the fields and then realised they'd clicked the wrong choice in a drop down menu?"

"I don't know," Griffith admitted, "but I guess there must be some way of amending that part of the entry."

"But not removing it altogether," Reason added.

"Definitely not."

"Hang on, Ieuan, didn't you say that if the online form isn't completed, the search is refused? No form no search."

"Yes," Griffith confirmed, "I made the same point to Mister Jones. Apparently, it is possible for DVLA staff to search without a request from the outside."

Dawson pulled a face, "Why would they do that?"

"Occasionally it's to find out more about an attractive driver they've seen but more often it's to make a bit of money on the side. There are people who do not have clearance who are prepared to pay decent money for information."
"Criminals?"

"Possibly, but much more likely private detectives acting for suspicious spouses."

Dawson conjectured that it wouldn't be worth the risk of losing their jobs, to which Griffith said that getting out of working in such a dreadful place would make it all worthwhile.

Reason recapped what they had, "So, no referral record, no single console being used, but the possibility that all the searches were carried out by one person."

"And that brings me to the slightly better news, Steve. One of the DVLA boys went AWOL shortly after Jones informed the staff meeting of what was occurring."

Reason was incredulous, "What?! Tell me I didn't hear you right." He put his head in his hands.

"Sorry, Steve. Believe me, I wish my next words were 'you need a hearing aid' but sadly you heard me loud and clear."

"What a twat!" Dawson cried.

"What a twat, indeed," Griffith echoed. "Jones has almost certainly given the heads up to whoever carried out the searches."

"At least he seems to have flushed him out in the process," Reason said.

"Yes, that's the silver lining I was alluding to earlier."

"Who's the member of staff who's gone missing?"

"One of yours," Griffith remarked chirpily, "name of Greg Cuthbert. You simply can't trust the English!"

"If you take Jones into account, I make that a score draw, Ieuan. Have you picked him up yet?"

"No, a patrol car's on its way to his house in Maesteg. I'll let you know as soon as we've got him, should have him within the next twenty minutes."

51

"It's turning out to be quite a roller coaster of a day for you, Inspector Plod. Your performances in the media spotlight are getting worse. This morning's was positively cringe-making. I am as nauseated by your abject failure to do your job properly as I was before.

But you won't feel vulnerable right now, will you? Thanks to a lucky break in Wales, I expect you're starting to believe that you've almost got the case cracked. Your excitement is understandable, but don't count your chickens before they hatch. For every step you take, I'll always be at least one in front of you. And at the end of the day that's the difference between us. I know what I'm doing and you don't."

52

"Ieuan! Thanks for calling back!"

"That's a bit premature, Steve," disappointment dripped from the Welsh detective's words.

"Don't tell me he's got away."

"Well, he had at least an hour's start on us."

"Shit! Shit! Shit!"

"If he's our man, that is."

"I thought we had no doubt about that. Jones the Twat lets everyone know there's police interest in the searches and the next thing we find out that Cuthbert has done a runner. Could it be clearer?"

Griffith replied that there were some unexplained threads including the fact that none of Cuthbert's neighbours had seen him arrive home.

"That doesn't put him in the clear. He's probably headed for a port or airport," Reason suggested.

"He'd need his passport and how many people carry that around with them just in case they win an immediate holiday in the works raffle?"

"Given what he's been up to, I would've thought that keeping travel documents to hand would be a smart precaution," Reason argued.

"I'm with you on that one, Steve, or I would be if it weren't for the other fly I've found in the ointment."

"Which is?"

"Greg Cuthbert's car is still in the car park."

"Perhaps he took a taxi?"

"We've already eliminated that possibility, Steve. Our bird, Greg Cuthbert, hasn't only flown, he's completely disappeared."

Having advised Griffith to get in touch day or night with any developments, Reason put the phone down. He knew what it must feel like for a football team to be winning with moments of a match to go, only to concede twice in injury time.

Dawson did his best to keep his spirits up, but, having assessed the depth of the DI's mood, he invented a pretext for withdrawing to a safe distance.

Reason mulled over the events of the day so far. If it wasn't the worst day he'd ever spent on the force, he couldn't think when the worse one might have been. Being becalmed in the middle of an investigation he could cope with, being blown off course just as he was entering a port was a different matter. "And why the hell are you using sailing metaphors?" he accused himself, "You don't like fucking boats!"

His frustration and anger were making it difficult for him to think straight. Cuthbert ... his car .. perhaps an accomplice...? He needed a break both within the investigation and from it. The second of these could be achieved by a walk down to Fiesta. A step back from the case and sustenance, yes that might help.

His plan was disrupted by his mobile's ring tone.

He picked it up without looking at the number displayed on the screen, "Ieuan?" he asked.

"No, Isobel."

Driven To Murder

"Oh, what do you want?"

"Hello darling yourself," she teased, "A little bird tells me that you're having a shitty day and I wondered if I can help."

"Not unless you can magic up the mole at the DVLA who has been aiding and abetting our mass murderer," he thought.

"What have you got in mind?" he said, "I'm not in the mood for sex."

"Which is just as well," Isobel replied, "as I don't think our bosses would be too pleased if we started bonking at work. I was thinking more along the lines of a cup of tea."

"Great minds think alike," Reason was starting to feel a little brighter, "I was just on my way to Fiesta. Can you meet me there in fifteen?"

"It's a date, Steve."

Dawson was pleased to see that his tip off had brought an almost immediate improvement in Reason's state of mind; however, he was left wondering if the strain was getting all too much for his boss when he had called him 'Wren' as he exited the office.

"Little bird, indeed!" Reason snorted to himself as he strode along Grove Road.

"I'm really worried about you, Steve," Isobel said softly stroking his hands across the table, "So is Peter."

"Ah yes, Super grass!" Reason mocked.

249

"Peter contacted me because he cares about you. However bad things feel right now, you must try not to lose sight of who your friends are."

"Or I'll lose them, is that what you're saying?"

"No, we never lose true friends, but we can hurt them."

"There was me thinking that you were here to cheer me up," Reason murmured.

"Sorry, you're responsible for your own feelings. All I'm trying to do is give you a reality check."
"You think I'm losing sight of reality, becoming delusional?"

"Of course not, I'm just reminding you of other people's interpretations of reality."

Reason knew he was probably heading towards another round of apologising, but, right now, that would feel like weakness. If he had to cut people off and go into his cave for a while in order to regain his strength, so be it.

His mobile phone rang.

This time it *was* DI Griffith, reporting that Greg Cuthbert had been found.

"Great news, Ieaun. Well done."

"Hold your horses, Steve. He's been found dead in the DVLA office toilets."

"Shot, I suppose?" Reason asked wearily. That would top a marvellous day!

250

"No, poor bugger seems to have died of a heart attack."

"He could still be our man, the killer's accomplice," Reason said hopefully.

"Yes. I'd be happy to pursue that avenue down here and let you know the moment it looks as if we might have a lead."

"Thanks. That would be very helpful." He looked across at Isobel and smiled, "You're a true friend, Ieuan."

Although Greg Cuthbert was no longer in a position to be of direct assistance, Reason had been in no doubt that Griffith and his colleagues would come up with detailed information about his contacts. This would certainly help narrow down the search for the elusive killer. The first part of the DI's assumption proved well founded, as the South Wales Police responded smartly with a comprehensive dossier on the dead DVLA worker. However, to Reason's dismay, there was nothing in the account of Cuthbert's bland life that pointed to any criminal associations. He had been happily married for over twenty years, the doting father of three children. Born and educated in Bristol, he had held down a succession of office jobs, culminating in ten years with the DVLA. Reason wondered whether he had become frustrated by his lack of meaningful promotion and prone to bribery as a result, but none of his performance management reports gave any hint of this. On the contrary, Cuthbert was universally viewed as a safe pair of hands, unimaginative but intensely loyal and reliable. His family's move to Wales had enabled them to afford a larger property than in the Bristol area and they enjoyed a comfortable, though not extravagant lifestyle. While the possibility couldn't be ruled out that he was the operative responsible for the peculiar searches, his track record of informing managers of anything untoward in his colleagues' behaviour seemed to suggest that such a possibility was very slight.

Dawson desperately tried to make light of the situation, "Looking on the bright side, Cuthbert's untimely end means that the statistical odds of identifying the rogue operative have shortened a little" but his words fell on the DI's deaf ears. And, any marginal improvement in the odds was rapidly dissipated when Griffith provided an update the next day, "About dozen of Cuthbert's colleagues have taken the day off as a mark of respect. More like an easy way of grabbing some extra leave away from that bloody mausoleum of an office, if you want my opinion. My team will do what we can to interview the ones who aren't work shy and trawl through records of computer activity, but it's a bloody big job. It'll take days. Besides, I would be surprised if the one we're after isn't among the lot who are taking a sickie."

Reason, who had been chewing his pen while listening to Griffith, came back with his thoughts, "Far be it from me to tell you how to go about your end of the investigation, Ieuan, but wouldn't it be easier to focus on the absentees? I agree that although our man, or woman played it cool yesterday, they won't be in work today."

"Good thinking, Steve, "Griffith said quietly, feeling a little foolish that he hadn't spotted the flaw in his intended strategy.

"How long will it take for you to chase them all up?" Reason wondered.

"They're scattered far and wide, but with three officers available to me, I've got a good chance of wrapping this up today. I'm tempted to round them all up and bring them in for questioning. That way, the mole wouldn't be able to burrow out of this," Griffith replied.

"Sounds like a guaranteed way of stirring up industrial action from the civil service unions," Reason laughed. "In any case, I don't think you'll find the fishy one in your net."

"No," Griffith agreed, "If I were him, I'd be putting as many miles between myself and Swansea as I could. Perhaps he'll show up on your patch, Steve."

"Unless he or she is panicking, that doesn't seem too likely, Ieuan, but we'll have our antennae up as soon as you can give me some idea of who's in the frame. If it helps speed things up, don't worry about verifying the absentees' computer activity, just account for their whereabouts."

"That's exactly what I had in mind," Griffith fibbed, "Now, if you could be so good as to get off the line, perhaps I can get on with my job. I'll keep you posted, Steve."

Reason was impressed by the speed of Griffith's response, "He's done us proud," he said to Dawson as he browsed at the list of names that had been emailed in the wake of Ieuan's latest phone call, "Shit, there are *three* unaccounted for."

"At least it narrows it down," Dawson said optimistically.

"I was hoping that there'd only be one name," Reason remarked pensively "and nothing stands out from these three. All are men under the age of thirty, all with solid work records."

Dawson continued to remain optimistic, "I expect Griffith will track them all down."

"Two out of three would be enough, Peter. Mind you," he added gloomily, "it might not do us a lot of good. Whoever's been up to no good at the DVLA will already have been in touch with the killer."

"Unless he *is* the killer," Dawson idly commented.

Briefly, Reason was taken aback by the constable's throwaway line as this possibility had eluded him.

"Either way, that should put a stop to the killing," Peter stuck to his attempts to help Reason climb out of the pit.

"Or have the opposite effect completely. It wouldn't be the first time a serial killer has reacted to the net tightening by going on a final rampage."

53

Reason continued to take his cloud with him over the next twenty four hours, until Ieuan's next call brought a sunny interval.

"Good news, Steve," Griffith's voice danced, "we have accounted for two of the workers we couldn't find yesterday. Only one hasn't made it into the DVLA this morning and he was neither due leave nor did he call in sick. His name is Nigel Llewellyn. There's no sign of him at home, but I've got his place under surveillance. We'll nab him when he returns."

"Excellent," Reason responded, his mood lifted, "but as you said before he may not be planning to go home in the near future, He may take some finding."

"I've already circulated his details to all forces in the UK and to ports. I hope you don't mind, me acting on my own initiative like that."

"No, I'm grateful for all the help I can get on this one."

Griffith advised that he was waiting for a recent picture of Llewellyn from his personnel file at the DVLA. "I've told our Mister Jones that I'll throw the book at him if he doesn't get it to me within the hour. I'll send it as a postscript to the description I circulated earlier, unless you want to take a look first."

"No need, but it would be helpful if you could send me my own copy of his description and mug shot. I'd expect my HQ to bounce it all onto me without delay, but I'd prefer not to leave it to chance."

The moment DI Griffith was off the phone, Reason instructed Dawson to get back in touch with Barry Jones at the DVLA, "I want details of

Llewellyn's working pattern over the last three months, just in case he wasn't in Swansea on the dates of the murders." Then he took the latest development to Superintendent Shaw, who was happy to accede to the DI's request for him to take sole responsibility for communications with the media.

"Things on the ground could move pretty fast now and I don't want to be tied up with all that nonsense," Reason had said.

"But it's all right for a senior officer like me to waste his time on it?" Shaw asked sternly.

"I didn't mean..." Reason began, before noticing that the super had cracked a smile.

"You're quite right, Steve. You need to be freed up to respond to events at short notice; however, I do expect to be kept informed at every twist and turn. I don't want you indulging your fascination in maverick behaviour, leaving me facing the press without knowing where you are and what the hell you're up to."

With Reason's reassurance in his pocket, Shaw laid out his plans for briefing the media. "Out of courtesy to the news people on the spot, I'll hold a brief conference this afternoon, but my main tack will be to ensure that the evening news programmes receive all the available information on Llewellyn directly from this office. I'll also make sure we get another slot on *Crimewatch*. Fortunately for us, its next broadcast is due tomorrow evening. You must let me have a copy of Llewellyn's picture as soon as it arrives."

When he returned to his own office, Reason was greeted by Dawson, who had not been idle while awaiting the DVLA manager's response, "Jones promised that he'd send over details of the work roster in a few minutes. I don't doubt that he'll be true to his word, 'cause Griffith seems to have put the fear of God into him. In the meantime, I've made a start with my own fishing expedition on Llewellyn's background."

"Anything interesting?"

"He has a sister," Dawson replied.

"*Interesting*" Reason emphasised the word to indicate that he wasn't interested in irrelevant snippets of family history.

"Who served in the Army," Dawson added.

"Interesting!" Reason's reiterated, now with a very different stress on the word, "Tell me more."

"That's what I'm in the middle of trying to find out, guv', though the military might not be in a hurry to release information to a humble DC."

"You can pass that upstairs, Peter. I've every confidence in the Super."

"You've changed your tune, guv'. I thought you couldn't stand him."

"I've come to see him in a different light recently. Perhaps being in a position of leadership has a damaging effect on some people," Reason said sagely.

"I've noticed that myself," Dawson smiled.

"Be careful, Detective Constable Dawson," Reason reacted with mock severity, "My impression of people can go down as well as up. Now, take me through the rest of the low down on Mister Llewellyn and his sister."

Dawson flicked through his notes, which were not yet extensive, "It's still work in progress" he said ruefully.

"Suzanne Llewellyn is thirty, three years older than Nigel. They were both born and grew up in Cardiff where their father worked in the docks and their mother in a school kitchen. Both parents still alive, divorced fifteen years ago. The father emigrated to Spain eight years ago."

Reason interrupted him, "Don't tell me that he knows Karpov" he said with a mixture of hope and sarcasm.

"No, at least, I haven't dug deep enough to confirm or deny that one."

"Well, given some of the setbacks I've had, I think I'd prefer you not to look further into Mister Llewellyn senior for a while," Reason grinned. "What else have you got on Nigel and Suzanne?"

"Nigel seems to have plodded his way through school and college, keeping his head down along the way and emerging with the sort of grades that until recently guaranteed a kid steady employment. He worked for an IT company before joining the DVLA in 2006. It appears that he learned from his big sister's mistakes."

Reason was intrigued, "Go on, Peter."

"Suzanne Llewellyn seems to have been a bit of a wild child, kicked out of a couple of schools, left at sixteen with grades well below what she was capable of. A string of dead-end jobs interspersed with unemployment, a string of dead-end relationships, had a baby when she was twenty, father unknown. Evidently this changed her life and she was determined to do the best she could by her son. She took two jobs to ensure that his material needs were catered for while her mother, who gave up her own part-time work, looked after his upbringing."

Driven To Murder

"So, Suzanne didn't see a great deal of ..."

".. Rhodri. No and in 2007 she joined up."

Reason expressed his scepticism, "What, she just upped and left the son she supposedly cared about?"

"By all accounts, she wanted to take him with her, but the army refused. She had to choose between him and a career that would continue to provide for him financially. By this time, her mother had come to view Rhodri as her own so it wasn't altogether out of altruism, that she encouraged Suzanne to make something of her own life. She could always spend her leave with the boy."

Dawson indicated that this was as far as he'd got.

"You've done astonishingly well. How did you manage it in such a short time, Peter?"

Dawson winked and tapped the side of his nose with an index finger, "It's not what you know, it's who you know," he said mysteriously.

Reason beamed, "Like you, I've also come to regard Ieuan Griffith as a reliable source of assistance."

"You've always told me not to jump to conclusions," Dawson responded, "but that's exactly what you're doing, guv'."

"Are you trying to tell me that you found all this out without Griffith's help?" Reason's voice was thick with surprise.

"Let's just say, it's time you stopped underestimating the ability of Detective Constables."

Reason contemplated tearing his subordinate off a strip for being so cheeky, but he quickly dispelled that thought. Dawson had made an excellent start with his line of enquiry and Reason reckoned he was man enough to trade a little rudeness for useful information.

"OK, sir," he said, "I'd better stop wasting your valuable time and allow you to get back to your invaluable endeavours."

Dawson smiled broadly, "All right, Reason," he said in a passable impersonation of Shaw, "that will be all."

"Exchange being no robbery," Reason said from the doorway, "It may be time that you stopped overestimating the tolerance of Detective Inspectors."

54

For the next couple of hours Reason and Dawson charted parallel courses, the DI remaining in regular contact with Griffith, while the junior officer continued to glean information on the Llewellyns' backgrounds from *his* opposite number DC Karen Phillips. Of the two detectives, Reason fared worse, with Nigel Llewellyn continuing to be off the South Wales Police radar. While awaiting the suspect's picture, the DI had to content himself as Dawson's personal assistant, taking *his* call back from the DVLA. Llewellyn had been in work on all but one of the murder dates, which, Reason concluded, not only ruled him out of four killings but also made it highly improbable that he had been directly involved in the execution of the fifth.

Much to his boss's chagrin and relief, Dawson's delving into the Llewellyns' back story progressed smoothly and when they caught up with each other, the constable again had more to contribute.

"Mrs Llewellyn, the mother, moved from Cardiff in 2009. It seems that Suzanne was able to save a substantial proportion of her army pay and she was keen for her son to grow up somewhere nicer than the grotty area that she'd lived in. Although no palace, at least her parents' house was mortgage free and as a condition of his wife not complicating his liberation plans, Llewellyn senior conceded his share of the equity in the matrimonial property. Between them, Suzanne and her mother were able to make a fresh start."

"Do we know where?"

"Somewhere in the South of England, but Karen, er, I mean my contact in the South Wales Police, wasn't able to provide an address. I'm hoping to find electoral registers online that will enable us to trace her.

"Assuming Mrs L was interested enough to vote. After all, we don't get many Plaid Cymru candidates in these parts," Reason mused.

"I'll put out feelers to the Royal Mail as well."

"Multi-tasking, eh, Peter? Very impressive. So, we may have a local connection, but that still leaves a giant leap to Suzanne Llewellyn being our killer."

"True, but I've also heard back from the military. "Thanks to your suggestion to involve the Super," Dawson added sensitively, not wishing Reason to feel completely outshone. He read out the key phrases from the email he had received, "An exemplary soldier, ... totally committed to all aspects of her training, ... thoroughly dependable, ...single-minded in her determination to advance her army career, three promotions ... excellent marksman ... honourable discharge 2011...."

"The reason she left?" Reason pressed.

"Compassionate grounds," Dawson read on.

"Meaning what exactly?"

"That's the sticking point guv'. They wouldn't divulge the precise circumstances of Suzanne's discharge, something about protection of personal data."

"Utter bollocks!" Reason erupted, "Some bloody army clerk wants to put one over on us, that's what that's about. Kick it back upstairs and see if Shaw can unblock the drain a bit more. I'll also give Tom Redfern a bell."

Dawson looked askance at him, "You're the boss, but is it such a good idea to involve the press at this critical stage?"

Reason batted his protest aside, "I know you don't like reporters and, to be frank, I share your general dislike, but Redfern's a good 'un. He's already helped us once and I trust him not to screw things up by publishing information without our say so." He could see that he hadn't won Dawson over yet.

"I need *you* to trust *me* on this one," he appealed, "And if I've made an error of judgment I'll apologise to you and let the top brass know that you were right and I was wrong. How's that?"

Dawson considered the offer for a moment. Whatever his disquiet about journalists, he trusted Reason implicitly, "Throw in a lunch at *Fiesta* and you've got a deal."

"I've also got Llewellyn's picture," the DI produced an A4 sheet from a folder and brandished it in the air. "It's being sent to forces up and down the land as we speak. Hopefully, Nigel Llewellyn's cover will be blown soon and we'll be able to get a crack at him."

Whether confident or hopeful, both men felt that they were getting close to a tipping point and they were reluctant to knock off when their scheduled shift ended.

"I'll hang around a while," Reason had played his hand first, "just in case something crops up."

"I'm staying too, guv'."

"There's no overtime for this, Peter. Besides Heather will be expecting you home shortly."

Dawson was not to be dissuaded, "I'll give her a ring, she'll understand."

Reason travelled back in time to the numerous occasions on which he had made similar calls to Rebecca, "What if she doesn't?" he asked.

"Then I'll try to find ways to make it up to her," Dawson smiled, "a dance that will go on until she feels that she has exacted suitable reparation."

Concerned as he was for Dawson's domestic situation, Reason was pleased that his colleague was determined to stay late.

An hour and a half ticked away with nothing to show for their patience but two rounds of coffees and a plate of tired sandwiches from the canteen. They wondered whether to call it a day when one of the phones rang. Like two squabbling schoolboys, they both dived forward to pick up, Reason narrowly winning the race at the cost of sending the handset flying onto the floor as he held the receiver.

"What was that?" Isobel asked in a startled tone.

"Only me knocking the phone over," Reason replied.

"Hello, Steve, it's Isobel."

"Yes, I recognised your voice."

"You didn't answer your mobile."

Reason padded his pockets with his free hand, "I must've left it in the other office."

"You've forgotten, haven't you?" Isobel said sharply.

"Yes, I said, I've left it ..." Then it dawned on him. They were supposed to be going to Devonshire Park Theatre. She had persuaded him that the brief respite of an Ayckbourn comedy would do him the world of good.

"Isobel, other than 'sorry', I don't know what to say," he said sheepishly.

"Apology accepted," Isobel's response lacked warmth, "but I don't think I could make a habit of putting up with this sort of treatment."

They disengaged awkwardly, him feebly floating the idea of calling round later, she curtly advising him of the poverty of that suggestion.

Reason turned to Dawson, "If you are as good at placating Heather as you claim, perhaps you could give me a lesson."

"That would be a first," Dawson chuckled, "me teaching the great Detective Inspector Reason something!"

Reason's uncomfortable feelings in the aftermath of the brief exchange with Isobel were short lived thanks to three more calls in quick succession.

"North Wales Police," Dawson said handing the receiver over.

Llewellyn still hadn't been detained, but his car had been located close to Wrexham General railway station. "We've already checked that he's not holed up in the Ramada Plaza nearby," said the sergeant on the other end of the line. "For my money he's hopped on a train to London, but we'll be keeping a weather eye out up here."

Although this snippet didn't advance their cause greatly, Reason and his partner took as positive the fact that their prey was apparently still on the move, possibly without a clear strategy.

The DI instructed Dawson to contact both the Met and British Transport Police, "If Llewellyn's heading for London that will give us two bites of the cherry."

"Do you think he's heading for his mother's, guv'?"

"A bloody long way round if he is. Perhaps it's a deliberate ploy, but more likely running scared. Isn't it about time we had something on the family address."

"I've been checking my emails every ten minutes," Dawson said wearily as he started dialling Scotland Yard.

While he was alerting colleagues in London to Llewellyn's latest movement, Reason fielded a call on his mobile from Tom Redfern, who was in what the DI had come to be recognise as his natural exuberant state. Reason stepped out of the office to avoid distracting his colleague.

"I'm glad you're still there, detective inspector," Redfern opened, "because I've got something here that I think is highly significant."

Suppressing the desire to say that he would prefer to do the thinking, Reason waited for the reporter to continue.

"I caught the news feature about the man you suspect of being involved in the killings and decided to see if he showed up in my system. I know we don't have much of a readership in Wales, but putting two and two together I assumed that he had a connection with Eastbourne."

"And judging from the excitement in your voice, I take it that your assumption was sound, Tom," Reason noted, biting his tongue to hold back the command to 'fucking hurry up and spit it out!'

"Partially," Redfern replied, "I've only got a passing reference to him. He attended a family funeral in our neck of the woods last year."

"His mother's?"

266

Driven To Murder

"That would be Megan Llewellyn," the journalist added for clarification, "No, she was another mourner. It was his nephew, Rhodri, who had died. He and his grandmother were picking wild daffodils on Butts Lane, when a driver misjudged his speed on a bend and collided with the boy. He died in Megan's arms."

"What about the driver? Anyone we know?"

"No way of telling," Tom answered, "He or she didn't stop and still hasn't been identified."

Reason reflected on the tragedy of losing a child under any circumstances, of which a hit-and-run death had to be one of the worst imaginable. Even with the miniscule amount of contact he had with them, the thought of either of his kids failing to outlive him sent a shudder down his spine.

"Are you still there, inspector?"

"Sorry, just thinking. I take it the boy's mother, Suzanne, surfaced in your search?"

"Yes, she was an army corporal, serving in Afghanistan at the time. She was flown home as soon as the news reached Camp Bastion."

"And never returned to active service."

"You already know all this?" Redfern sounded almost hurt.

"I only had some of the jigsaw and your latest assistance has enabled me to get a better idea of what the puzzle as a whole depicts."

He re-joined Dawson, whose intelligence had been well received by the other two forces and who had turned his attention back to his computer.

"At last," he cried, "a result on the Llewellyn family home!"

"Polegate," Reason interjected calmly.

"Yes, how did you know?"

"Maybe an informed guess or perhaps I'm psychic" the DI smiled.

Dawson retaliated with a challenge, "If you're so bloody smart, guv', you'll know the full address, then?"

"Things are becoming foggy, I am losing connection with the other side," Reason wailed like a demented medium.

The detective constable shook his head, "So, that was Redfern on your mobile and the best he could come up with was the town!"

"Don't be too harsh on the lad, Peter," Reason sanctioned him. "He's doing his best to help us and whatever you think he isn't in competition with you. So, stop acting jealously and tell me the address."

In response to Dawson's call for urgent action, "Let's pay Mrs Llewellyn a visit tonight," Reason counselled caution.

"Even if we could find a way through the red tape to summon an armed response unit, they won't be too keen to mount an operation in the dark."

"This is the twenty first century, guv'" Dawson countered, "They have night vision equipment."

"Still too risky in my book," Reason held his line, "though I'm happy to set things in motion for first thing tomorrow morning."

"By which time, we'll have another one or two members of the Llewellyn clan on the run," Dawson remarked impatiently.

Reason refused to budge, pointing out that if either or both women had anything to hide, they would've taken to flight the moment that Nigel got in touch. "A few hours won't make a difference on that score, so why don't you call it a day. I don't intend to stay here much longer myself once I've tried to arrange protection for tomorrow."

55

Whatever possessed Reason to take a detour and drive past Isobel Perry's flat on his way home, he immediately regretted the manoeuvre. For, as he approached her block, he could see her and a man in a warm embrace by the front door. Reason applied his brakes as smoothly as he could and was relieved to find a parking space near to hand. He pulled into the kerb from where he watched Isobel go inside while the man drove off.

Reason played out a number of possible scenarios. To use an obsolete expression, had Isobel been 'entertaining' and the clinch on the doorstep marked her lover's departure? Had she been to his place for a fuck? Was it the end of an innocent evening between friends or colleagues? Reason swiftly dispelled this, the least unpleasant option. "We were meant to be at the theatre, so this has been arranged hastily," he said to himself. "Perhaps she's picked him up in a bloody bar!"

Somehow common sense returned to him in time to divert him from his knee-jerk inclination to march up to Isobel's front door and refuse to leave until she had explained what the hell was going on. For all the progress he and Dawson had made with the case that evening, his mood had taken on a deeper shade of darkness.

Reacquainted with past failures with relationships, Reason tried to drink himself to sleep, but, already drained by the emotional charge of his elongated day, he crashed out on the sofa part way through his third tumbler of malt.

56

Pleased though Reason was to escape without a throbbing head, the next day started painfully for him with a text from Isobel, demanding to know what he thought he was playing at, spying on her the night before. He knew that he couldn't hide his head in the sand; he would have to face her and try to put things straight or, failing that, strive to restore some of his integrity as their relationship ended. But that would have to wait. This morning's priority had to be the trip to Polegate, even though he was resigned to leaving there empty handed.

Shortly after he had arrived for work, the front desk rang up to confirm that the armed response unit's 4x4 BMW had appeared. He and Dawson went downstairs to meet their colleagues.

"Good morning, sir," the Specialist Firearms Officer leading the team greeted Reason and introduced himself, "Clive Dunlop." "I'll need you both to wear ballistics vests and helmets. Vests on now, because we don't want you faffing around when we get there. You can slip the helmets on at the scene. Are you travelling with us in the Bimmer or taking your own wheels?"

Reason indicated that Dawson and he would be driving an unmarked car.

Dunlop was not concerned about which vehicle would lead, "providing we both arrive together." He eyed Dawson with suspicion, "I don't want you getting carried away by the thrill of the moment and zooming ahead."

Dawson dismissed the suggestion as never having crossed his mind.

Reason knew him better and was glad that the SFO had reined in his enthusiasm a little.

"Hear what the nice man said, Peter, "he laughed, "you must drive carefully."

Dunlop was singularly unimpressed with the banter between the two detectives and put it down to nerves. As a veteran of many armed deployments and false alarms, he had developed a degree of immunity to the tension of such situations.

Mrs Llewellyn's property was in a neatly laid out but largely nondescript close of modern semi-detached houses.

"Not the sort of place you'd associate with a rabid killer," Dawson observed dryly.

Reason pointed out that no one socio-economic group had the monopoly on murder. "Think Harold Shipman if you need to be convinced," he added.

Two patrol cars were already in position to seal off the close and their occupants were on standby to shepherd any of the neighbours back into the safety of their own little boxes.

Dunlop made it crystal clear that he was in charge of the event, "Put your helmets on now and wait over there while we obtain entry," He pointed to a lamp post a couple of doors down from the Llewellyns. "PC Beech will be at the rear of our group and he'll signal when it's OK for you to join us."

With everyone kitted up, Dunlop led his unit up the short path to the front door. He rang the bell and stepped to one side in case the door was being targeted from within.

No reply.

He rang again, this time adding a heavy rap on the door with his fist.

Still nothing.

Through the frosted glass pane, the Specialist Firearms Officer could detect no movement and confident that a gun was *not* trained on the entrance, he stooped to call through the letter box.

"Mrs Llewellyn, this is the police. We are armed, repeat, we are armed. Please acknowledge us. I will give you thirty seconds to respond at which point we will have no option but to force entry."

The deadline passed and Dunlop gestured to one of his colleagues to step forward with the Enforcer, the steel ram. Moments later the door burst open. The firearms team waited for a few seconds either side of the opening and in the absence of any sounds from inside they entered stealthily in a thoroughly rehearsed and perfectly executed piece of choreography.

Outside, the noise of the Llewellyns' door being caved in had drawn some of the neighbours from their beds or breakfast cereals. The uniformed officers responded quickly and ushered them back indoors.

At number seven, Dunlop and his men picked their way through the building, room by room. The beds were cold and drawers and wardrobes looked as if they had been attacked by incompetent burglars.

The initial search complete, Dunlop relayed the 'all clear' to Beech who waved Reason and Dawson over.

"No-one's been here for several hours at least, inspector," Dunlop reported, "and there's plenty of evidence that the place was evacuated hastily."

Reason was neither surprised nor dismayed by this revelation. It was as he had expected. "Are we OK to carry out a detailed search?"

The SFO gave him the green light, "There's not much more for us to hang around for," he said coldly, "but keep us in mind when you're closing in for the kill."

The detectives handed back their protective clothing and watched the BMW pull away. Reason mulled over Dunlop's words. Had he used the word 'kill' loosely to describe the end of the investigation or was it a conscious statement of bloodlust?

Dawson broke his chain of thought, "Ready, guv'?"

"Yes, Peter, let's go," the DI replied. In the final analysis, he wasn't sure that Dunlop's intended meaning mattered all that much. On occasions like this Reason welcomed the additional safety afforded by armed back-up so who was he to judge the firearm officers' motives?

Although Dawson grumbled about the thoroughness of their search, sure that they would find nothing of great consequence, the demands Reason placed on him paled into insignificance when Ray Miller and another member of the forensics team arrived at nine.

"Hello Ray," Reason greeted his old friend, "I want you to go over every square inch of this place for any trace of weapons having been kept here. If there's the tiniest trace of powder or grease I want to know about it." Then as an afterthought he added "or metal filings."

Miller happily accepted the commission, "We love a challenge, don't we Bill?" he laughed. His colleague drawled "Yes, boss" like a primary school pupil mechanically answering the class register.

"There is one condition, though," Ray halted Reason's progress out of the room, "You'll take any flak for the size of our overtime claim."

276

"How about payment by results, Ray?" Reason parried, "You find the evidence and I'll sign your claim."

"Fuck off, Steve. Carry on down that track and you'll have a full-scale mutiny on your hands. Now, the meter's running, so if you want to avoid being hauled over the coals for extravagance, why don't you and Robin go and do something useful and leave this place to the experts?"

"He's a cheeky sod!" Dawson complained as he and Reason stepped outside.

"But bloody good at his job, Peter. The service will be all the poorer when he retires."

Dawson guessed that Reason and Ray were of a similar age and wondered if, subconsciously, his boss was referring to himself as well.

With the close now fully awake and the exclusion zone reduced to the immediate area around the Llewellyns', the detectives joined the door-to-door enquiries that their uniformed colleagues had already commenced.

Megan and Suzanne Llewellyn had left fully twenty four hours earlier. The neighbours' accounts conflicted in their description of the car – anything from a silver grey Ford to a white Vauxhall – but were unanimous about the vehicle being unfamiliar. They identified Megan Llewellyn's ageing Citroen parked a few yards from her drive, although there was no sign of Suzanne's Mazda. None of the witness statements mentioned Nigel being present.

"A hire car, maybe?" Dawson surmised.

"Good thinking, Peter. Call the station and ask them to check rental firms in the area."

"What radius, guv'?"

Reason pondered for a moment, "Get them to start with Eastbourne, then fan out a few miles at a time. Tell them to be methodical, rather than simply going through the firms in telephone directory order."

Leaving the detective constable to pass on his instructions, Reason returned to the house, where he called for the forensics man.

"Up here, Steve. Wait a minute."

"No need to come down, Ray. There's a set of car keys on a hook in the cupboard under the stairs. I think you'll find they're for the Citroen parked in front of next door. I could do with you running your rule over that too."

Ray made the sound of a cash register opening to accept a deposit, "My pleasure!" he called back.

57

Reason simultaneously reached for his mobile and blearily looked at the green display on his Pure clock radio. Three fifteen. Who the hell was calling him at this hour?

The night shift at the station with the breaking news that Nigel Llewellyn had been apprehended in London!

Reason sat bolt upright in bed, his brain in overdrive. He peppered the sergeant with questions about Llewellyn's arrest and with instructions about getting ready for his interrogation.

His colleague didn't have the sort of details that Reason craved leaving the DI frustrated. His frustration grew even greater when he heard that the fugitive would not arrive in Eastbourne until late morning.

"You know as well as I do, Steve," the duty sergeant said, "that if we drag him down here in the middle of the night, his lawyers will be all over us."

Reason reluctantly accepted this and also realised that a tired and hungry interviewee would also be less productive. A similar observation applied to the interviewer, but there was no way he could get back to sleep after the phone conversation. He wanted to share the news with Dawson but figured that Heather wouldn't be too impressed. Instead, he spent the remainder of the night drinking coffee and rehearsing his strategy for tackling Nigel Llewellyn.

Despite his lack of sleep, Reason went to work high on a cocktail of adrenaline and dopamine and by the time the Metropolitan Police Volvo drew up in the station yard he felt razor sharp.

He made a beeline for the front desk as the arrested man was led in. Although he had become familiar with the Welshman's description, Reason studied him closely as the formalities of the handover were being completed. Tall and slim, the word 'angular' came to the DI's mind, Llewellyn had light auburn hair the waves of which gave the contradictory impression of being slightly wild but neatly arranged. His skin was pale but free of the freckles that often went with that hair type, gold wire glasses rested slightly below the bridge of his nose and his lips were thin. He was unshaven but his stubble lacked coarseness. He blinked nervously as he was signed in and taken along to the interview room. "At least he appears to have managed to get some sleep" Reason said to himself as he noted that alertness accompanied fear in the prisoner's eyes. To the detective's dismay, Llewellyn had arrived without a legal representative. That would mean a further delay while the suspect had the opportunity to discuss *his* strategy with an appointed solicitor.

It was almost midday before they were in a position to proceed. Superintendent Shaw had the good grace to allow DC Dawson to be alongside DI Reason in the interview, "It's only fair that you do the honours, Peter. I can watch the show through the one way mirror." Dawson welcomed Shaw's expression of faith in him. Would he look back on this as the pivotal moment at which he really had arrived as a detective?

The two detectives entered the interview room where Nigel Llewellyn was already seated with the duty solicitor, Brian Manning, an old but not unfriendly adversary of Reason's.

Reason nodded towards Dawson who dropped a tape into the recorder and switched it on. Reason swallowed hard. He had gone through this procedure on myriad occasions, but each time there was a sense of anticipation, which was heightened in big cases like this.

The formal announcement of who was in the room over, for the benefit of the tape Reason restated that Llewellyn had been arrested and was being interviewed under caution in connection with the murders of Conrad Gilligan, Danny Young, Alan Morrissey, Geoff Allen, Marion Allen and Mike Jarvis. Reeling off the list of the dead brought home afresh to Reason the shocking extent of the killer's activities.

"I didn't do anything," Llewellyn blurted out the second that Reason completed the roll call.

"I'm confused," Reason said gently, "because I can't square you going on the run with your claim of innocence."

"My client means that he didn't kill anyone" Manning interjected.

The DI ignored the solicitor, conveying with the minimum of words his expectation that the arrested man would speak for himself, "Mister Llewellyn?"

"You know I haven't killed anyone, you'll have already checked that I have an alibi on all those dates," Llewellyn said with a mixture of agitation and confidence.

"I know you were at work on all but one of the dates and I have no doubt that you will have a secure alibi for the other one."

Nigel Llewellyn smiled and nodded in an 'I told you so' way.

Reason smiled back. He felt encouraged to see a small chink in Llewellyn's armour so early in the process, "I'm intrigued by your reference to your alibi 'on all those dates'. Are you saying that you have committed to memory precisely when each of the murders took place?"

Llewellyn looked blankly at him. Manning leaned towards his client and advised against a response.

"Because if that is the case, Mister Llewellyn, I find that remarkable and significant," Reason moved metaphorically towards the suspect's jugular and turned towards Dawson. "Detective Constable Dawson, can you tell me the dates on which six murders took place?"

Dawson paused and Reason feigned irritation with him.

"Come on, man. You've been involved in this case since day one. Surely you must know when the crimes took place!"

Dawson tuned into the ruse, "I'm sorry, sir," he said with mock remorse, "I can't remember them all at the drop of a hat."

"Nor can I, DC Dawson, nor can I." He faced Llewellyn again, "Which is what makes your reference to the dates so interesting."

Manning stepped in again, "As you are well aware, Inspector Reason my client was making a general reference to his alibi when the killings took place."

"And I could've easily remembered the dates from all the news coverage," Nigel leapt in, "there's been enough of it."

Reason waved his acceptance, content in the knowledge that he could prompt such animated responses with so little effort. He looked at Llewellyn, who was rocking very slightly in his chair, his gaze averting the detectives' eyes.

"Is it all right for me to call you Nigel?" Reason asked softly.

Llewellyn focused in on the DI's face and he shrugged, "If you like."

Driven To Murder

Another little gain, imperceptible to the uninitiated, the informality of using a forename juxtaposed with the formality of the interview, the possibility of lulling Llewellyn into a false sense of security.

"OK Nigel, I am fully prepared to accept that you have not killed anyone..."

"..Good..." Llewellyn sighed with relief.

"..so that brings us to you being an accessory to murder, before and after the fact."

Llewellyn's face turned ashen. Manning whispered to him.

"You know the identity of the killer."

"No comment."

"It is your sister, Suzanne."

"No comment."

"You assisted her by providing information that would enable her to track down her intended targets."

"No comment."

"You were fully aware that she intended to kill these people."

"That's not true."

Another chink, Llewellyn was becoming agitated again, perhaps confused.

"Good, at least you're now admitting to providing the information."

"That's not what I said. No comment."

"You weren't aware that Suzanne planned to kill."

"No, that's what I said, isn't it?" Llewellyn was now shouting.

"OK, Nigel. Calm down. I accept that you didn't know what Suzanne had in mind ..."

Dawson looked puzzled. Was the DI going to let the bastard off the hook so easily?

Reason picked up the thread and swiftly disavowed his colleague of that interpretation,

"... at first, but you continued to provide information after she had started her killing spree."

"No comment."

"That makes you as guilty of most of the murders as the person who pulled the trigger."

"I know what you're trying to do," Llewellyn said cleverly, "You're trying to catch me out by bombarding me with questions. Well it won't work, 'cause you're just stabbing in the dark. You know I've got alibis and you can't prove any of what you're accusing me of."

Reason leaned back in his chair and rested his palms on the back of his neck. He puffed out his cheeks and tilted his head up, his eyes flicking from side to side across the ceiling.

The pose he had adopted had the desired effect.

"That's right, inspector. You've got nothing on me and you know it."

Reason came into land again and looked across at Llewellyn, "We'll see, Nigel. It's still early days. If you have nothing to hide, can you explain why you've been on the run ever since it became clear that there was a connection between the DVLA and the murders?"

Llewellyn clearly emboldened by his recent experience of victory answered smugly, "Wrong again, inspector. I remained at work on the day that Mister Jones, my manager, made his announcement about the murder enquiry. I remember it clearly enough, one of my colleagues died of a heart attack."

"Ah, yes," Reason said, "Greg Cuthbert. I stand corrected on the precise timing, Nigel. So, can you explain your movements from the next day onwards? Why did you take to flight?"

"No comment."

"What was your sister's reaction when you told her that the net was tightening?"

"No comment."

"She must have been very angry with you."

"No comment."

"Did she blame you for being careless in your search for information?"

"No comment."

"But that was so unfair," Reason's voice dropped almost to a whisper, "because you hadn't done anything wrong, had you Nigel?"

"No," Llewellyn realised that he may have left himself open and quickly added "comment" but too late to deny Reason the sense that he was a step further along the path towards Nigel's breaking point.

Manning tried to come to his rescue, "I think my client needs a break, inspector."

"No comment," Reason said firmly.

He enjoyed that.

"You can see Mister Llewellyn is stressed," the solicitor vainly attempted a rear-guard defence.

"In my experience, Mister Manning, stress is ninety per cent self-induced. I'll put my hand up to the ten per cent, the rest is down to your client and what he's been up to."

He didn't wait for a riposte and went back to work on Llewellyn.

"Are you all right to carry on for a little longer, Nigel? Then we'll sort you out some lunch."

Llewellyn shrugged his ascent.

"Tell me about what happened to your nephew, Rhodri," Reason set off on another tack, "he was killed in a road traffic accident wasn't he?"

Llewellyn's response was explosive and he banged on the table as he shouted, "It wasn't a fucking accident! Some bastard ran him over."

"You mean deliberately?"
"No, of course not," the Welshman angrily spat out his words.

"Then it was an accident, Nigel," Reason remained cool.

"The bastard didn't stop, he didn't fucking stop, but he must've known what he'd done. You can't do something like that and not know!"

286

Driven To Murder

"I agree, Nigel. You can't do something terrible and not have any awareness of the consequences. You must know that more than most."

Llewellyn saw through the ploy, "Think you're clever do you? Well, I'm not going to fall into your little trap. If you're so fucking smart, how is it that you never found the bastard that killed my little nephew?!"

"We weren't involved in that case," Dawson tried to explain in response to feeling personally under attack.

Reason waved away his comment and kept his focus on Llewellyn, "That must have hurt you all almost as much as Rhodri's death."

Llewellyn did not respond.

"No-one would blame your family for feeling as strongly about our failure to apprehend the hit-and-run driver as you did about the driver himself."

"It's your job, isn't it?" Llewellyn's question had an accusatory ring.

"In those circumstances, it's understandable if someone takes the law into their own hands."

"No comment."

"But you had no more joy identifying Rhodri's killer than we did."

"No comment."

Reason raised his voice a little, "So Suzanne decided to take her revenge elsewhere."

"No comment."

"On anyone who had transgressed while behind their steering wheel," Reason's voice continued its upward curve.

"No comment."

"In however small a way."

"No comment."

Reason, almost shouting now, "And you helped her!"

"No comment."

Reason sharply brought his decibel level back down, "I understand. It's important that families stick together." A momentary sadness at the erosion of his own family's glue, then back to the fray, "I can tell that you really care about Suzanne and right now the best way of demonstrating that care is to help us find her before she kills again."

"No comment."

Reason signalled to Dawson, who recorded the time of the suspension of the interview and noted the details on the ejected tape.

"Let's all do some thinking over lunch," Reason said from the doorway.

The two colleagues waited for Llewellyn to be escorted to the cells before emerging from the interview room. Shaw had laid on sandwiches in his office, to optimise the amount of time available for a debrief. He invited the junior detective for his views first.

"He's doing a good job of frustrating us with his stonewalling. I think he'll try to keep up the 'no comment' bollocks until we've exhausted the time limits." He wasn't much more positive when Shaw said that he anticipated no problems in securing an extension, "Let's just say if he were at the crease in a game of cricket, he'd probably bore his opponents to defeat."

"I thought I was the negative one on the team," Reason smiled. "What happened to your optimistic outlook, Peter?"

"We know the bastard's involved up to his neck and it would be a choker if he slips through our fingers," Dawson responded glumly.

"It won't come to that, Peter," the Superintendent reassured him. "If it looks as if we're running out of time, we'll charge him and I don't think there's a magistrate in the land who would agree to bail in a case of such importance and interest. What do you think, Steve?"

"Peter's right about the stonewalling, up to a point, but there are already little signs that the cement in that wall is crumbly."

"Then let me have a crack at him after lunch," Dawson said enthusiastically, "If you think he's weakening, it's time to go onto the offensive."

"You mean the old 'good cop, bad cop' routine?" Reason smiled again, "I think he's more likely to put up the shutters if he feels under sustained attack. I'd prefer to maintain the same line as before lunch."

Dawson wasn't happy with this, but knew he would have to defer to the Detective Inspector. His mood lightened a little when Reason added that if they ended the day without making further progress, he would throw Llewellyn to the lions for the next day's morning shift.

58

When the group re-assembled, Reason briefly engaged Llewellyn in small talk, checking that he had a decent lunch and a rest, before instructing Dawson to set up the recorder for the next phase of questioning.

"I am concerned by your lack of co-operation, Nigel," Reason kick-started the session, "not from my own point of view. I'm confident that we'll get a result. No, I'm concerned for you, Nigel. If you don't assist us with our enquiries, when things are wrapped up, you'll be facing a stiffer sentence. The difference between playing ball with us and running off with the ball could be as much as ten years." He looked for a glimmer of fear in Llewellyn's eyes, but before he could assess the impact of his comment, Manning stepped in, "Inspector, I do not expect you to make veiled threats to my client. I don't doubt that you are crudely knowledgeable when it comes to sentencing, but can I remind you that Mister Llewellyn hasn't been charged, let alone convicted and that it is for the judiciary not the police to determine punishment in our legal system."

Reason thanked Manning for his contribution but not without a degree of retaliation, "Mister Manning, I know you are only driven by your client's best interests and I admire you for that. I hope you will counsel him wisely in what those best interests might look like."

His short joust with the lawyer over, Reason faced Llewellyn again.

"On reflection, before lunch I was probably running before I could walk. You know, pushing you too hard without giving you a chance to explain yourself, Nigel. Let's go back to your last day at work before you went walkabout. I'd like to hear what happened after Mister Jones told you and your colleagues about the investigation." Reason held his hands up and picked at the cuffs of his shirt, "Look, nothing up my sleeves, no tricks, just genuine interest in your account of events. Are you OK with that, Nigel?"

Manning wanted to remind him that he didn't have to say anything, but the Welshman seemed comfortable enough. He described how everyone, including him, had returned to work. The police had become particularly animated over Cuthbert's disappearance. Then he was discovered dead in the toilets and a lot of people were upset. He had known Cuthbert quite well and was saddened by his death.

"So, along with some of your other colleagues, you decided to take the next day off, a mark of respect?" Reason prompted.

"Yes."

"Was it a co-ordinated gesture?"

The lines on Llewellyn's forehead tightened, "How do you mean?"

"Did you get together with the others to decide on the absence?"

"Not exactly. On the way out of the office, one or two people mentioned that they were thinking of doing it and I decided to follow suit."

"You didn't think to phone your absence in?" Reason asked gently.

"I tried a few times" Llewellyn explained, "but the line was engaged, so I guess I gave up."

"You guess you gave up," Reason repeated. "I don't suppose you know how many lines there are into the DVLA exchange, do you Nigel?"

"No."

"Nor do I, but I'd guess that there'd need to be several, for the volume of business the office does."

"That's my point," Llewellyn added confidently, "things get so busy that all the lines can be in use at any one time."

"But surely not at the time of day when people are phoning in sick for work. Anyway, don't you have a separate personnel line for that?" Reason persisted with his matter-of-fact curiosity about the DVLA telephone system.

"Yes, that's what I meant. I assumed that lots of us were staying off work for the day and the absence line couldn't cope," Llewellyn seemed flustered and, to Dawson's horror, Reason didn't press home his advantage. "I expect you spent the rest of the day quietly at home, reflecting on what a good bloke Greg Cuthbert was and contemplating mortality. Or, at least, that's the sort of thing I would have done."

"Yes, something like that."

"It must have been difficult," Reason offered a vague prompt.

"Yes," Llewellyn agreed.

"What was?" Reason asked without adding a degree of sharpness to his tone.

Llewellyn felt confused, "What was what?!" he demanded impatiently.

"What was difficult?" Reason clarified. "Staying at home all day when you're used to being out and about? Losing a colleague? Thinking about life and death? Or was it difficult because a witness saw you drive away from your house the evening before and you didn't return there on the day of spontaneous mourning."

"The witness must've been wrong," Llewellyn countered.

"Oh, did I say 'witness' singular. I meant to use the plural. How many corroborating statements do we have, DC Dawson?"

"Five, sir."

"Added to which my colleagues in the South Wales Constabulary had your place under surveillance the day after Mister Cuthbert's sad demise. Nigel, it's not looking very good for you. I'm going to suspend the interview now at one fifty three p.m. ...." he waited for Dawson to press the switch ".. and give you some quality time alone with Mister Manning. My hunch is that you and he have got a few things to discuss." He waited for Dawson to write the time on the tape and the two officers stepped outside and rendezvoused with Shaw, who drew on the benefit of hindsight to say that Llewellyn had looked scared and vulnerable from the minute he entered the station.

"I'm sure he did," Reason commented doing his best to play down the sarcasm, "but I don't think it's us he's afraid of."

"A long stretch inside," Dawson opined.

Reason acknowledged that possibility although he remained open to other explanations.

"Either way, we've got him," the junior officer trumpeted.

Reason was more measured, "We're getting there, Peter, but it's advisable not to assume that he hasn't finished twisting and turning yet. We'll need to be prepared for more bullshit, keep cool and take it in our stride."

The deliberations between Manning and Llewellyn lasted much longer than any of the officers had foreseen, which Reason took as an encouraging sign of them being involved in some wrangling over what to do next.

Nearly an hour had elapsed when the solicitor appeared at the door to advise the uniform on guard that they were ready to resume.

The tape was set in motion for the third time and Reason offered the two men opposite the opportunity to speak first. He wouldn't have bet on it, but he hoped against hope that Llewellyn might simply come clean.

Manning declined their invitation, "My client is happy to field your questions."

Reason took a deep breath, "Nigel, we've established that after coming home on the day Greg Cuthbert died, you drove off and didn't return. Why was that?"

"I panicked," Llewellyn answered, with what for Reason was a disappointing lack of panic in his voice.

"Tell me more, Nigel."

"With the police crawling all over the office, I thought I'd be found out."
Reason waited in silence.

"I've been making a few quid on the side, you know, unofficial searches, that sort of thing."

"I see and you were afraid that we would stumble across this and you'd be for the chop."

"Something like that."

Reason rested his chin on his fingertips while he appeared to chew things over. This was solely for effect, to make the man opposite think he was struggling to work out his next step. This was already mapped out in Reason's mind.

"There's something I don't understand about the technology at the DVLA. By the way, don't be surprised if DC Dawson pulls a funny face or two during this part. He's s whizz kid with computers and, not without good cause, has me down as a bit of a dinosaur. If you were worried about detection, couldn't you simply flit from computer to computer to cover your tracks?"

Llewellyn smiled almost sympathetically, "You weren't kidding when you said you were completely ignorant when it came to computers." Reason interrupted him to say that he hadn't put it that strongly and that he'd appreciate Nigel going a little more gently with him.

"Unless someone forgets to log off, which would leave you with instant access, you have to go through the log on procedure. In old-fashioned speak," he smiled sarcastically at Reason, "like clocking on and off. It must be the same with your system." Dawson affirmed this.

"I'm slowly catching up," Reason said with faked pain, "So you're telling us that you didn't bother to use other computers for your moonlighting. You did it all at your own desk?"

"Yes."

Reason shook his head, "I'm really struggling to make sense of your behaviour, Nigel. Running off like that has resulted in the very thing you said you wanted to avoid. We'll have to check your story out and that will mean uncovering your illicit activity. You could be booted out of the DVLA for certain."

"Better than being done for conspiracy to murder, inspector."

296

Driven To Murder

They took another break while Reason made contact with Ieuan Griffith to request further checks on the DVLA system.

"It'll take a while to verify your story," he advised Llewellyn on his return.

"I don't see why," Llewellyn responded authoritatively, "It's a straightforward enough procedure and my activity will show up on my computer."

"Your colleagues at DVLA are a bit under strength at the moment so we've got to be patient. In the meantime, I'd like to ask you some more questions."

Llewellyn shrugged in his already familiar fashion.

"Have you had contact with your mother in the last seventy two hours?"

"I ring her a couple of times a week."

"That's a yes, then?"

"I suppose so."

Dawson had had enough of the pussy footing about, "If you're in regular touch, you must know when you last spoke to her, so stop acting mysteriously and tell us the bloody truth."

Unexpectedly Reason threw the interviewee a life line, "I think I understand the pressure you've been under, Nigel. It's not so unusual to lose track of little things in such circumstances."

"Exactly," Llewellyn sneered in Dawson's direction.

"I'd like you to try to remember, Nigel," Reason came back, "You see, I'm a little concerned about her safety."

Llewellyn was startled, "What do you mean?!"

"Well, she's not been seen at home for a couple of days, but her car is still at the house."

"Perhaps she's taken a break for a couple of days."

"Gone somewhere with Suzanne, you mean?"

"Probably, they go off for weekends sometimes."

"Seems strange that they didn't tell you where they were off to, you being so close, Nigel."

"No comment."

Reason suggested leaving it there until he'd heard back from South Wales. Manning negotiated a temporary return to his office on the clear condition that Reason would summon him as soon as he was ready to pick up the interview again.

"Which will be tomorrow morning at the earliest, regardless of when I hear back from DC Griffith," Reason said to Dawson once the solicitor had left.

"That's more like it guv'" Dawson gave his approval, "Let's make the bastard sweat."

"As if I'd be so cruel to a fellow human being," Reason rebuked his colleague, "No, I need to gain a little more thinking time."

Dawson saw through him, "Whatever you say, you're the boss."

298

For what seemed like the first time since he had started out on the bloody trail, Reason reflected on a more or less wholly progressive day. Not only did he sense that Nigel Llewellyn was pinned on the ropes, but uniform came up trumps with their search for Suzanne's car. Dawson had made a chalk mark in the air when it was confirmed as being parked near to a car rental base in Hastings. Reason smiled as he visualised Ray Miller rubbing his hands with glee when he heard that he had another site to examine. The hire car would not take long to detect, although Reason suspected that the Llewellyn women would probably abandon it and hire another. No doubt they would keep swapping in this way until they reached their destination, but Reason could not get his head around where that might be.

Although it had been a very good day, he opted out of a drink with Dawson, "If you don't mind, Peter, I'll put it on hold until we're ready to celebrate. I don't want to take anything for granted."

His words came back to bite him later that evening in the form of another text from Isobel,

"Still w8ng 4 ur apology. Don't take me for granted!"

He replied with what he intended as a holding position, "Sorry, snowed under at present. I will get back to you when I can."

"Damn texting," he said to himself, as Isobel's response flashed onto his screen, "Some apology! Cant w8 4 ur nxt offer!"

Reason didn't like texts at the best of times, they were one down the evolutionary chain from emails, but he was in no mood for getting embroiled in a protracted argument tonight. "If you can't wait, Isobel," he thought out loud, "so be it. It's been nice knowing you."

He went to bed wondering whether his callous streak would still be in working order for the next round with Messrs Manning and Llewellyn.

59

On his arrival, Reason found an email from Griffith providing everything he needed from the latest trawl through the DVLA systems. Perhaps he'd been a bit harsh. When emails were this good he wouldn't hear a word said against them.

The two pairs of adversaries settled down around the table. Reason did his best to convey genuine sympathy when Llewellyn said he had not slept well, but he was itching to get stuck in, "I'll take that into account, Nigel. I'll be gentle with you."

Dawson grinned broadly. He was looking forward to seeing Llewellyn squirm.

"You said yesterday that the reason you panicked and ran was because of your moonlighting," Reason recapped.

Llewellyn nodded.

"For the benefit of the tape, Mister Llewellyn answered with an affirmative nod," Dawson commented.

"I've now received verification of that, based on analysis of your work station. On two occasions you unilaterally waived procedure to accommodate unofficial requests. As a matter of interest, can you remember how much you received for these?"

"Fifty pounds."

"In total or each?"

"Each!" Llewellyn exclaimed in a way indicating astonishment that Reason could have thought that he would settle for less.

"And you said you only conducted this business from your own computer?"

Another nod from the Welshman, who didn't wait for Dawson this time, "Yes."

"So you've only dabbled with the dark side twice, yet the appearance of the police on a wholly unrelated matter sends you running for cover, a move that is guaranteed to draw attention to you in the precise way you say you were trying to avoid. You can see why I might be having trouble making sense of that, can't you Nigel?"

Llewellyn started to become restless, "I've already told you, I panicked. People do some strange things when they panic, they stop thinking straight."

"Indeed," Reason said cheerfully, "I almost ended up there myself." He sat back with a contented smile and waited.

The silence could only have lasted for four seconds, but that was too much for Llewellyn, "What do you mean?"

"I mean when you confessed to moonlighting, you nearly threw my entire chain of thought into a nose dive. There was I thinking that you were in abject denial with your 'no comments' when out of the blue you admit to being on the make. If only you hadn't been in such a hurry to own up, I might have joined you in Panic Alley."

"What the fuck are you on about?" Llewellyn hissed, "You're doing my head in with your silly mind games."

"I can empathise. You're explanation of computer log-ins was having the same effect on my brain, but happily DC Dawson had no difficulty grasping what you were saying. Roughly translated, 'look for the petty stuff on my computer and keep away from the other consoles'."

302

More waiting to allow the meaning to sink in, then Reason invited Dawson to lay the last card, "Obviously it took a few hours, but with your colleagues and ours working through the night, we've identified the computers from which you searched on your sister's behalf and the dates and times of those searches."

Reason took the baton back from his colleague, "Nigel Llewellyn, I am hereby charging you with conspiracy to murder, accessory to murder and assisting an offender to avoid capture. You do not have to say anything. But it may harm your defence if you do not mention something which you later rely on in court. Anything you say may be given in evidence."

Reason recorded the termination of the interview and instructed the uniformed officer to take Llewellyn back to the cells.

"Wait!" the Welshman pleaded. "If I tell you everything I know will I be treated with leniency?"

"That won't be my decision," Reason said sternly. "A court may take the view that you could have been more forthcoming earlier in the piece, but if you help us now, that is really help us, Nigel, I'll be willing to put in a word."

Manning advised Llewellyn to think things through before carrying on.

Llewellyn rejected his advice and for good measure said he would manage without him from now on.

"As the solicitor appointed to protect your interests in a very stressful and confusing context, I cannot overstate the risks of continuing unaided."

"You've done what you can and I'm grateful, but the rest is down to me. I know what I'm doing."

Manning gathered up his papers and placed them carefully in his briefcase, "You know where I am if you change your mind" he said as he scurried out.

"Do you think Superintendent Shaw should take over from me at this stage, sir?" Dawson showed uncharacteristic deference before they entered the last lap.

"No, I think Mister Llewellyn will be happier to work this out with familiar faces. Nigel?"

The accused concurred, "Better the devil you know, eh?"

The recorder whirred into action.

"In your own time and your own words, Nigel," Reason encouraged, "take us through what happened."

Inevitably, Llewellyn viewed Rhodri's tragic death as the start line. "You can't begin to imagine the grief that swept through the family. Our mother was inconsolable, she felt as responsible for his death as the person who drove into him. I suppose people handle loss in different ways, Suzanne's default position was anger, not with mum, just the person who had deprived her of her only child and ..." he paused.

"Us," Reason filled in the gap.

"Yes, she couldn't come to terms with the police's failure to find the culprit. She compared you lot to her colleagues in the military. 'They don't know they're born' she would say, 'fucking police wouldn't last a day in Afghanistan, no room for incompetence there, unless you plan to come back in a body bag'. It became a sort of mantra for her, fuming about Rhodri's killer and slagging you guys off for letting him get away."

"How about you, Nigel? How did you cope with the loss?"

"It was different for me. Don't get me wrong, I loved my nephew, but living so far away, I didn't get to see that much of him, so perhaps the loss wasn't as intense for me. But I paid for that lack of intensity, boy, did I pay for it?"

"How?" Dawson picked up Reason's lead and prompted Llewellyn gently.

"Suzanne turned on me. She couldn't understand how I could express so little emotion about Rhodri. I tried to tell her that I was hurting inside, that his death was gnawing away at me, but she was having none of it. Called me every name under the sun, she did. Even managed to turn our mother against me. The two of them were always on the 'phone to me, goading me, taunting me about what they saw as my weakness. It was hell, I couldn't eat, I couldn't sleep, my concentration at work started to go."

"It sounds as if you had an awful time, Nigel. What did you do?"

"I told Suzanne that nothing we could do would bring Rhodri back but that I'd do anything to restore our family cohesion."

"And that's when she asked you to do some research for her?" Dawson checked.

"Yes, I didn't know what she wanted the information for, not at first. She persuaded me that it was such a small thing to ask of her brother so I gave the names and addresses of the people whose car registrations she provided."

"Do you really expect us to believe that you didn't suspect what it was in aid of, that you weren't even curious?" Dawson pressed, reverting to a less patient frame of mind.

"It's the God's honest truth. I was too immersed in the loss, not only of my nephew but also my sister and mother, to take account of what lay behind Suzanne's requests."

"When did the penny drop, Nigel?"

"I think it was after the third murder," Llewellyn tried to recall.

"Alan Morrissey?" Reason tried to jog his memory.

"Yes, that's the one. I hadn't followed the news before that, but when his name was mentioned, I made the connection."

"And went on supplying Suzanne with more names and addresses! That's unbelievable!" Dawson cried.

"Go easy, DC Dawson," Reason intervened, anxious that Llewellyn might clam up again if under fire.

"You don't know Suzanne, DC Dawson. If you did, perhaps you'd understand that I was trapped and didn't dare stop assisting her."

"She threatened you?"

"Indirectly. If I didn't help her she would make sure that I never saw our mother again."

Dawson took this to mean that Suzanne would kill her own mother in order to despise Nigel, but he swiftly corrected the DC. "Mum had already joined Suzanne's attack on me and my sister wouldn't need to push her very hard before she cut me out completely."

"You were worried about your share of the family inheritance?" Dawson persisted.

"Of course not. This was more important than money, constable."

"Parental affection and sibling rivalry," Reason suggested. He knew first-hand about the effects of a family splintering. "This has proved most helpful in mapping out the background, Nigel," he continued, "but what we need most of all right now is to know how the land currently lies. I take it that you tipped Suzanne and your mother off about our activity?"

"Yes."

"Do you know where they are at present?"

"No."

Dawson threw Llewellyn a black look.

"Honestly, I don't have a clue. After telling you what I have so far, I've got nothing to gain by holding back other information."

Dawson wasn't going to be shaken off that quickly, "You were picked up at Victoria station so we can assume that you were planning to travel to Polegate."

"I wasn't sure what I was doing or where I was going," Llewellyn defended himself, "I wasn't able to think straight. Yes, I was probably heading for mum's place, but with no expectation that she'd still be there." He was visibly agitated as he struggled to convince Dawson that he was telling the truth.

Reason picked this up and continued to talk calmly, "Nigel, can you tell me if the murders have followed the same sequence as Suzanne's requests for information?" Llewellyn shut his eyes as he recalled the order of the killings, "Yes," he said assuredly.

"Was Mike Jarvis's the last registration plate that Suzanne asked you to check out?"

"No, she's recently asked for one more."

"Can you remember the details?"

Nigel Llewellyn shook his head, "Sorry, my mind's scrambled at the moment." Then he remembered that the car registration was written on a piece of card in his wallet.

Dawson told the recorder that he was leaving to fetch Mister Llewellyn's wallet. He had only just left the room when Llewellyn's face lit up, "The name has just come to me, or part of it anyway," he declared. "Being Welsh myself, I wondered at the time whether the person was a compatriot. Her name is Owen."

60

Reason didn't wait for Dawson to return. He'd rather forewarn Harriet and find out that the next target was a different Owen than delay a second longer and run the risk of losing a colleague. His hand was shaking as he scanned his mobile for her number. It rang five times then the voicemail message kicked in. "Shit!" Reason shouted and grabbed the landline handset, "Put me through to DCI Owen in Lewes!" he ordered, hurting the switchboard operator's feelings in the process.

Stockbridge picked up at the other end.... No, the DCI wasn't in the office.... No, she wasn't on leave so there was no point trying her home number.... She had received a call some while back and left the building shortly afterwards .... No idea where, but it might be worth trying the main reception where everyone signed in and out ... fire safety and all that .... No need to be aggressive .. putting you through now.

The receptionist at Police Headquarters was helpful, to a degree. The DCI had said she was heading over Eastbourne way. She knew it wasn't to the police station, but she had only half caught the name of Owen's destination. "If you pressed me I'd say it was something like Babylon but that can't be right," she laughed nervously. She heard the phone being slammed down at Reason's end and became the third person in the space of a few minutes to comment on his rudeness.

Babylon Down! A short walk from the car park at Butts Brow and not much more than a stone's throw from where the Llewellyn boy had been run over!

Reason almost collided with Dawson as he dashed into the corridor. He demanded the number. "It looks famil...." He didn't let his colleague finish but snatched the card from his hand. "Just as I thought, it's Harriet Owen's. I think she's been lured to Babylon Down by Suzanne Llewellyn. I'm heading up there. Peter, get onto Shaw for a chopper and Dunlop's crew. Keep me posted on my mobile." He continued on his way.

"But you haven't got hands free guv'" Dawson shouted after him.

"No time for a bloody road safety lecture, Peter!" his voice tailed off as the double doors swung closed behind him.

As he sped towards the exit, Reason felt in urgent need of an unmarked car. His own Audi, a reliable old friend would not be nippy enough for the task at hand. He was in luck, Frank Graham was on duty and he handed over the keys to a new Astra without the formality of booking it out.

The three mile drive from Grove Road to Butts Brow was a white knuckle affair, made worse by an unexpectedly heavy shower of rain. With the portable light flashing and the horn locked on, Reason's fellow road users had plenty of warning of his approach. That didn't mean he had a completely clear run up the climb out of town as a couple of nervous and elderly drivers were thrown into a state of dithering by the sight and sound of the Astra closing fast. Reason fought his impatience. He had to stay cool, focus on the road, but also try to envisage the scene that might greet him at Babylon Down. What a time to have to multi-task!

The speed cameras on Upperton Road flashed as if saluting his progress. By the cemetery he swept past a bus that was labouring up the hill, narrowly avoiding a startled taxi driver on his way to the station. He could see the lights ahead at the Eldon Road junction turning to red and cursed. "Hold your nerve!" he heard himself say, as he again veered onto the wrong side of the road to overtake the double

310

file of parked and halted vehicles. A brief hiatus at the junction as one of the cars coming from the Rodmill Drive froze part way through its turn into Eldon Road, then dramatic acceleration away with the world shrinking rapidly in his rear view mirror.

His mobile buzzed and he struggled to keep control of the car and take Dawson's call at the same time.

No joy with the armed response team, a major security alert at Gatwick Airport. The helicopter was also involved elsewhere but would be diverted. It would be with him in ten minutes all being well. Not soon enough!

Reason was pleased to clear the lights at Victoria Drive without a repeat of the last delay and the rain had stopped which gave him a further edge. As he careered up Wish Hill he calculated that the only remaining hazard might be in the narrow twist in the road as he hit the historic centre of Willingdon Village. A sharp left into Butts Lane and as he embarked upon the final steep climb, he killed the horn and beacon. He slowed to pull into the car park, hoping that his arrival would pass unnoticed. Two other cars were parked up. Reason immediately recognised the DCI's, which he approached with stealth. He got out and felt its bonnet, which was hot to the touch. She hadn't been there long. Perhaps he was not too late. No heat from the other car which must have been there longer or travelled a much shorter distance. Suzanne Llewellyn? Lying in wait to ambush Owen?

His body had trouble unscrambling the mixed messages from his brain as he headed for Babylon Down. Get there fast! Make yourself small! Use speed! Use stealth! He had only gone a few steps along the track when he met a short woman walking a black Labrador. Small and bespectacled, the woman was wearing a tweed skirt, a gilet and a head scarf. Fleetingly he thought it would be more fitting for her to be walking corgis. Breathlessly he asked if she had seen two women ahead. Yes, to his left, by an outcrop of trees. They'd not returned her 'good morning'.

Before he had parted company with the dog walker, his eyes were scanning the area to pick out Harriet and her contact. What if the woman with the Labrador *was* the contact? Shit! Would Suzanne go to the trouble of a disguise? A swift calculation, the least likely option.

A second later and his eyes fell on the two women, now barely a hundred yards away. Little cover between him and them. Staying as low as he could, Reason carefully picked his way from one scrubby bush to another, never taking his eyes off Owen and the other woman. They seemed to be in animated conversation across the few feet that separated them. Reason's heart hammered against his rib cage as he closed in on them. It nearly broke free of the cage when he saw the second woman, whom he now recognised as Suzanne from the picture that had been circulated, pulled a gun.

No time to think, Reason broke cover and screamed like a banshee as he hurtled towards them. Suzanne turned, the gun now trained on him, but only briefly. In the split second of distraction, Harriet Owen launched herself at Llewellyn. The gun went off at the moment of impact, so close to Owen's head that she was left temporarily deaf in one ear. Under normal circumstances, the police woman would have no chance in combat with the physically tougher ex-soldier, but catching Suzanne off guard she was able to knock her to the hard ground, hand cuff her and immobilise her legs with plastic ties while she lay winded.

Disoriented by the awful ringing in her ear, in her moment of triumph Owen had forgotten Reason. Then, his non-appearance at her side registered in her consciousness and she turned to see him lying still a few yards away.

She picked up Suzanne's weapon and shakily kept it pointing at her as she went to her colleague's assistance. Reason lay unconscious with blood seeping through the front of his shirt. The bullet had hit him high up in his chest. Owen pulled out her mobile, but the need to call for an ambulance was rendered unnecessary as the police helicopter came into view. Unbeknown to her, the pilot had already spotted the group and Owen frantically waved her arms around to signal their whereabouts.

As she sought to reassure Reason that help had arrived, she struggled to understand why the chopper was standing off, not coming into land. Then it dawned that they might not be in a hurry to put down near a woman, whom they didn't recognise, waving a gun in the air near to two prone bodies. She signalled again in as exaggerated fashion as she could invent and threw the weapon to the ground.

This and her obvious concern for one of the people on the ground did the trick and the pilot brought the helicopter down onto the flattest available spot, abut twenty yards away. Owen flashed her ID and left the crew to tend to Reason while she returned to complete the arrest of Suzanne Llewellyn, who, to the detective's surprise, was lying still and apparently calm.

Owen summoned a squad car to collect her prisoner and once more went back to Steve. The helicopter team had already got him onto a stretcher, attached him to a drip and were ferrying him the short distance to the aircraft. "We've already got the District General Hospital standing by. He'll be in their care within five minutes," the pilot reassured her.

Dawson arrived on the scene just in time to see the helicopter lift off. He joined Owen as she stood guard over Suzanne Llewellyn. "The guv'nor, will he be OK?" the DC asked, undisguised anxiety shrouding his words.

"I hope so," Owen replied pensively.

The storm of the last few minutes having passed, her conscious self began to take over. Why had she been so stupid in accepting an unknown caller's invitation to meet for vital information about the recent murders? Why hadn't she notified Reason? Her only conclusion was that she was driven by a need to restore her hurt pride in the wake of losing the case, losing Boronin and losing Steve, although he wasn't even hers to lose. She had put herself in danger, but, much worse, had put him in the firing line, literally. Unnecessarily and avoidably. He had saved her life, but how would she live with herself if he lost his? She suddenly felt a deep chill coursing through her entire body, in defiance of the warmth of the late summer morning. She shivered and a lost her battle to hold back a tear.

61

Over the next three days, DC Dawson experienced new depths of anxiety and tension. Although Reason had been 'lucky', in that the bullet from the Browning pistol had missed his heart, he was in a bad way and yet to regain consciousness. This weighed heavily on Dawson's mind and he seized every opportunity to get to the DI's bedside. Invariably, he met either Harriet Owen, who carried an even greater mental burden over the turn of events, or Isobel Perry. It struck Dawson that the pathologist seemed less self-assured around the living than the dead, although, in fairness to her, he shared her sense of helplessness.

As Dawson had expected, Superintendent Shaw announced that he would take an active part in the interviewing of Suzanne Llewellyn. The constable had instantly heard Reason in his head, "There you go, Peter. Just as I told you, when it comes to the glory end of things, you can rely on Shaw to be there," only for the Super's stronger voice to intrude with the news that he, Dawson, would be leading the interrogation. He could hardly believe his ears, but affirmation came swiftly in the form of encouraging noises and slaps on his back from colleagues.

For all his astonished pride in being given the lead, Dawson's anxiety had now opened up on a second front. And in the process, he had been presented with a dilemma. How could he do justice to his new role *and* sustain the frequency of his vigil at the hospital?

Once the celebration of his appointment had subsided, Dawson wasted no time in taking the problem to Shaw, who thankfully was very understanding, "I *could* relieve you of the interviews, Peter," he said, "but, DI Reason apart, no-one has your depth of knowledge of this case. Of course, it's a foregone conclusion that Suzanne Llewellyn will be convicted, so a trained chimpanzee could probably wrap this one up, but there's an issue of ownership of the case. This is your investigation, Peter. Yours and Steve's, that is, and you must ask yourself whether he'll be happy when he finds out that you had backed out of this."

Dawson agonised for a moment. He sensed that whatever he decided would simultaneously be right for one reason and wrong for another. While he very much wanted to tie such a big case up, he didn't want his ambition to be seen as a callous disregard for the colleague whom he most admired. Shaw broke his tangled chain of thought.

"Besides, Peter," he beamed, "do you want to be harangued by DI Reason for the rest of your career for letting that bastard Shaw take the credit?"

As Shaw and Dawson prepared themselves for the interview, Suzanne Llewellyn and her solicitor did likewise in their parallel universe. Whereas the police rehearsal reflected their heightened state of arousal, Llewellyn's was calm and understated. The hapless Brian Manning, who had again drawn the short straw when Suzanne had indicated her openness to whichever legal representative was available, felt uneasy in her presence. At first he thought that this was because of the near certainty that she was a mass murderer, but after a while deduced that it was the dispassionate sense of control that she exerted over their briefings.

"Let's be absolutely clear, Mister Manning," she said, as they were about to set off for the interview room, "I don't want any of that whispering in the ear crap, no interruptions supposedly on my behalf. I am not some dippy little teenage shoplifter who can't think for herself. If I need your assistance, I'll ask for it. Otherwise, you are to sit there taking notes and saying nothing. Right?"

Manning nodded.

"Right?" Suzanne reiterated, this time more forcefully.

"Right," Manning replied timorously.

"Excellent, Mister Manning," Suzanne smiled thinly, "I can see we're going to be a great team."

The solicitor shuddered at the thought. Yes, from a legal perspective, he was required to be on her side, but this wasn't a voluntary association. He was with her under duress.

In the build-up to the interview, to have said that Dawson had butterflies in his stomach would have been a gross understatement. There were enough in there to set a convention of lepidopterists fluttering. However, once the formalities were over, and he had commenced his interrogation, Dawson's nerves immediately abated. What Shaw had forewarned could be a difficult encounter turned out to be almost alarmingly straightforward. Suzanne Llewellyn had evidently decided to play everything as straight as a die.

From a professional perspective, Manning found her candour alarming. She was providing him with no opportunity to fight so much as an inch of her corner. His personal view was entirely different, being one of relief that the process would be relatively short and he could escape from this wretched woman's company much sooner than he had feared.

"Ms Llewellyn," Dawson had opened, only to be advised that she would prefer to be addressed by her forename, "Until such time as you upset me, when I will expect things to become cold and formal," she had added with a hint of malevolence.

Dawson was not fazed by this, but merely nodded calmly, while holding her gaze. "You might be a crazed killer, capable of instilling fear into an entire population" he said to himself, "but you can't put the shits up me, not on my patch."

"Suzanne," he started again, "In the course of this interview, my aim will be to establish that you committed the murder of Conrad Gilligan."

She jumped in, "I admit it."

Slightly caught off guard by her dramatic capitulation, Dawson moved to the next name which he stated with a questioning inflexion, "Danny Young?"

"Yes, I killed him too," Suzanne answered calmly.

Manning made as if to intervene, but remembering his client's unequivocal injunction, did not go through with the action.

"Alan Morrissey?"

"Yes."

"Geoff and Marion Allen?"

"Yes."

"Mike Jarvis?"

"Yes."

"Suzanne, I need to be certain about this. You are confessing to all six murders?"

Llewellyn stared hard across the table, her eyes locked onto Dawson's face, "I thought I had made myself crystal clear, Detective Constable Dawson, but if you are too thick to assimilate my words, perhaps I should change my tune and simply deny everything. I'm sure my friend Mister Manning would feel a lot happier if I put the 'No Comment' cracked record on."

"Nothing could be further from the truth," the solicitor thought, hoping that Dawson would not get bogged down in a search for an elusive affirmation from his client of what she had already affirmed.

Dawson got the message, "That brings me to the attempted murders of Detective Chief Inspector Harriet Owen and Detective Inspector Stephen Reason."

Suzanne Llewellyn sneered, "So, you want to have your cake and eat it, do you, DC Dawson? Is that wise? After all, doesn't greed come before a fall?"

Dawson chose not to correct her over the proverb and simply sat and waited for her to make the next comment.

"I can't deny that I threatened the policewoman with a gun, but 'attempted murder'? I don't think that will stick. And as for poor Inspector Plod, well, I think a jury would see that as self-defence. They'd understand that when he charged at me, I naturally reacted to a perceived threat. That's what I've been trained to do."

While she was finishing, Superintendent Shaw whispered something into Dawson's ear.

"How fetching," Suzanne mocked, "His Master's Voice! Come on, Detective Constable, isn't it about time you asserted your authority and demonstrated who is in charge here?"

"Well, Suzanne," Dawson smiled, "I appreciate your backing on that score. At least we have established that *you* are not chairing this meeting."

"Very clever," Llewellyn spat, "but then it's easy to be clever in a cosy little hole like this. Another matter altogether when it comes to tracking down a killer."

"We've got you, haven't we?" Shaw stepped in.

"I was talking about the person who killed my son!" Suzanne cried angrily.

Dawson tried to soothe her, "Losing Rhodri must've been dreadful."

"Have you got children?" she asked accusingly.

"No," Dawson admitted.

"Have you ever had someone you loved ripped away from you like that?"

"No," Dawson repeated, although he wondered whether DI Reason might soon fall into that category.

"Then, you can't even begin to imagine how dreadful it is!" Suzanne snapped, "So you can shove your false sympathy."

By this stage, she was shaking quite violently. The DC contemplated the need for medical assistance, but her storm ended as abruptly as it had begun.

"I want to take a break," Suzanne Llewellyn said quietly, almost meekly.

"But we've only been going a few minutes," Shaw protested.

320

Driven To Murder

Suzanne turned to her solicitor and made a gesture with her head back towards the other side of the table.

Brian Manning took his cue, "Gentleman, you must realise how harrowing this is for my client. Ms Llewellyn has co-operated with you and, unless I am mistaken, she intends to continue with that co-operation. Respecting her need to collect her thoughts seems a small favour to ask."

With ill-disguised reluctance, Shaw led the withdrawal. He feared that Suzanne would use the hiatus to back track on her previous admission and was unimpressed by Manning's part in that possible outcome, " 'Harrowing for his client'!" Shaw scoffed, "'Harrowing' doesn't begin to describe the impact of her actions on others."

Belying his lesser experience, Dawson tried to see the situation from Llewellyn's angle, "I don't think the interview in itself is at all upsetting for her, but any reference to her son is off the scale in terms of distress. I hope I never experience anything like that."

"Such a wise head on young shoulders, Peter," Shaw said in genuine admiration and astonishment. "I owe you an apology, because I never had you down as being so thoughtful."

"Let's just say I've had a good teacher," Dawson smiled, "and on that note, would you mind if I use this break to call the hospital to see if there's any change with the guv'nor?"

Returning from the news that Reason's condition was still the same, Dawson was pleased to find that Suzanne Llewellyn's position was also unchanged. As Manning had hoped and prayed, she indicated that she would co-operate as fully as their approach allowed her to.

Dawson thanked her then picked up the thread of the attempted murder of two police officers.

"With regard to Detective Chief Inspector Owen, we have irrefutable evidence and your brother's confession that he procured her details on your behalf in the same way that he did the details of the six people you have admitted to murdering. That and the statement that DCI Owen has provided should be sufficient to show that you meant to kill her too. Are you denying this because you know that the courts are particularly harsh on those who murder or attempt the murder of police officers?"

Suzanne slowly shook her head, "At the time, I didn't even know she was a police officer. When she answered her mobile by saying her rank, I nearly rang off." She paused, "Oh, not out of respect. After your failure to catch the person who killed my son, respect for the police is the last thing I have, no, I thought the risks were too great."

"But, you went ahead anyway?"
"Yes, I backed my hunch that she would be willing to comply with my request to come alone in exchange for the quality of information I could give her."

"You misunderstand my point, Suzanne," Dawson responded, "You went ahead with your plot to lure Harriet Owen to her death, even once you'd established that she was a police officer."

The woman opposite conceded the point, but wondered whether what she had done constituted attempted murder, given that she hadn't fired a shot at the DCI.

"That'll be for the Crown Prosecution Service to decide," Dawson observed, before turning to the shooting of DI Reason.

322

"Your claim that you were acting in self-defence won't hold water, Suzanne."

"I don't know," she frowned. "As I said before, I've been trained to respond to ambushes. In Afghanistan if it doesn't become second nature or even a sixth sense, you don't last long."

"Yes," Dawson mused, "that training must equip you with the ability to react with incredible speed and accuracy."

"It does."

"And enable you to distinguish immediately between an armed insurgent and a harmless peasant?"

"Of course!"

"And between an armed and unarmed policeman," Dawson said triumphantly.

Suzanne Llewellyn thought for a moment, "I heard the sound of the advancing helicopter, and started to panic. So when Inspector Reason appeared from nowhere, I no longer had my usual high level control over the situation."

"Are you denying that you intended to kill DI Reason?"

"I am."

"So you shot to wound him?"

Suzanne held her ground, "No, I shot as a reaction to being attacked."

Dawson said he was having difficulty coming to terms with her coyness in respect of the incident at Babylon Down. She had admitted to six killings and must know that denying culpability with regard to the two detectives made no sense.

"Including the intended murders of DCI Owen and DI Reason in the prosecution isn't going to make any difference to your probable sentence," he said, "In this case, I'd be surprised if 'life' didn't mean 'life'."

Manning started to utter his mantra about judicial responsibility for sentencing only to be cut off sharply by his client, "I shouldn't have to remind you, Mister Manning, that you're here at my beck and call. I don't remember telling you to talk." She gave him a hard stare, before responding to Dawson.

"Only a few minutes ago, you were reminding me how gravely judges and juries view offences against police officers. Now, you are telling me that owning up to the attempted murder of Owen and Reason won't make a difference. It's all very confusing, DC Dawson," she said quietly, before raising her voice unexpectedly, "Or is this yet another example of your incompetence?"

Dawson allowed the dust to settle on her mini outburst before continuing with what was fast becoming his trademark introduction to a new avenue, "Suzanne, although it's incredibly painful for you, can we establish that your motive for murdering six people was revenge for Rhodri's death?"

There was no disputing this, although Suzanne pointed out that, strictly speaking, it was displaced revenge, "Thanks to your failures, I was unable to avenge my son by killing his killer. I suppose you could say it was also 'once removed', as my initial impulse was to make you pay for what you had failed to accomplish."

"You considered killing police officers?"

324

"Briefly, yes," Suzanne said firmly, "then I realised that it would be more appropriate to remove people who have shown themselves capable of doing what that bastard did to Rhodri!"

"So, you scoured the local newspaper for reports of convictions for motoring offences?"

"Yes."

"Not just convictions," Shaw added from the side-line, "Mister Gilligan was charged but acquitted."

Suzanne said nothing but gave a snort of derision.

"The Allens weren't even charged, Suzanne. Mister Skinner's death was clearly an accident."

"They killed someone with their car," Llewellyn parried, "and that put them in the same league as my son's hit-and-run assassin. Lower down the ladder, admittedly, but still the same league."

"And Alan Morrissey? We found no evidence of him having committed offences, or being cautioned. Where does he fit into this?"

"He nearly ran over a pedestrian," Suzanne declared.

Dawson and Shaw blinked their disbelief.

"I saw the incident. I was out for a walk along the seafront. It's one of the few places that I can find so much as a single grain of solace. A car, which I later found out was Morrissey's, swung out of the gateway to that big apartment block towards Holywell and almost wiped out a woman on the pavement. Luckily she had the presence of mind to fall backwards. I guess she got away with a few bruises."

"You didn't go to her assistance?" Shaw asked severely.

"She had a friend with her. Once I was sure that my army first aid training wasn't required, I went on my way, but not until I'd noted the car registration."

"I see," Dawson responded thoughtfully, "Are also you saying that Alan Morrissey was in the same league as the person who killed Rhodri. If so, that's one giant leap in logic."

Suzanne scowled, "I was being far too optimistic when I expected you to be able to understand! Of course, Morrissey is as bad as the others, on the same page as Rhodri's murderer. Don't you see? It's like drug addicts. You're always telling us that they start with a little weed, then once hooked, they're soon into hard Class A stuff. It's the same with these people. A bad bit of driving today, a traffic offence tomorrow, killing someone's son next week."

Dawson somehow managed to stay calm and focused, "And Detective Chief Inspector Owen?"

"I saw her speeding to get through lights at Polegate."

"But you managed to get her number," Dawson noted, "so how can you be sure what speed she was doing?"

"To be a good marksman, you need three things," Suzanne explained as if instructing a raw recruit, "a steady nerve, A1 eyesight and the ability to compute contextual data in a fraction of a second. I possess all three in abundance," she crowed. "On this occasion a blind man could've told you that she was breaking the speed limit, just by the roar of her engine."

It was the detectives' turn to call for a break.

326

"Good going, Peter," Shaw congratulated his junior colleague when they were back in his office.

"Thank you, sir," Dawson accepted the praise awkwardly, "but apart from her occasional outburst, she's not making it particularly difficult."

"Don't underestimate yourself. I know plenty of officers who would have flipped in the face of some of Ms Llewellyn's comments. You're staying calm is a big factor in us getting this far this soon."

Dawson alluded to the swan, gliding serenely above the water while paddling furiously below.

"Well, whatever you're feeling, what you're doing is clearly working, so stick with it."

When they reconvened, Dawson followed the agreed strategy to explore the parts played by Suzanne's mother and brother.

"Did you pressure your mother into assisting you, Suzanne? If you did, the consequences for her will be less severe."

To his surprise, Llewellyn made no effort to come to her mother's defence, "She felt responsible for Rhodri's death, but that was nonsense. In my absence, she was responsible for his *life!*" she spoke harshly. "Having failed to discharge that responsibility, she had no choice than to assist me."

"You mean you gave her no choice?" Peter asked softly.

"No!" Suzanne reacted crossly, "I meant what I said. My mother knew that she had to help me. It was the only way in which she could remove the weight from her conscience."

"She knew that it was you who killed Gilligan?"

327

"Of course."

"And made no attempt to stop you killing again?"

"Of course not! She had a duty to Rhodri's memory."

"Can you tell us where she is now, Suzanne?"

"I don't know."

She noticed Shaw pull a face.

"I don't give a damn whether you believe me or not, Superintendent, but it's the truth. When Nigel informed me that you were closing in, we quit mum's place in Polegate."

"In a hire car," Dawson recalled the moment that he had impressed Reason with his deduction.

"Yes, the first of a few. The plan was to abandon each one, not far from a rental firm, where a replacement could be hired. Not that I can tell you anything about the others. She dropped me off on the first day and I went into hiding on the Downs."

Momentarily, Dawson felt some admiration for the diverse skills of the woman across the table from him, before reminding himself that she had killed six times.

"Suzanne, Nigel claims to have been forced into getting information for you. What do you say to that?"

"What is there to say?" she huffed. "My brother is a spineless piece of garbage," she hissed, "and totally lacking in passion. He was always destined to be an office boy!" There was venom in her tone as she recounted how Nigel hadn't managed to express deep sorrow or deep

328

anger when Rhodri was killed. At first, he didn't even have the guts to help me, but once he realised mum would never have anything to do with him again if he didn't, he came around to my way of thinking."

A brief non-verbal exchange with Shaw and Dawson took a final step towards completion, "One final question, Suzanne. Whose idea was it to carry out the revenge killings, yours or your mother's?"

"No comment," Suzanne said through a thin lipped smile. She had assisted them enough for one day and was determined that they should do some of their own work.

She persisted with her stubborn refusal to provide the last piece of the puzzle, for which Dawson had less than twenty four hours to wait. The arrest of Megan Llewellyn in Lichfield and her subsequent admission to all bar one of the offences, of which she stood accused, left him convinced that Suzanne had been the authoress of plot.

"Not that it makes a huge difference to the end result, sir," he had said to Shaw, "but if I've learned anything from DI Reason it's that it is always best to have no loose ends."

With the Super's commendation that he appeared to have learned a great deal more than that ringing in his ears, Dawson hot footed it back to the hospital.

62

Detective Inspector Reason had never imagined that death would be this wonderful. He stood alone but unafraid in a vast hall, decorated in pastel shades, white and gold. A mist was swirling around at floor level, a warm, comforting vapour, not the camouflage of a hidden threat. He recognised the music that was playing in the background, but couldn't name it. He liked the sound and felt a gentle embarrassment as he hoped it wasn't the muzak that they played in his local supermarket. He smiled.

No longer alone, he had become aware of two figures, one either side of him. Without turning his head he could sense, even see their feminine forms. Two beautiful women, dressed in diaphanous togas. Simultaneously, they took hold of his hands. The mist slowly rose up and engulfed the three of them, before dispersing again.

Reason opened his eyes and stared up at the pure white ceiling. He didn't think he was in the wonderful hall anymore. This was a much colder, harsher place. But the sensation of his hands being held had lingered on. He moved the fingers in both his hands. Gentle squeezes in return. Keeping his head still, he looked to the left and saw the concerned but beaming face of Isobel Perry. "Eyes right!" he commanded himself without words. Harriet Owen, anxiety and relief etched in her thin smile.

"Oh," said Dawson arriving at the end of the bed a moment later, "I see both hands are taken. Where does that leave me?"

Without attempting to raise his head, Reason answered his colleague, "Unless you want to destroy my reputation with the ladies, don't even think about touching my genitals, detective constable."

The party burst into laughter.

Reason joined in, "Sod the pain!" he grimaced, "it's great to be able to laugh again."

63

During the two weeks of his hospitalisation, Reason proved to be the most impatient of patients. At best, whenever his consultant or a member of her team indicated the slightest progress, Reason immediately wanted to push the limit of what he might be able to manage. At worst, he didn't even wait for a medical opinion, simply launching himself into self-set challenges. Invariably, these acts of bravado ended in failure, discomfort or embarrassment, sometimes all three.

He welcomed the news that he could sit up in bed, with an attempt to get *out* of bed and sit in the adjacent armchair, which resulted in the various tubes and wires to which he was connected becoming entangled, causing his drip stand to fall over. For good measure, the wound in his chest opened up again.

On another occasion, Reason's disdain for the cardboard bed pans and flasks prompted an earlier expedition to the toilets than he was ready for and he ran out of steam at about the same point as his urine ran out of him, namely some thirty feet short of his intended destination.

Having tired of antics like this, the ward sister, a flame haired Irish woman with hard features and, on a good day, a sparkling smile, had given him the mother of all bollockings. *He* might think he was being clever, but he was alone in the whole world as far as that interpretation of his actions was concerned. She didn't give a toss, if he wanted to put back his recovery by taking no notice of the collective knowledge of the entire medical profession, on condition that it didn't inconvenience her already hard pressed staff. In order to achieve this unlikely balance between his ambition and their workload, she suggested than when he next had it in mind to impersonate Scott of the Antarctic, he was to give her notice, so she could arrange for a porter to take him into the middle of the bloody car park and leave him there to his own devices.

In answer to the question with which she ended her tirade, Reason said that she had indeed made herself clear.

Thereafter, Reason largely did as he was told, which did nothing for his mood; however, he had to admit that his less adventurous, more compliant approach confirmed the consultant's prognosis of a speedier recovery. The process was further aided by the regular visits from colleagues, of whom Dawson seemed to spend all his spare time at the hospital. Reason started to grow concerned about his junior colleague.

"My name will be mud with Heather," he commented on this particular occasion, "You're not to screw things up at home on my account. I wouldn't want that on my conscience."

Dawson smiled.

"I'm serious, Peter," Reason responded, "deadly serious. I know what I'm talking about. I've been there, done it, got the tee shirt."

Dawson kept smiling, as if taking no notice of his boss.

Reason lowered his voice, "For Christ's sake, Peter. You're not on something are you? You'll get booted out of the force if you're found out."
More smiles.

"Detective Constable Dawson, tell me what the hell you're up to. That's an order. If you don't comply I'll summon the sister and have you sectioned!"

Dawson continued to ignore him. Instead he nodded towards the other side of the bed from where he had engaged Reason, who turned to see three new visitors. Rebecca and the children!

He threw his arms open and first Ellie, then Liam embraced him tightly.

Rebecca declined his invitation to do the same, opting to kiss him gently on the forehead. Dawson collected three more chairs but the children chose to perch on the bed, so as to be closer to their dad.

Rebecca had seen the news report of the shooting and she had established and maintained contact with Peter, biding her time to bring the children to see Steve, once it was clear that he was either on the mend or at death's door.

"Do I take it that it's bad news, then?" Steve asked gravely.

Overhearing this comment, Sister O'Malley joined the group, "Will you listen to your father, kids? He never stops joking. Well, for the record, I've got some very *good* news. You're almost fit enough to be transferred to a police convalescence centre somewhere near Oxford. They're sorting out the arrangements, should be ready to go in a couple of days.

And what makes that news especially good is that you'll be out of my hair at last!" With that she left them to enjoy a couple of hours together. The children were anxious to hear what had happened and Liam in particular wanted to know the gory details even if they didn't exist. For his part, Steve was even more anxious to catch up with their progress towards or through teenage life.

Well into the official visiting hours, for which Reason had established a healthy disregard, Isobel Perry arrived. When she caught sight of the family tableau, she turned on her heels, but failed to escape Reason's attention.

"Isobel," he called to her and with obvious discomfort she changed course again and joined the happy group.

Reason introduced everyone and made a point of singing Isobel's praises as one of the best pathologists he had ever worked with. Liam was fascinated by her work and started to pepper her with macabre questions.

Reason intervened and told his son to give Doctor Perry a break, but she didn't seem to mind the boy's inquisition. If anything, it helped lance the awkwardness of being an interloper at the family reunion.

After a while, Isobel indicated that she had to make a move, "I'm heading back to Surrey later today."

Reason assumed that this was another social interlude, but she corrected him, "Doctor Erickson's back, so my tour of duty is at an end."

The DI made no attempt to hide his disappointment. He still had unfinished business with her.

Isobel got up from the chair in which she had been interrogated by Liam, took the two steps to the bed, leaned over and kissed Steve on the cheek. "I've enjoyed working with you," she said.

As she broke away she placed her business card on the bedside table, "In case you need a second opinion," she smiled. A round of uncomfortable "nice to have met you" and she was gone.

"Dad," Ellie said, picking up Perry's card, "what does this mean?"

She handed it to her father, pointing to some writing on the reverse.

336

Driven To Murder

"The man you saw that night was my brother!" he read to himself and smiled.